I0615410

Lucifer

BY THE SAME AUTHOR

The Marvelous Story of Claire d'Amour
The Call of the Beast
Priscilla of Alexandria
The Angel of Lust
The Mystery of the Tiger
The Poison of Goa
The Blood of Toulouse
The Albigensian Treasure
Jean de Fodoas
Melusine
The Brothers of the Virgin Gold

Lucifer

by
Maurice Magre

Translated, annotated and introduced by
Brian Stableford

A Black Coat Press Book

English adaptation and introduction Copyright © 2017 by Brian Stableford.
Cover illustration Copyright © 2017 by Mike Hoffman.

Visit our website at www.blackcoatpress.com

ISBN 978-1-61227-676-2. First Printing. November 2017. Published by Black Coat Press, an imprint of Hollywood Comics.com, LLC, P.O. Box 17270, Encino, CA 91416. All rights reserved.
Except for review purposes, no part of this book may be reproduced or transmitted in any form or by any means, electronic or mechanical, including photocopying, recording, or by any information storage and retrieval system, without permission in writing from the publisher. The stories and characters depicted in this novel are entirely fictional.
Printed in the United States of America.

TABLE OF CONTENTS

Introduction 7
LUCIFER.. 17
THE NIGHT OF HASHISH AND OPIUM 249

Introduction

This is the seventh volume of a twelve-volume set of translations of Maurice Magre's prose fiction. It contains translations of the novel *Lucifer* (1929) and the novella *La Nuit de haschich et de l'opium* (1929), as "The Night of Hashish and Opium."

Volume One, *The Marvelous Story of Claire d'Amour and Other Stories*, contains translations of early short stories, including the collection *Histoire merveilleuse de Claire d'Amour suivie d'autres contes merveilleux* (1903) and six other stories from various sources, published between 1901 and 1913.

Volume Two, *The Call of the Beast and Other Stories*, contains translations of his first three works of prose fiction in volume form, *Les Colombes poignardées* (1917), as "Stabbed Doves," *La Tendre camarade* (1918), as "The Tender Comrade" and *L'Appel de la bête* (1920), as "The Call of the Beast."

Volume Three, *Priscilla of Alexandria and Other Stories* contains translations of the original version of the story collection *Vies des courtisanes,* first published in *Oeuvres Libres* 23 (1923), as "Courtesans' Lives" plus the additional story added to the version published in volume form in 1925, and the novel *Priscilla d'Alexandrie* (1925), as "Priscilla of Alexandria."

Volume Four, *The Angel of Lust*, contains translations of the novella, *La Vie amoureuse de Messaline* (1925), as "The Love Life of Messalina," the novel published as *La Luxure de Grenade* (1926), as "The Angel of Lust," and the chapter from *Magiciens et illuminés*

(1930) entitled "Christian Rosenkreutz et les Rose-croix," as "Christian Rosenkreutz and the Rosicruians."

Volume Five, *The Mystery of the Tiger*, contains translations of the novella *Le Roman de Confucius* (1927), as "The Story of Confucius," and the novel *Le Mystère du tigre* (1927), as "The Mystery of the Tiger."

Volume Six, *The Poison of Goa*, contains translations of the novel *Le Poison de Goa* (1928), as "The Poison of Goa," and the prose poems contained in *Le Livre des lotus entr'ouverts* (1926), as "Lotus Blossoms."

Volume Eight, *The Blood of Toulouse*, contains translations of the novel *Le Sang de Toulouse* (1931), as "The Blood of Toulouse," and the chapter from *Magiciens et illuminés* entitled "Le Maître inconnu des Albigeois," as "The Secret Master of the Albigensians."

Volume Nine, *The Albigensian Treasure*, contains translations of the novel *Le Trésor des Albigeois* (1938) as "The Albigensian Treasure," and the collection of vignettes "Communication avec la nature" from *La Beauté invisible* (1937), as "Communication with Nature."

Volume Ten, *Jean de Fodoas*, contains translations of the novel *Jean de Fodoas: aventures d'un Français à la cour de l'empereur Akbar* (1939) as "Jean de Fodoas" and the chapter from *Magiciens et illuminés* entitled "Le Mystère des Templiers," as "The Mystery of the Templars."

Volume Eleven, *Melusine*, contains translations of the novel *Mélusine, ou le secret de solitude* (1941) and the collections of vignettes "Le Côté d'ombre des âmes" and "Révélation des mondes invisibles" from *La Beauté invisible*, as "The Dark Side of Souls" and "The Revelation of Invisible Worlds."

Volume Twelve, *The Brothers of the Virgin Gold*, contains a translation of the novel *Les Frères de l'or vierge*, first published posthumously in 1949.

After a sequence of exotic historical fictions, which had made gradual progress from the fifth-century Alexandria of *Priscilla d'Alexandrie* and the Imperial Rome of *La Vie amoureuse de Messaline* to the nineteenth century settings of *Le Mystère du tigre* and *Le Poison de Goa*, Maurice Magre's fiction returned to the present day in the two works of fiction he published in 1929, *Lucifer* and in *La Nuit de haschich et d'opium*; in the former—which was not necessarily written earlier—he also returned after a long gap to contemporary Paris, the setting of *Les Colombes poignardées* and *L'Appel de la bête*, and the focal point of the reminiscences contained in his two volumes of autobiographical reflections, *Pourquoi je suis Bouddhiste* [Why I am a Buddhist] (1928), and *Confessions sur les femmes, l'opium, l'amour, l'idéal*, etc... [Confessions regarding Women, Opium, Amour and the Ideal, etc.] (1930).

In fact, like *L'Appel de la bête*, which similarly has a first-person narrator who never reveals his name, *Lucifer* reads as if it were a kind of confession, and although it is very obviously fictitious, exploring a demonic possession consequent on a casually-made diabolical pact—which might or might not be entirely subjective and psychological—it does have marked affinities with the supposedly honest confessions of the autobiographical texts that bracketed it, in which it is similarly unclear as to whether the various supernatural agencies detailed therein are purely metaphorical and symbolic, the narrators remaining profoundly uncertain as to their objective reality.

Although the existential circumstances of the narrator of *L'Appel de la bête* were not those of the author at the time he wrote it, and the events of the plot are clearly fictitious, there is an obvious temptation to read those invented events as a superficial disguise permitting the author to contemplate and examine certain real feelings that he had. *Confessions* certainly endorses that view; there too the author speaks about the sensation that there were two selves competing within him, one an inferior self obsessively orientated carnal pleasure, whose sexual obsession was akin to a form of possession, continually undermining a relatively intellectual superior self interested in spiritual and intellectual development. Certain specific incidents in the narrative of *L'Appel de la bête* are also akin to anecdotes related in *Confessions*, not in the sense that they reproduce them straightforwardly, but in the sense that they seem to be reflecting on the lessons to be learned therefrom.

Given that, it is tempting to regard *Lucifer* as a kind of continuation of the literary and psychological exercise begun in *L'Appel de la bête*, similarly indulging in reflections, albeit considerably more melodramatically, on matters that would be discussed in a more sober fashion in *Confessions*. To some extent, it undoubtedly is such a continuation, and in that regard, its near-hysterical extrapolation and exaggeration of the motif of demonic possession introduced in the earlier novel offers an intriguing insight into the psychological ground that the author had covered in the intervening nine years. Those were years during which his amorous adventures had been severely curtailed, when he was diagnosed with syphilis, occasioning a permanent change in his attitude to his inferior self. In *Lucifer* however, that troublesome personal conflict is set in a broader historical context, the malignity of the possessed inferior self being hypothetically mirrored on a much larger scale in organizations of worshipers of evil whose objects of adoration are capable of supernatural influence.

Magre had broached that notion before, most explicitly in *La Luxure de Grenade*, where the Spanish Inquisition becomes just such a organization, sending assassins to murder philosophers, although its central Antichrist, Tomas de Torquemada, convinced of his own twisted virtue, seems unaware that he belongs to the Devil's party. In *Lucifer* it appears to be assumed that the quest to eliminate the virtuous opposition has been successful; the Rosicrucians and their kindred virtuous organizations have not merely been driven into hiding, but they seem to be extinct, leaving the narrator with nowhere to turn for spiritual succor except the Church—which proves, as might be expected, to be at best impotent, and at worst in tacit alliance with the forces of evil. The narrator is, in consequence, forced to find his own way out of his predicament, if he can—but that was certainly a conclusion that Magre reached in his life, all of the later works of fiction and non-fiction published in his lifetime being insistent on the fact that every individual has to find his own way to spiritual enlightenment, based on personal experience of contact with the divine.

As a philosophical novel, *Lucifer* has a certain amount in common with Joris-Karl Huysmans' classic novel of contemporary Satanism *Là-Bas* (1891; tr. as *Down There*), which must have been one of its models. Like Huysmans' novel it features a climactic "black mass," albeit one addressed to a pagan deity rather than to the Christian Devil. However, Huysmans' hero and *alter ego* Durtal finds a refuge within orthodox faith that the narrator of *Lucifer* tries out and finds utterly vain,

11

forcing him to orientate his efforts in a different direction. Durtal's involvement with Satanism is also primarily and quintessentially scholarly, a derivative of his escapist Medieval studies, and of a particular fascination with the personality of Gilles de Rais. Unlike Magre however, who had a strong scholarly interest himself in the Middle Ages, the narrator of *Lucifer* only pretends such an interest, and thus has no such intellectual refuge. He is entirely focused on the present day, and on his amorous projects, and is unable to take any real interest in the obsessive historical and philosophical research of his *bête noire* Kotzebue, whose academic pursuit of the legend of Simon Magus enables him to give form to the ritual that he wants to enact, partly and perhaps entirely in pursuit of his own amorous objectives.

That difference might seem surprising, but it is less so when one considers that the particular historical figures in which Magre took an intense interest were Messalina and Isabelle de Solis, and that those he invented, such as Priscilla of Alexandria and the various heroines of *Vies des courtisanes*, were all variants of the archetypal femme fatale modeled at the very beginning of his career in *Claire d'Amour*. In *Lucifer*, the central element of the narrator's perceived predicament is his obsessive pursuit of two half-sisters, who divide the attractive aspects of female beauty between them, one essentially carnal and the other, at least ostensibly, pure and entirely orientated toward spirituality. Insofar as the novel is exploratory and experimental, it is an examination and evaluation of that duality. To the extent that the analysis in question reaches a conclusion, it is deeply and poignantly frustrating, although—in fact, because—it is evidently and painfully honest.

Partly in order to supply a sense of conclusion that its central analysis cannot provide, the story told in *Lucifer* is supplied with an epilogue that steps outside the main narrative and reveals that narrative to be the confession of one "J.N***"—which any reader familiar with Magre's earlier contemporary fiction would unhesitatingly decode as Jean Noël, the poet featured in four of his Paris-set narratives, who seems in those works to be a fictitious device enabling the author to take a wry look at his himself, sometimes in parallel with an unnamed narrator who also seems to be a stand-in for the author. The decision made in *Lucifer* to obscure the name, while leaving its interpretation obvious, at least to *cognoscenti*, is odd, and it is not obvious why the author did it. It might be simple playfulness—there was always a playful element to Magre's creativity, even when he was at him most intensely earnest—but it might also reflects a genuine uncertainty as to the extent of the identification that the author wanted to make with his character, and with the existential situation in which the narrator finally, winds up as a result of his tortuous endeavors.

Seen simply as a story, perhaps *Lucifer* does not reproduce the full force of the colorful flamboyant melodrama of such historical romances as *Priscilla d'Alexandrie* and *La Luxure de Grenade*. In dramatic terms, even the climactic black mass might seem somewhat weakened in its plausibility by its contemporary setting, less dramatic than the mass of Saint Sécaire featured in the later historical novel *Le Trésor des Albigeois*. If that is the case, it would not be surprising that having got through the retrospective self-analytical phase represented by *Pourquoi je suis Bouddhiste*, *Lucifer* and *Confessions* Magre made a swift return to gaudy historical romance, in no uncertain terms, in the brilliantly extravagant *Le Sang du Toulouse*. Within the context of the phase of intensive self-reexamination, however, *Lucifer* is a very striking exercise in transfigurative symbolism, and as an intimate horror story it functions very well indeed—considerably better than *L'Appel de la bête*. As an account of metaphorical possession, it is detailed with a persuasive conviction, and if one regards its essential purpose as that of sowing a discomfort in the reader's mind similar to one experienced by the author, albeit exaggerated by poetic license, it certainly succeeds, aided rather than undermined by its protagonist's ultimate frustration. In its own terms, therefore, the novel is a fine and memorable piece of work, as well as a very unusual one.

La Nuit de Haschich et de l'Opium, set in India, is a far more conventional narrative than Magre's two previous works of fiction set in the Far East, *Le Mystère du tigre* and *Le Poison de Goa*. Like the latter novel, it begins by placing its female protagonist in danger of rape, but the tone and manner of the story are completely different. Unlike Rachel Jehoudah in *Le Poison de Goa*, the narrator of *La Nuit de Haschich et de l'Opium* is extremely naïve, and takes an implausibly long time to accept the realization that she has walked into a trap, in spite of receiving all manner of supernatural and explicit warnings. Thereafter, the narrative unfolds is a conventional manner, in spite of its bizarre magical and hallucinatory trappings, and deliberately embraces exactly the kind of stereotyped conclusion that Magre usually made it a point of principle to avoid, making the story a striking anomaly within his canon in that regard.

The novelette was first published by Ernest Flammarion in 1929, and was probably commissioned by its editor, but that does not explain its determined, albeit doubtless ironic, conventionality. *La Vie amoureuse de Messaline* had probably been written to commission in the same way, but there is nothing conventional about its elaboration and its depiction of the conclusion already specified by legend. Superficially, at least, *La Nuit de Haschich et de l'Opium* looks more like hackwork than any other work of fiction Magre signed, recycling erotic elements from "Bagawali" (in *Vies de courtisanes*) and the full-length version of *Priscilla d'Alexandrie*, as well as making much of the hallucinatory effects of opium.

In the latter regard, *La Nuit de Haschich et de l'Opium* has obvious affinities with *Le Mystère du tigre*, collaborating with that predecessor in subjecting the effects of opium to a quasi-clinical re-examination, a decade after Magre's first literary examination of the drug's effects, carried out in *Les Colombes poignardées* and *La Tendre camarade*. It seems probable that, from the viewpoint of both the commissioning editor and the commissioned author, the plot of the story was merely a container, casually contrived for the convenient representation of the effects of opium—here combined with hashish—and the associated pontifications of the philosophically-inclined Rajah, who is less enslaved to his carnal appetites than his competitors in the scabrous game of cards that supplies the fulcrum of the plot.

As in *Le Poison de Goa*, the strength of the *La Nuit de Haschich et de l'Opium* is as much in the setting as the plot, and perhaps more so. The temple of Chillambaram featured in the story is fictitious, but is obviously based on reports that Magre had read of the actual temple-complex of Chidambaram, removed from the city of that name into a different and more isolated location for the convenience of the narrative. It is easy to understand why Magre would have been impressed by a description of Chidambaram' five Shiva temples, and the symbolism of the incarnation of the elements in their five lingams; in its gaudy exoticism, however, his Chillambaram is very much a product of his own imagination, especially when it is transmogrified by the imagination of the hallucinated and terror-stricken heroine.

Whereas the hallucinatory effects of opium on the anti-hero of *Le Mystère du tigre* seem to assist in his redemption, however, they are purely problematic for the hapless narrator of *La Nuit de Haschich et de l'Opium*, and that probably offers a more accurate account of Magre's final judgment of the drug than the nostalgic reminiscences of *Confessions*, which deliberately attempted to return to the mind-set of his early experiments, and to explain his initial hopeful enthusiasm for opium-smoking. Although calculatedly trivial, therefore, the novelette is not without interest in the context of the author's work as a whole, and if viewed in isolation it does have a certain depth behind its obvious artificiality and its breezy fluency. At any rate, it provides an interesting frivolous counterpoint to the earnest intensity of *Lucifer*, and might have been written with that purpose in mind, as an item of light relief from intense introspection.

The translation of *Lucifer* was made from a copy of the 1929 Albin Michel edition of the book. The translation of *La Nuit de haschich et de l'opium* was made from a copy of the reprint published in Pondicherry in 2009 (as *Nuit de haschich et opium*) by Kailash.

Brian Stableford

LUCIFER

I almost uttered a cry of surprise. The coaching entrance to the small house, the two symmetrical illuminated windows and the plastered wall with its coiffure of tiles represented an enormous and bizarre face looking at me.

It's a warning, I thought.

And I strode back and forth with satisfaction along the sidewalk of that solitary street in Passy without worrying about what the nature of the warning might be. My appetite for mystery was so great that I populated the world with enigmas, not in order to solve them but in order to delight in marveling at them.

I darted a further glance at the house, and perceived to my surprise that the crude representation of a face had been modified, and resembled another image, also created by a secret society, at the time of my twentieth year.

I saw once again the distant station in winter, the innocent eyes of the friend who was accompanying me. I was on the point of boarding the train. I was struck by the designs that the frost had made on the windows. In the midst of those polar landscapes there was a representation of a devil with his horns and his demonic laugh on the glass of my compartment. The eyes, under obliquely inclined eyebrows, were staring at me with an embarrassing fixity. I was so surprised that I thought it was a hallucination, and I said to my companion:

"Can you see anything on the window?"

"Nothing at all," he replied.

A whistle resounded, I closed the door, and as the train pulled away I heard my friend on the platform shout:

"Yes, yes, I see. There's a devil on the window."

At first I had admired the subtle art deployed by hazard, but at length, I had suffered a sight irritation. The face paid no heed to the three or four other people sitting in the compartment, and was obstinate in looking at me. I passed my hand over the glass in order to get rid of it, but it was on the other side that the mysterious artist had worked. Then I put my face close to it and projected my moist breath. I only succeeded in magnifying the eyes and rendering the rictus of the mouth more intolerable.

I remember that I was about to brave the protests of the passengers and open the window in spite of the cold, in order to escape that obsession, when I was saved by the stopping of the train.

I had had difficulty forgetting that incident. It would, however, have disappeared along with the millions of cinematic images that constitute our lives if the ridiculous figure that had just appeared had not revived it suddenly.

I shrugged my shoulders. I blinked. I no longer had before me anything but Monsieur Saint-Aygulf's house, which I had come to consider on that warm night in June.

I looked at my watch and resumed my walk. It was a little after eleven o'clock and the two sisters must be in the process of going to bed in the room that they shared and where they both slept. Perhaps they were already in bed and reading, each on their side, by the light of two lamps.

Two young women. Two lamps. My double amour. Good and evil. How harmonious it all was, and mysterious at the same time!

I stopped and passed my hand over my face as if to wipe away a certain expression of stupidity that sometimes settled there and remained there in spite of my efforts. I had just thought about the bodies of two young women, the grace of their bare arms, the contour and firmness of their breasts, which must appear under their nightdresses. It was June and the heat was excessive. Perhaps they had thrown back the sheets and were reposing with the abandonment that summer evenings procure.

At that moment I was brushed on the sidewalk by a man with a wooden leg, who was walking with a singular rapidity for an invalid. I thought that if I reached out with my cane with the curled-back handle toward the stem of his foot he would fall; he would cry out, think it an aggression, and the noise would make the shutters of the two windows open like eyelids. I would catch a glimpse of the origin of shoulders, the hollows of armpits, and a surge of slender upper bodies above the stone sill.

Folly! The fast-moving invalid had disappeared at the extremity of the street and I remained open-mouthed facing windows whose illumination had been abruptly extinguished.

Why had I come to prowl in that street? I was no longer at the age of such escapades. Monsieur Saint-Aygulf, the father of Eveline and Laurence, might emerge abruptly, see me and be astonished by my presence outside his house. For him, I was not a friend but a relative who attempted by constant effort to enter further into his intimacy. He believed that we were linked by our common appetite for mystery, and the admiration that I supposedly had for his ides. He always exposed them abundantly before me and I had hidden from him, thanks to a fashion of rounding the eyes, nodding the head and thinking about something else, the absolute scorn that his stupidity inspired in me. Many men, enveloped by the cloud of their vanity, do not perceive that it is their wife, their daughter or their mistress that one comes to seek out in their home.

Since I was there, I was in love. But with which of the two? I had never reached an understanding with myself regarding the significance of the word love. What I experienced could, strictly speaking, be called that. But to love two sisters at the same time! There was a sort of mystery in that.

It was Eveline that I desired more, first of all because I thought her inaccessible to all desire. She was a mystic. If she had been Christian she would have gone into a convent. He father had put the most foolish ideas into her head. I was not far from believing that she attributed a spiritual mission to herself. As if a spiritual mission could devolve to such a desirable body! But whether she was a missionary or not, that had no importance for me.

Eveline secretly considered that a man who has surpassed the age of thirty-five, who has attained that advanced age, ought to retire from life, become a hermit, what do I know? And I knew, without her ever having expressed it, that she deemed that I, in particular, ought not to permit myself to raise my eyes either to her, her sister or any other woman. I had understood that by the way she considered my temples, the attention she paid to counting my hairs, although numerous, and measuring the thinness of my neck, where my age was betrayed.

That disdainful examination was not the act of someone who has a spiritual mission. She hated me, I was sure of it and I had also sworn...

But that oath was buried in the depths of my heart.

Laurence loved me. I declared that to myself without vanity. She had said several times, intentionally, in my presence, that young men did not interest her. That was a certain sign, not to mention the pressures of the hand, remarks with double meanings and the scene in the dining room. But if there was a balance and immaterial weights for weighing love, I loved Laurence less than Eveline. She was certainly not as pretty as her sister. Her features were irregular, her mouth too large and too sensual, her dazzling teeth evoked images of bites, and she had a slight bodily sway that made me think of a panther I had seen the previous year in a menagerie.

Then again, she was brunette and an invincible taste attracted me toward blondes. There were certainly glints of tawny gold in her hair, but not enough for my taste. Her principle fault was her lack of intelligence, or rather, the kind of intelligence that I like. There was nothing mysterious about her. It was said of her that she was an absolutely material creature. I had seen her eat with an astonishing appetite.

She made fun of the efforts of her father and sister to communicate with the beyond; she considered as scatterbrains the members of the group of Essenes and students of ancient religions and their mysteries. She made an exception for me because in her presence I was able, by raising a corner of my mouth or by a skillful wink, to make her suppose that I was only a false believer, a slightly ironic enthusiast who only came to her father's house for her.

I loved Laurence less than Eveline, but when I thought about her natural independence, a kind of rebellion against everything that she allowed to burst forth in her speech and was betrayed in her movements, I loved her more, because I have always been seduced by rebellion, although personally rather servile to the prejudices of society.

I knew that Laurence did not have the same mother as Eveline, and that Monsieur Saint-Aygulf had collected her at the age of eight in order to save her from poverty. Like a plant whose roots are steeped in a fecund compost, she had retained from her early years something vivacious, audacious and unhealthy, which rendered her more attractive to me The virtuous monster, the flat-haired torturer that Madame Saint-Aygulf was, had martyrized her on the grid of family duties, with the wheels of good intentions. She had even had her locked up for a few years in a house of correction.

But Eveline the pure and proud had received from nature elevation of mind as well as the gift of a perfect body. I could not think without shivering about her ash-colored hair, which she had not cut, about the curve of her neck, the radiation emanating from her person, which stole the quality of transparency from the fabric of dresses, rendering them as heavy and unliftable as the veil of chastity.

If I was here it was because a presentiment had pushed me, in which case it was necessary that something would happen. The idea of returning home after the futile contemplation of a house whose two illuminated windows had just been extinguished was utterly insupportable to me. I nearly launched myself toward the door shouting: "Laurence! Eveline!" careless of the possible appearance of an irritated and amazed father.

It was a perfume of acacia that stopped me. A flowery branch emerged from a wall and allowed to fall upon me an insipid odor of sex and spring. I wanted to cut that branch, but it was too high. For the second time in a few minutes I experienced the utility of the crooked handle of my cane. I held it by its extremity, congratulating myself internally for the poetic idea of at least bringing back a flower from my nocturnal excursion.

It was at that moment that I heard a slight noise at the door of Monsieur de Saint-Aygulf's house. I stood there motionless. The door opened, and while the flowering branch returned skywards, the silhouette of a woman appeared on the threshold.

I was in the shadows and I could not be seen. My first thought was joyful. Then I had a presentiment. It was a secret warning that had impelled me to come. A counselor full of wisdom was hidden in my unconscious. My second thought was anxious. What ought I to do? Ought I to run? And first of all, who had just come out of the house?

The door had closed again and the silhouette—Eveline or Laurence—slid along the street rapidly. Instinctively, I hastened behind her. The summer mantle that I saw floating in the distance prevented me from seeing which of the two sisters I was dealing with. Might it not, in any case, be a chambermaid? I rejected a hypothesis that negated the value of the presentiment. Then again, the family resemblance that the two sisters had was visible in the gait.

It was only at the corner of the street that my heart began to beat faster, as at the announcement of some disagreeable news. Why was a young woman leaving her house furtively like that in the middle of the night? The precaution she had taken in not making the door click indicated that she wanted her father to remain ignorant of her departure.

I thought about turning right, reaching a lighted avenue that I had crossed in the evening, and then doubling back. I would find myself face to face with the person I was pursuing and would seem to be encountering her by chance. I reflected on the breathlessness that would result. And there was a risk of losing her.

As those thoughts succeeded one another, a taxi emerged slowly from the shadows and I saw the young woman signal it. She opened the door and climbed in, with a feline movement that allowed me to recognize her. It was Laurence.

Hazard dictated that a second taxi emerged from the same shadows, into which I climbed, and which launched in pursuit of the first on my order.

What I experienced comprised an equal mixture of dolor, because Laurence might be about to escape me, and delight because I was on the track of an enigma.

On the way, I tried to deceive myself: Women are all the same. Fundamentally, I had divined that. And in any case, what did it matter?

I had divined nothing. I found that that event was very important. My bitterness was increasing. I saw as if in a dream the wine-shops with their terraces overflowing on to the pavement, the busy waiters, the consumers mopping their brows. One sensed the atmosphere of sad joy that the first heat wave spreads over Paris. I suddenly perceived that one of the taxi's windows was raised. I brought it down with and irritated gesture, but without looking to see whether a mist had traced some design thereon.

"It's really that," I murmured, without knowing why, when I saw that we were approaching Montmartre. A fairground was in the process of installation there. I saw wagons with minuscule windows, square masses covered in gray canvas, dismantled wooden horses lying on the ground. A crowd was dispersing outside the hippodrome.

Who knows? I said to myself. *Her father or sister might be ill, the telephone might be out of order and she's gone to fetch a doctor to bring him back immediately.*

Alas, slightly before arriving at the Place Blanche her vehicle stopped. I made a sign to my driver to stop too. I noticed from a distance that Laurence seemed entirely at ease and, while waiting for her change, she looked to the right and left with a tranquil curiosity. She crossed the boulevard with a light step and headed for the Moulin Rouge.

I had the feeling that he heat was increasing. The café orchestras evoked in dying away the languors of a casino. A rotating fire, which came from I know not what luminous advertisement, launched regular flashes. I was brushed by a late night tram. It was overflowing with petit bourgeois who, because they had spent their evening at the cinema, gave the impression of weary party-goers. A murmur of drunkenness rose up around me and I suddenly felt tired and futile. The sky was riddled with indifferent stars.

Laurence did not go into the Moulin Rouge. Without any hurry, she was now going past cafés full of frightful men whistling at the women who went past them on the sidewalk. The Rue Lepic was cluttered with creatures selling newspapers, buying or eating oranges, hirsute bohemians, hunchbacks and women with the faces of ghosts. Laurence went through that bizarre population, to which theater exits give birth on the pavements of Montmartre as if it were part of them. Her manner was so casual that I would not have been surprised to see her exchanging handshakes of greeting right and left.

Abruptly, she disappeared into a café. It was a rather ill-famed establishment, a meting-place of prostitutes and drug-dealers. I was struck as if by a beam of light. Cocaine! Was it not that for which she had come in search? I strove to peer over the heads of the customers sitting on the terrace and I saw Laurence marching through the tables inside, supple, her head slightly tilted forward, looking at the people in the process of drinking beers like a panther about to pounce, a hooker on the point of sitting down next to a man who gives her a sign.

Curiosity suppressed anguish within me. Two louts, fairly good-looking fellows with shaven faces, made her an inviting gesture. One of them half rose to his feet, pointing to the banquette beside him with his reversed index finger, and I glimpsed in his eyes and laughter the idiotic expression men have when they are making a proposition to a woman they do not know.

Laurence did not even twitch her shoulder. Having looked them in the face, she passed on, with a total absence of response to the invitation, as if the material image of the two louts had been imperceptible to her senses.

There had been no purchase, no sale, no furtively slipped package.

I was obliged to step aside abruptly, and it was by chance if Laurence did not see me. She went past me and I sensed that she darted a long glance at the people distributed outside the café, as if to examine them.

She was looking for someone. But who? Who had been able to give Monsieur Saint-Aygulf's daughter a rendezvous as singular as that café haunted by shady individuals, policemen and drug-dealers? But then I realized that the rendezvous was not in that specific place—that it was a vague rendezvous in one of the cafés surrounding the Place Blanche, for I saw her push a door a little further along. She hesitated in the doorway for a moment, darting a circular glance around a smoky interior, and then she resumed her course on the sidewalk.

A little further on, she stuck her face to another window. She stopped outside an almost-empty wine merchant's, and as a short fat man with a ruddy race and a jovial expression looked at her slyly and opened his arms to bar her way she turned round and crossed the boulevard again. She retraced her steps and walked on the other side of the avenue, which as almost deserted. She went past two motionless hookers, standing side by side, and I noticed that she looked at them without any embarrassment, and even with a persistence great enough to attract insult—but that did not happen. The whores did not emerge from a stony immobility and Laurence passed slowly before the café at the corner of the Place Blanche, brushing the tables, examining the seated couples.

I suffered from her tranquility. I told myself that the best thing to do was to present myself abruptly in front of her. First of all, I would have the satisfaction of putting an end to that ease, which was unbearable to me. Then, I considered as possible a cry of surprise, a favorable greeting, and plausible explanations. Perhaps she needed a guide for a perfectly natural enterprise. I immediately imagined confidences, an intimate chat in a taxi taking her home, perhaps the sensuality of her lips, which would be greater because of a shared secret.

But Laurence undoubtedly made an abrupt resolution, for she suddenly started going along the Rue Blanche with a disconcerting rapidity. A crowd hindered my acceleration. I lost sight of her momentarily, and then rediscovered her a long way away. She was almost running. Had she perceived me behind her and was it me she was fleeing? Determined to catch up with her, I started running too. She had turned into the Rue Ballu.

When I arrived at the entrance to the street I had the sensation that it was entirely deserted. I ran along it, careless of the ridiculousness of what I was doing, the lack of any right I had to pursue the young woman. A vague form to the right disappeared somewhere, and I heard the muffled sound of a door closing.

She's just gone to find her lover! I thought, reaching the post office. I turned round, and found a sinister character in the Rue Ballu. I remembered having heard that many of those small houses were brothels. I embraced the Square Vintimille with a glance, and murmured: "What a landscape of crime!"

I sat down on the deserted terrace of a win merchant where there was only one small round table and a rickety chair. I ordered a beer and waited.

Ready-made phrases came to mind, such as "That's young Parisiennes for you!" or "And I was about to take that adventure seriously!"

I have always remarked that the lowest forms of thought naturally find the most banal means of expression to translate them. But that evening, I set that observation aside.

Eveline had just retreated, almost disappearing in a mist of indifference. I had a scornful smile on my lips again, addressed to Laurence, and already I saw clearly all the importance she had acquired in my eyes in the last hour. Rapidly, a series of questions and answers succeeded one another within me.

Had I thought about marrying her? No, never. But I might have thought about it. I professed the opinion that one ought only to marry a woman who has been one's mistress, with whom one has experimented in amour. I had paid court to Laurence, haphazardly, to see what would happen. No concern of responsibility had weighed upon me, even for a second. Now, here was the event that proved me right. First of all, is the concern of responsibility not an absurd trap that tends to restrict any agreeable action? One would never do anything if one thought about the consequences of one's actions. Then too, who can tell how things are linked together. Is not the greatest service one can render someone that of ridding them of the burden of family?

Is it even possible, I said to myself then, to feel love for someone? No, no, sensual, purely sensual. And I started tapping with my fingers on the greasy marble of the table, darting a long glance into the obscurity of the Rue Ballu...

And then, finally, her mother. It was necessary to think about heredity...

And I reconstituted what I knew about Laurence's history.

A few years earlier, Monsieur de Saint-Aygulf had been struck by a sort of spiritual revelation. The dead had suddenly started talking to him through the intermediary of small tables, by means of raps in the walls. That had led to a complete change in his character and way of life. He had abandoned the women for whom he had always had an excessive taste, in order to devote himself entirely to his wife, a lay saint who lived in the worshipful amour of her own hearth, and a merciless hatred for everything she placed under the label "immoral." And a notion of duty, new for him, had abruptly irrupted into his soul. It was necessary to tell the truth, to accomplish disinterested actions.

Monsieur de Saint-Aygulf confessed to his wife the existence of a natural daughter that he had had with a casual mistress he had immediately abandoned, and of whom he had not wanted to hear any further mention. He had decided that the child, who was then eight years old, would be reclaimed from her mother in order to be regenerated by good examples and contact with the moral perfection of Eveline, her half-sister. It appeared that the mother had consented without difficulty and had renounced all her rights over her daughter, doubtless thinking, like everyone else, that she would ensure her daughter's wellbeing by assuring her of wealth.

Between the little girl "with bad instincts" and the virtuous Madame de Saint-Aygulf a struggle had been engaged—a struggle of which I only knew details by way of a few conversations with Madame Saint-Aygulf or brief confidences on Laurence's part. In that struggle, Laurence had been vanquished and tamed. It seemed that Madame de Saint-Aygulf had seen to it with a redoubtable solicitude that the soul emerged from "the most abject depths of society" was recast and reshaped in accordance with her law.

"It's justice that has the most action on children," she said to me once, talking to me about that period of her life. "I've never made a gift to Eveline without making exactly the same gift to Laurence."

But she did not tell me whether she had been able to do so with the same love.

Madame de Saint-Aygulf had no other religion than that of the family, but she believed in a kind of Providence that punishes the wicked and recompenses the good.

"It's in watching those two children grow up," she said to me on another occasion, "that I've seen most clearly how equitable Providence is for everyone. The moral purity of Eveline is transformed into facial beauty and bodily grace, whereas all the ugliness of original sin took possession of Laurence's features."

That ugliness was to be transformed, however. Contained desire magnified the eyes. Luminous teeth gave the flesh of the lips a lightness of laughter that animated the excessively wide visage over the excessively short neck. The hair grew in all directions and brightened with ruddy gleams.

"At fourteen," said Madame Saint-Aygulf, again, "Laurence developed with her breasts a light tawny down on the arms and the perpetual mobility of her features, an expression of disquieting animality that caused me to experience the sentiment of a pollution in her presence. It was at that moment that it was necessary for me, at all costs, to triumph over the Beast."

Madame Saint-Aygulf had thought that the irremediably bad instincts of the Beast could only be vanquished by the iron discipline of a house of special education, where manual labor was incessantly alternated with that of the mind. She had placed Laurence there, and she had remained there until her seventeenth year, only emerging therefrom because Monsieur de Saint-Aygulf had thought he discerned in certain raps struck by a table the indication of that deliverance.

It was at that moment that I saw her for the first time. The contact with brutality, the suffering and the absence of pity had taught her hypocrisy.

Madame de Saint-Aygulf said of her: "It's necessary to beware of dormant waters." And she added, with an anxious expression: "What might become of her later?"

But she had another source of anxiety much graver. Monsieur de Saint-Aygulf, increasingly stunned by what he did not understand, had made his house a center for all spiritualist, Rosicrucian, Gnostic and neo-Platonist groups. Seekers of the philosopher's stone, Hindu mages, and passing fakirs had been welcome there. He had just founded, with my old friend Michel Kotzebue and myself, a new group, that of Essenes, and we were ardently laying down the foundation of a new religion.

Until then, Madame de Saint-Aygulf had endured, as a hostile and patient spectator, what she called her husband's follies. She had thought that those follies had a normal character, since they had brought Monsieur de Saint-Aygulf back to the true God, which was the family. But she saw with alarm her daughter Eveline sharing her father's reveries, falling into a mysticism incomprehensible for her.

At first she attempted to struggle against an enemy more redoubtable than Laurence's bad instincts and only found allied therein what she still called the Beast. She sought belatedly to penetrate the secrets of the Essene religion in order to be able to demonstrate its absurdity to her daughter. Reading a few books, a few conversations with me and Michel Kotzebue, struck her with a dolorous surprise by informing her about the first Essenes.

Hermits who lived on the shore of the Dead Sea! So-called saints who, in certain epochs, sent Messiahs into the world to instruct it. She retained above all the fact that they practiced communism, and she attached herself to ridiculous details in order to try to laugh at it. A patch of oil on their white robe was considered by them as an opprobrium! They only ever spit while turning to the left! Doubtless crackpots of the same kind as her husband. But they were also revolutionaries. Did the world have any need for the instruction of a Messiah? Were the established rules not sufficient?

She perceived that those primitive Essenes, those ascetics whom one might have believed forever dormant on the shore of the Dead Sea, in the stony earth of the land of Moab, had conserved through the centuries a strange power over her daughter's mind. For them alone,

Eveline had amour. Did they not offer her a veneration that was not due to her parents?

Eveline sometimes forgot herself in her mother's presence and pronounced mysterious words, such as "I'm a candidate for baptism." And when she was told that the Essenes of the time of Jesus Christ had disappeared a long time ago, she smiled, shrugged her shoulders and made it understood that they were still present, and that they might appear at any moment to those who believed in them.

It was for some time a curious characteristic of that house, and also its charm: that possibility of seeing a grave old man in an immaterial linen robe appear behind a curtain or by the movement of a door, come to deliver some sage instruction.

Madame de Saint-Aygulf was exasperated by only having Laurence to support her in her attacks. She also suffered in thinking that her invisible enemies had professed a purity far above the one she flattered herself in having. Thus, she had gone backwards. By a change of direction whose mechanism she could not grasp, she, the apostle of all the virtues, had become in her own house a coarse creature, the ally of the Beast.

She was unable to measure for long the extent of that monstrous contradiction. Hazard determined that I was a witness to the last scene of the drama, which coincided with the first of another story far more important to me: the dining room scene.

Madame Saint-Aygulf, afflicted for a long time by a malady of the heart that was treated by her husband, had had two successive crises and seemed to be at the final extremity. I had gone to obtain news of her several times, in spite of my habit of writing a letter in such circumstances in which I announced that I was leaving Paris for a while. I had thought that, in the disarray of the house, I might find an opportunity to talk more intimately with Eveline or Laurence.

It was a Friday at six o'clock in the afternoon. I had been shown in immediately. I had understood from something in the urgent attitude of the domestic, the fact that the electric light on the staircase was not lit, as usual, and the troubled quality of the already funereal atmosphere, that something serious must be happening.

Monsieur de Saint-Aygulf joined me in the drawing room. He needed to talk to someone, he said, to respire other air than that of the sick-room. I saw in his eyes that he regretted having allowed too much pleasure to show on seeing someone from outside. I understood that he was breaking his voice artificially and doing it very poorly, and I sensed his absence of real grief so strongly that I nearly told him to speak like everyone else.

"I was warned long ago by my guides; I'm going to lose my dear wife," he said.

That was not true; the malady was unexpected for him. He did not cherish his wife at all. He had always feared her, as an angel without grace, of a hearth without joy.

He was very impressed by the fact that Madame de Saint-Aygulf was considering death without terror. He professed the simplistic idea that only those who have faith are capable of not fearing death. He had even made use of the threat of the beyond to diminish the power of the flat-haired tyrant. Well, he could not get over it. In those solemn moments, Madame de Saint-Aygulf had not ceased to dismiss as culpable nonsense the theories of the immortality of the soul that he thought it his duty to formulate anew. Thus, the annihilation that he feared so much for himself did not frighten his wife. I understood that he would have preferred to see her final hours poisoned by terror. He almost allowed his disappointment to burst forth.

He begged me to stay. He went out and then came back. He made me party to his astonishment. Madame de Saint-Aygulf had, it appeared, taken Eveline's hand in hers, raised herself up slightly, issued in a changed voice the peremptory order to expel all the gardeners who had invaded her room, and wanted to force her child to labor the earth like peasants.

We only had an explanation of that order later.

A few days before, Eveline had described to her mother the life of the Essenes between their monasteries of stone and the shores of the Dead Sea. When they were not plunged in meditation, she had told her, they devoted themselves to the work of gardening, which they considered as the best exercise for elevating the mind. Madame de Saint-Aygulf had had a vision of sordid workmen carrying spades and rakes drawing her beloved daughter alongside the somber waters and bituminous cliffs in an accursed landscape.

A great physician called in consultation had just arrived. I tried to take my leave. Monsieur de Saint-Aygulf, desirous of keeping with him someone who was not wearing on his person the uniform of dolor that he had donned himself, said to me as he pushed me into the dining room: "Laurence will keep you company."

Laurence was indeed sitting there, beside a large somber sideboard, reading a book that she closed when I came in. She stood up. The ennui painted on her features disappeared on seeing me. She spoke to me without giving her voice the grave tone that everyone else in the house had. I knew what a grim and justified hatred she nurtured for Madame de Saint-Aygulf, and I was secretly grateful to her for not allowing a conventional sadness to appear.

Night had fallen completely. It was the commencement of spring, and it was warm enough for the window to be open. That window overlooked one of those little Parisian gardens surrounded by walls in which there are four trees and two flower-beds. A vegetal odor emerged from the ground that we sensed at the same time. All our words had been banal. I even thought it appropriate to attenuate by the tone anything that might have been interpreted as amiable or tender. I am sure that Laurence had no hidden agenda until the moment when we approached the window together. Then, without knowing why, I put my arm around Laurence's waist, but scarcely touching it. That gesture, strictly speaking, might have passed for a mark of the amity, slightly more affectionate than usual, that one ought to show in dolorous circumstances.

Abruptly, Laurence slid into my arms. She was against me, and I hugged her without knowing quite how it had come about, and what was personal to me in the gesture. Her lips crushed mine, melted, and I then felt materially something that was her joy, her terrible and inadmissible joy, which no one ought to know, but which took for its form of expression that kiss full of delight.

During the few months that had followed the death of Madame de Saint-Aygulf, Laurence had scarcely given the appearance of remembering the bond that that rapid embrace had created between us in the dining room, between the somber sideboard and the odorous garden. And now I was here, at the corner of the Rue Ballu and the Square Vintimille, and Laurence was perhaps embracing someone other than me with the same ardor.

It was scarcely half an hour since I had sat down and reflected when a taxi stopped some distance away. I perceived someone confusedly who descended from it. As if the arrival of the taxi were a sort of signal, a wave of discouragement passed over me. I summoned the waiter and paid for my beer. Laurence would doubtless only emerge at an advanced hour of the night. I was tired. I was sad. What was the point in waiting?

I had risen to my feet, hesitant as to what I ought to do, and in the same second, Laurence's face glided past me, framed by the window in the door of the taxi. She was alone. She did not see me. Doubtless someone had sent the taxi to fetch her. It was going extraordinarily quickly, for I was scarcely conscious of its passage and it had already turned into the Square Vintimille and disappeared.

I was discontented with myself. I thought about the lie of certain novels in which one sees heroic policemen following other individuals for entire days without ever being in default. I went back up the Rue Ballu. All the doors were silent and mute. Deep inside, a joyful voice was beginning to formulate vaguely the thought that a passionate mistress, if she comes to see her lover at midnight, stays for longer than half an hour.

My fatigue had increased abruptly, at the same time as a desperate desire not to go home. I went back in the direction of the Rue Blanche and sat down on the terrace of the Brasserie Romano with I know not what hope of diversion. At the table next to mine a woman was writing a letter on lined paper, of the format that makes one think of anonymous letters. All the men had taken off their hats, as if for a ceremony, but it was only because of the heat. A beggar was staring at me as if he knew me.

Someone touched me lightly on the shoulder with a fingertip. I do not like such unexpected contacts and I almost bounded in my chair.

I had before me Michel Kotzebue. He extended a limp hand to me, and as was his habit, instead of looking me in the face, he examined my right shoulder as if a precious object posed there were on the point of falling off.

I was motionless. I had heard mention several times that he lived in the vicinity of the Place Blanche. Was it not the Rue Ballu?

For a long time Michel Kotzebue had worn the vulgarity of his features like a mask scarcely suitable for a sensitive and religious individual. One grew accustomed to it at length. I had known him long ago in the Latin Quarter, poverty-stricken, when he arrived from Austria, his country of origin, and was preparing for examinations in theology. I had met him again fifteen years later, living in style and having become the great man of an entire milieu in which a few people even addressed him as Monseigneur. It was said that he gave himself the title of Bishop of the Essene religion. An enormous amethyst that he wore on his left hand was the evidence of it.

My presence never seemed to be agreeable to him. I thought that he did not like to rediscover a witness of a forgotten time in which he had sometimes been a joyful companion, very different from what he was today. We had addressed one another as *tu* in that era. He had asked me to say *vous*, deeming that it was more appropriate because of his title of Bishop. I had accepted, and he had been sufficiently indelicate to continue to address me as *tu*. He knew, however, how to talk very loudly and for a long time. He was reputed to be a charlatan and I had come to believe that he was one, but he had a faculty of losing himself in a certain sadness of an elevated order that enabled him to be considered as a superior man.

His face had not darkened, as usual, on seeing me and he sat down rather heavily on a chair before I had even said: "Would you like to have a drink with me?"

He ordered a liqueur, specifying that he wanted it in a wine-glass, and he murmured in a low voice, with a sideways glance that did not escape me: "Nothing is sadder than a failed evening."

Failed is a word that I cannot abide. It immediately caused me to look back on myself, over the stages of my life, on my fruitless attempts to succeed in the various arts that I had, by turns, loved passionately and abandoned. I thought that he had pronounced the word deliberately. But no, he was looking to the right and left at the people around him.

Then I asked him the only important question: "You live near here, don't you?"

He would normally have replied "Yes, in the Rue Ballu," if my fears were well-founded, or pronounced the name of a different street.

He pretended not to have heard, and said, as if it were a matter of reanimating a conversation that was almost extinct: "Is it a long time since you've seen the Saint-Aygulfs?"

I almost called to the waiter to bring me a *Tout-Paris* in order to search it ostentatiously for his address. I contented myself with saying that I had seen Laurence that day. He did not ask me whether it was in the morning or the evening. I had said Laurence by design, while watching for a movement of his eyelids. They did not flutter any more rapidly.

He ordered another wine-glass, sipped it, and I saw that he was increasingly uninterested in what I might say. He was following a private train of thought, and from time to time, with a gesture of his astonishingly white hand and well-manicured hand, which he waved in my direction, he deigned to allow me to participate in the conversation that he was having with himself.

"Conform one's life with one's ideas! Yes, one should. But it's difficult. Everyone would like the existence of another, but is too cowardly to obtain it for himself."

And he darted a glance at me that went from my hat to my shoes, as if I synthesized the host of those cowardly and exigent men.

"There are people who would be indignant if they saw me on the terrace of a café after midnight. And yet the search for wisdom does not deprive us of desire." After a pause, in a toneless voice, he added: "And the desire is sometimes all the greater the further one goes in pursuit of spirituality."

Those words appeared to me to be insupportable. Since we had been sitting face to face I had reviewed certain attitudes of Kotzebue's in Laurence's presence. The prestige with which he was surrounded authorized familiarities that would have appeared extraordinary in another I remembered that he had once held the young woman's hand in his for a rather long time, repeating: "my dear child," with an ecclesiastical unction.

And abruptly, I also remembered certain gazes, accompanied by a moistness of his thick lips, in Eveline's presence. All that had not struck me at the time because I believed, like everyone else, that Michael Kotzebue was uniquely occupied with occult research, orientated exclusively toward spiritual joys. I suddenly understood that it was nothing of the sort, and a violent indignation gripped me at the thought that he dared to pursue the two sisters with an equal desire—a desire that, as he had just declared, was greater than that of others. I might perhaps have allowed that indignation to explode if I had not suddenly thought that he was simply in the same condition as me.

Yes, but older, much older! cried the interior voice of my jealousy. In fact, how much older? Perhaps the age difference that separated us was not so great.

"How old are you?" I asked. And I prepared a phrase to tell him that the age is question ought to suffice to temper his passions.

Kotzebue did not attach any importance to that insignificant question.

"I sometimes wonder whether there are not individuals who have an innate predisposition to evil, who are touched by a reverse grace. They are filled with good intentions, they make just and elevated speeches, they aspire with all their hearts to rise, but it seems that a will that perhaps exterior to them organizes their existence for evil. And by evil I mean, naturally"—he made a gesture that seemed to sweep away all narrow conceptions of evil—"the retrograde force that diminishes the spirit. How, then, can that initial fatality be remedied? What should those predestined individuals do?"

He interrogated me with an oblique gaze, but I did not want the humiliation of a reply that would not be heard. He made a noise with his amethyst against the marble to the table and went on: "Perhaps the passions are creative. But it is necessary to know how to give oneself to them. They are like the fire that is useful and warms if one circumscribes it in the hearth. Perhaps we ought to allow ourselves to indulge our sensuality with the objective of engendering a sublime and hidden force."

He leaned toward me and he said, as if it were a confidence: "I've always thought that the physical act of amour was a magical rite of which humans had lost the secret. The man who rediscovers the ceremonial grandeur of dual pleasure, who renders it its character as a mystical mass, who makes a man and a woman lying together into priests coming closer to God would be more useful to humankind than Gutenberg or Christopher Columbus."

He touched me with a fingertip, perhaps to ask for my opinion. My thoughts were focused on the time that Laurence had spent in the Rue Ballu: scarcely half an hour. I hung on to the brevity of that visit like a shipwreck victim to a plank. Amour, especially if it is conceived as a magical rite, must demand infinitely more time.

There was a silence between us and I wondered why the great man of the Essenes was making me confidences that would have scandalized those who believed in him, if they could hear him.

I did not formulate that question. But undoubtedly, Kotzebue was only responding that night to questions that had not been asked. He started sniggering, and while looking me in the face, which he very rarely did, he said: "You're wondering why I'm telling you this? It's because there is something in common between us, because you, strictly speaking"—he shrugged his shoulders slightly, scornfully—"might be able to understand me, or at least try."

I suddenly saw what he was getting at, and I remained indifferent in order to deceive myself, but my heart beat faster.

"You remember the pact? We made a pact together. We never talk about it, but we haven't forgotten it."

I started to laugh. I put on a semblance of hilarity. "Oh yes," I said, as if I were suddenly remembering for the first time something long-forgotten. "The joke of the pact. What can have become of Lévy since that epoch?"

I didn't care about Lévy; I wanted to change the subject. It was in vain.

"It wasn't a joke," said Kotzebue. "We believed it at first. But either way, we accomplished the prescriptions, followed the rituals minutely. Lévy understood that. We did everything that was necessary to render the pact valid."

I had often thought, in the course of my life, about the evening spent with Kotzebue and that Lévy, and I had always concluded hypocritically: *A farce of the twentieth year! A happy time in the Latin Quarter when one could still find a comrade naïve enough to believe in the Devil!*

However, I knew full well that Lévy was not naïve and that the pact had exceeded the range of a farce.

I had met Lévy with Kotzebue in a little restaurant in the Rue Monge. None of us had any money, but there are degrees in poverty even when it is very great, and Lévy was the most wretched of the three of us. Short and ugly, intelligent and hostile to everyone, he spent his days in libraries. Possessed of an extraordinary erudition with regard to occultism and religious questions, he mocked my ignorance incessantly. I took my revenge to turning to derision his belief in the Devil, for he believed in the real existence of the Evil Spirit, the one that had borne the name by turns of Ahriman, Iblis and Satan. Sometimes we walked together after dinner, accompanying one another, in such a way as to avoid the expense of coffee and thus attain the reasonable hour when one can go to bed without shame.

Naturally, Lévy did not have the crude conception of the Devil such as the witch-trials of the Middle Ages represented him to us. He believed, even so, in a force opposed to good, active and conscious, susceptible of materializing and with which one could make a pact. He went so far as to claim that, in the same way that there are associations of monks coming together to pray to God and to do good, there are secret groups of egotistical men who augment their power by their union and strive ardently toward evil.

"It's logical," he added. "One cannot imagine a coin without a reverse side. Light only exists by virtue of its relationship with darkness."

That stimulated our bursts of laughter.

One day, we were talking about the ancient pacts that linked sorcerers with demons. Lévy firmly believed in them. According to him, humankind entire might have been damned with an extreme rapidity and had only been retained by the ignorance of a few details necessary to the formation of the pact and the ceremony by which it had to be surrounded. He, Lévy, knew those details of the ceremonial ritual.

Kotzebue and I protested. Why did he not emerge from poverty by making an alliance with the Devil? He replied that poverty was unimportant, but that he was thinking seriously about acquiring by means of a pact something much more precious than wealth. We immediately declared that we were ready to sell our future life in exchange for an immediate material advantage.

It was winter, I had a rather thin overcoat and I believe I said that I would gladly sign the pact in exchange for a hot toddy. Lévy was not astonished by the low price at which I evaluated my soul and said that he was delighted by our declaration. I remember that when he quit us, Kotzebue and I were astonished for a long time by a credulity greater in him than we had supposed.

A few days later he came into the restaurant where we were dining with a certain solemnity in his manner. He placed a little packet tied with string beside him and asked us whether we had the same intentions. We didn't understand immediately what he was talking about. Waitresses were running around us shouting in loud voices to invisible cooks to announce the requested half-portions. He raised his voice in order to make himself heard and hazard determined that the conversation fell silent just as he said: "It's a matter of the Devil."

Our joy—Kotzebue's and mine—was immense. We affected a gravity analogous to Lévy's and we followed him urgently after diner. It was in my lodgings that the thing took place.

Lévy made us remark that the moon was full, which was an essential condition. We lit three candles that were contained in the packet he had brought, along with a piece of charcoal, which he did not use, and the utility of which I only learned years later.

He told us that there was no need to thank him—which we were not thinking of doing—for it was for himself alone that he was acting, the power of pacts being in direct proportion to the number of those who made them.

"Three is a Luciferian figure, of which the Kabbalists are usually unaware," he added, gravely.

Kotzebue said to me then in a low voice that he was in the process of playing a trick on us. However, when we saw him unroll a large sheet of parchment, we exchanged a glance, deeming that it was not worth the expense of that parchment for a joke. He also called our attention to the fact that the name of God was written backwards in Hebrew characters on the parchment. That is always slightly impressive. I wondered why Hebrew rather than another language. He shrugged his shoulders slightly.

We almost declared that it was all a ridiculous comedy to which we would no longer lend ourselves when a slight prick was required, because the signature had to be traced in blood; but Kotzebue and I had a false shame in regard to one another. The three candles cast a sinister light and Lévy, in the middle, was prey to an emotion that the tremor of his lip betrayed. Whichever of us recoiled would have confessed by that action that he had the belief in the non-existent Devil that he had been mocking in Lévy for several days.

What the pact said we had scarcely asked. We did not know either what we had promised or what we engaged to pay, since it was only a matter of laughing. But in truth, we were no longer laughing. We signed as best we could by dipping a golden—or perhaps merely gilded—quill in a droplet of blood parsimoniously shed.

Lévy then set fire to the parchment and he blew out the three candles successively. The room was then only illuminated by the parchment, which crackled, and was consumed with difficulty; the minute during which its combustion lasted seemed very long to me.

Kotzebue touched me on the elbow and said: "Poor Lévy!" in order to try to dissimulate the sinister impression that he had, as I also had. Finally the ashes, carefully collected by Lévy in a napkin, were reduced to dust in the obscurity. He approached the window, opened it and threw them as high as he could in the direction of the moon, which was visible over the rooftops.

I uttered a sigh and finally relit the lamp, no longer having any ardent desire other than to see Lévy go away. He was significantly downcast. He fell into a chair saying that he was exhausted. He hoped that he had succeeded, he said—which is to say that he had succeeded in communicating with Lucifer—but he was not sure. He was astonished not to have obtained an immediate response, for which I secretly congratulated myself.

He explained to us at length that the pact was only a material sign to channel the force of thought. Perhaps the number three was insufficient. He regretted the great assemblies of the Middle Ages, the Sabbat and the entire crowds gathered to participate in the current of the power that animates the world. One could call him Lucifer if one wished; he had other names. The simple represented him with horns, hairy and holding a pitchfork. Everyone could give him another image, according to taste. Lucifer mighty be a bald philosopher, a young woman naked on a bed, or an officer emerging from Saint-Cyr.

He finally got up to leave. He was sad. Not as much as me, however. He looked carefully to see whether there was any fragment of ash on the floor that had escaped him. As was his habit, he wanted to say something disagreeable as he left.

"For you, Lucifer is a naked woman," he said to me, "beautiful but above all stupid. For Kotzebue he's an individual in religious costume—no matter which, provided that he has a chasuble and burns incense. Unfortunate beings both of you!"

In the following days I ceased to go to the restaurant in the Rue Monge. I only rain into Kotzebue at rare intervals. As for Lévy, I only saw him once more. He came to borrow ten francs from me. I thought privately that a pact with the Devil doesn't enrich its man. I gave them to him gladly, for I knew already that, however small a sum lent may be, it hollows out a ditch between the creditor and the debtor that no amity is able to fill in.

And now that scene, which the tide of memory had sometimes brought back to the edge of my soul, and which I had determinedly rejected, was revived in the presence of one of its actors. I associated with it for the first time the design that had once appeared on the window of a railway carriage and that I had subsequently given to the diabolical image that Monsieur de Saint-Aygulf's house had figured for me that very evening.

"I don't suppose you attach any importance to that story?" I said.

Faithful to his habit of not responding directly, he raised an excessively white and slightly plump hand and said: "How can I explain why I always wear my amethyst on my left hand? I can't do otherwise. The amethyst, in Christian symbolism, is the sign of humility, but on the right hand. Do you know what the amethyst signifies on the left hand?"

I did not know, and I thought that one could always put a ring on one's right or one's left hand, as one pleased.

Kotzebue went on: "How can I explain, also, that I tremble and enter into a kind of trance, every time I penetrate into a room where there is a host? Evidently, Lévy might have nothing to do with it. But if I told you about the Essenes..."

It was claimed that Kotzebue had received communications from invisible sages, whose last authentic representatives were reputed to live in certain Palestinian solitudes. He was normally excessively reserved on that subject. I lent an ear avidly. He stopped.

"And you—I don't ask you to admit it, but be sincere with yourself. Haven't you remarked something particular in your life since that evening with Lévy? Oh, almost nothing... First of all, no one knows what Lucifer is, exactly. Scarcely a nuance, and one is in his claws—

except that one doesn't know it; the claws are velvet. Personally, I called Lucifer egotism."

He got up abruptly after those words, throwing on to the table, to pay for the drinks, a hundred franc bill, for which he neglected to collect the change.

I wanted to make the remark that it was me who had invited him, but he was already crossing the Place Blanche with long strides and I was obliged to run after him to catch up with him.

He headed toward the café into which I had seen Laurence go. There were now very few people in it. Kotzebue remained on the threshold and inspected the tables with a circular glance. Then he walked along the boulevard a little way, looking at a few people sitting on the terraces. Then he retraced his steps, almost exactly as Laurence had done.

We found ourselves not far from the terrace of the Brasserie Romano, where we had been a few minutes before. A woman was curled up on a pile of unsold newspapers. A bartender in uniform hailed a taxi importantly. A fresh breath of wind that appeared to be coming from the Place Clichy, as a stroller might have done, brushed us in passing.

Kotzebue murmured, in a lugubrious tone: "I'm bored." Then he added: "I'm going home."

It was not to me that he addressed those syllables but to himself, as if to notify himself of his own decision. I started to walk alongside him and I murmured: "I'll go with you."

"I live close by, in the Rue Ballu," he said eventually, wearily.

I have heard it said that men wounded by a revolver shot or a shell-burst sometimes see their wound close up and heal without it having been possible to extract the bullet or piece of shrapnel. They live for many years in perfect quietude, with the illusion of health. And then, without any apparent reason, their organism enters into a strange battle with that foreign matter, which it had supported until then without complaint. It tries to reject it. The wound reopens and becomes a larger and more corrupt wound than the initial injury. Thus, after having buried the evening of the pact beneath a layer of indifference, my soul began to suffer from its existence, and to want to annihilate it.

When I woke up the day after the one when I had followed Laurence and met Kotzebue, I had the sensation that a misfortune had befallen me the previous day and that its consequences were about to modify my way of life. I sat up on my bed with the appetite for recapitulation that one often has when one awakens. It was as warm as the previous day, but it was raining. I took my head in my hands. I felt overwhelmed.

It was not because Laurence had gone by night to run around Montmartre and had spent half an hour in Kotzebue's house. Half an hour was too little. In any case, the latter's sadness, the absence of proud satisfaction and the nature of the things he had said to me set aside he hypothesis of a rendezvous in which amour had counted for anything. There was a mystery there. I would succeed in clarifying it.

My depression came from the memory resuscitated by Kotzebue.

"Lucifer!" I repeated, several times. And I summoned to my aid all my philosophical knowledge.

The Devil did not exist. He was a puerile imagination born of human terror and ignorance. So? A pact with nothing could not have a frightening character, under any pretext. Why, in that case, was a man like Kotzebue preoccupied in that fashion. His erudition in theology was very great, and if he was anxious in that subject, I could not neglect that anxiety.

I remembered having read or heard it said that even in the Middle Ages, many sorcerers did not believe in the person of the Devil in the ridiculous form ordinarily given to him. They already thought that it was only one of two currents of life, the one contrary to the orientation of the universe. They believed that certain symbolic actions could react upon us and push us henceforth in a retrograde direction. We discover so many things every day! Perhaps there is a law there that escapes us. If good, which is called God, is identical to love, Lucifer would then be hatred, and I, without any reason, by the caprice of a certain Lévy, had vowed myself to hatred.

I recapitulated the years that had gone by, and I saw a direction of hatred in all the actions of my life. Shortly after the evening of the pact, I had lost my mother and inherited her fortune. Had it not been me who had killed her by means of a demonic projection? Had not my friends and my mistresses been struck, without my intention, by sequences of ill luck, by misfortunes of which I was the cause without knowing it?

I told myself that when one makes a pact, there is an exchange. If I had renounced the growth of my perfectible soul, what had I received for that divine gift? And I believed that I saw then a kind of malign and organized protection that had extended over me over the years and had accorded me advantages that I would not otherwise have had. I argued with myself about that intervention, without being able to affirm whether it was real or not.

Money worries had abruptly disappeared. That came from my mother's death and her heritage. But had that abrupt death not had a singular character? I had not had any malady. The natural case of that was my good health. Yes, but before the pact, I had suffered from petty ailments, neuralgias, the commencement of rheumatisms, which had not developed. It would have been more logical that my health had declined, while its excellence seemed to have improved over time.

I had desired women, and Lévy had even specified that the desire in question expressed Lucifer within me most particularly. Well, there had been women who had abandoned themselves to me with a facility that I had never been able to comprehend. I found, on reflection, that my personal seduction was not sufficient to explain it. One of my friends, a professional Don Juan named Leubas, of whom I was scornful because of his donjuanesque conception of life, claimed to emit a fluid that forced all women to run after him. Certainly, I did not think I had possessed such a fluid; but it seemed to me that for a period of my existence, which began almost at the moment of the pact, women had changed their attitude in my regard.

It is true that that period had been the one in which my Latin Quarter poverty had changed into ease and an apartment near the Place Péreire had replaced my lodgings. Now, the quality of one's abode, the magnificence of apartments, has a great influence on the amours of women. On the other hand, the fact of desiring Laurence and Eveline without possessing them was also an argument. A man who, by means of a demonic pact, has acquired powers over creatures, is not obliged to go and prowl around furtively by night, launch himself into taxis, and make miserable stations at the corner of the Square Vintimille and the Rue Ballu.

And my life, the precious life of my body, how had it been so strangely protected during the war? It is true that, from the start, I had not solicited precipitate departures for the front. I had had some remorse about that. But I had said: *Let's let Destiny do its work. Let's not intervene personally. Let the mysterious laws that dictated this war retain all the responsibility for the life and death with whom I only have a poor unity.* I had confided myself to what it pleased me to call my lucky star. Had that lucky star perhaps been an evil star?

Why had I been sent to Morocco, where no antecedent colonial order had summoned me? What was the futile pretext of a license in law that the military administration had seized in order to make me a reporter to the Council of War? But on the other hand, was not that situation a glaring sign that I had been allied with the good against the evil, the defender of justice in everything that it has of the most sacred?

That thought dissipated by anxieties and I uttered a sigh of relief. Yes, for several months I had accomplished in Morocco the functions of a judge—a military judge, but in sum, a judge. If that war had taken place several centuries earlier I would have had witches burned. I remembered how I had taken my role seriously and that in a room with a niche in the wall where there was a Christ I had spoken with severity against deserters and criminals, not hesitating to make the end of my sentences resound, in order to obtain the most severe penalties, with the words justice, fatherland and God, above all God. In Morocco, therefore, I had been the representative of God, and a few old officers full of gravity united in tribunal had considered me as such. So? Could a Luciferian individual have played that role, allied with the Christ in his niche, having the true instruments of Satan condemned?

The sigh that I had uttered had not yet quit my breast when an interior voice spoke to me, and I recognized its tone of verity.

Have you not had remorse for your wretched judicial function? Do you recall the scorn you had for the members of the Council of War, for their professional faith, their incapacity to see the two sides of anything, their absence of pity? You had people condemned, but you had pity in the depths of your being. You were merely a coward. You knew what excuses those almost savage men had for not believing in a fatherland that was not their own. On which side was love and on which hatred? Do you remember the twenty-year-old Arab whose gaze was so sad that you dared not look at him in case your voice broke? Perhaps it was the Evil One, the principle of Evil that gave you that eloquence admired by the old career officers.

I leapt out of bed and I got dressed in haste. The rain had made a thousand designs, a thousand figures, on the window panes, but I drew the curtains in order not to see the strange imaginations of chance.

Ten years before, I had bought a vast library of works treating religions, their mysteries and the questions of occultism that interested me. I never touched any of those volumes, but I was reassured by their mass. I incessantly put off reading them, tell myself, by way of excuse, that intuition is superior to the study of books.

In the demi-obscurity of my room, I started searching feverishly for the authors who had dealt with pacts with the Devil. A certain Bergier had a great authority in such matters.[1] The secret of pacts was contained, according to him, in the Great Keys of Solomon. But what were those Keys? The great Larousse, to whom I referred, only spoke about "a long bone that joins the head of the humerus to the upper part of the sternum."[2] The eminent theologian Bergier, with an impressive sincerity, believed in the effect of those pacts. According to him, a wand of almond-wood cut at the precise moment of the first ray of dawn was necessary. It was also necessary to find an intersection of three roads, shed the blood of a chicken and trace a triangle with a bloodstone.[3] I could not discover what that stone was, which is not mentioned in the dictionary.

Lévy had made the pact, neglecting a part of the conditions judged indispensable by the learned Bergier. The pact was therefore not valid. On reflection, however, I estimated that Lévy might have been more knowledge-

---

[1] The reference is presumably to Nicolas-Sylvestre Bergier (1718-1790), a staunch defender of Catholic dogma against the skepticism of the *philosophes*, and co-author of an oft-reprinted dictionary of dogmatic theology. The dictionary does include credulous mention of diabolical pacts, but Bergier had no special expertise in the subject, and the employment of that dictionary and Larousse implies that the narrator's research must have been rather superficial.

[2] This wordplay does not translate. The Latin title of the notorious grimoire whose title is usually translated into English as The Great Key of Solomon is *Clavicula Salomonis Regis*, the first word being the root of the English and French words for the clavicle or collar bone.

[3] The original has "ématille stone," which is term only found in occult sources, but it is generally though to refer to the gemstone otherwise known as heliotrope or bloodstone, which is green with red spots, supposedly resembling spots of blood.

able than Bergier, who seemed to add faith to the worst stupidities. Lévy, a modern in the matter of the pact, had employed more scientific methods, and hence more efficacious.

I remained perplexed. The day passed in research of that kind. In the evening, I had the naivety to go to the Rue des Feuillantines, to the furnished hotel where Lévy once lived. It had been demolished and there was a modern building in its place.

A palace has replaced the hovel; that's logical, I thought. *It's seen all the time in tales where here's mention of the Devil.*

Yes, but the accursed fellow had not profited from that transformation. The concierge I interrogated did not know Lévy.

I dined no matter where. I went back to Montmartre and I went to sit down near the Place Blanche, in the drug-dealers' café into which I had see Laurence penetrate the previous evening.

I had only been sitting there for five minutes when I saw a heavily made-up woman come in whose skirt was too short and whose corsage allowed the birth of the shoulders to be seen. She came in swaying and looking to the right and left as Laurence had done the previous evening.

Almost immediately, I recognized that it was Irma Pascaud, or, rather, the caricature of Irma Pascaud. She perceived me; her face took on a joyful expression and she came to sit beside me. We exchanged the banal phrases that people exchange who have not seen one another for a long time and our affectionate conversation was a caricature of our former conversations.

"Well, I didn't expect to see you here," she said.

"I'm glad to see you," I repeated, for my part, coldly, as a hand was placed on my wrist and shoulder in order to pull the wool over my eyes and stimulate a familiar delight.

And around us wandered joyless waiters; a pipe-smoker's smoke made spirals; groups grimaced; mirrors reflected emptiness; and everything contributed to make me relive a caricaturish scene from the past. It is a singular law of life that, after an interval of a few years, reproduces what has been, blurring the lines, scoring the faces, deforming the images as if cinematic plates, worn away by usage, had an obligation to pass over it, in order to spoil the image.

Irma Pascaud caught my gaze and said: "It's like the old days. Do you remember? We hardly ever saw one another, except in cafés."

It is, indeed, in cafés that the joy and sadness of the amours of youth unfold. But I thought that the beer had a more delicate color then, the marble of the tables had been more delicately veined and the air reeking of tobacco had been easier to respire.

When I thought about Irma Pascaud, I said to myself: *Perhaps she's the only woman who really loved me.*

Her conquest had not been difficult and I had not attached any importance to it. I had been attracted to her because of her regularly pretty face and because of a mysterious chagrin that she had just experienced, which caused her to weep from time to time and which she never wanted to explain. Before me, Irma Pascaud had been the mistress of two or three comrades in the same Left Bank cafés, but that had not created a false situation between us. People said "How is she with you? With me, she was like this"—and we laughed about it. I had called her "the woman with no soul," and the nickname had been generally adopted.

Irma Pascaud claimed that she loved me much more than all the others and that with me "it was something else." I made a semblance of not believing her, but deep down I believed it, and I said to myself: *Well, nothing is more natural.*

I had announced to her one morning, quite simply, that we were soon going to part. She wept, but was resigned. "When?" she asked. It was decided that it would be in three days, and three days later, I declared solemnly to the café in front of a group of friends that the evening was that of our divorce.

"Who'll replace him?" people asked her. She declared, with dry eyes, that it was all the same to her and that since we were playing cards, she would go home that evening with the winner.

I was one of the five players. Hazard determined that I was the winner. A medical student named Méricant, whose head was posed on his shoulders without the intermediary of a neck and who had rectangular hands, was profoundly disappointed. On the other hand, I saw Irma's charming features suddenly light up. She thought that one final night might be susceptible of prolonging our liaison, because the hearts of men are subject to change. I turned my eyes away in order not to see that childish hope, and I was pitiless.

"I give my right to Méricant," I said.

The illumination of the visage was extinguished. Irma Pascaud went away with a coarse hand holding her arm, and I went home alone, with the sensation that I had just failed a happiness, unexpected for me and for a woman who loved me, that was perhaps the most precious thing in the world.

I don't think I had ever seen Irma Pascaud again since that epoch.

And now I was hypnotized by her puffy eyes, the extraordinary thickness her arms had on emerging from the shoulder, the weight of the once-light breasts glimpsed beneath the corsage, the maturity all the more visible because its possessor affected to be unaware of it. I thought of the number of lovers she must have had since me and Méricant, fixed an approximate figure, and felt sorry for her.

"And that great chagrin?" I said, in order to get a grip on a memory that was not dolorous for me. "It must have flown away with time, I suppose?"

She shook her head, apparently saying no.

She remained silent, and then became nervous and distracted. She gave me the impression of being irritated. She allowed it to be seen that she wanted to leave. I was vexed by that, as if I had hoped that her sentiments had not changed in my regard, in spite of the years. She stood up.

"I beg your pardon for leaving you so quickly. You understand..."

"Don't worry about it," I said, in a tone that was almost disagreeable.

"We'll see one another again, I hope," she said. "Where are you living now?"

And I saw from her inattention, when I replied to her, that she had only asked me that out of politeness.

I thought, for the same reason, that I ought to ask her the same question, I regretted it, because she hesitated, and appeared to be embarrassed to tell me that she was staying temporarily in a hotel at the top of the Rue Lepic.

I would have liked to be able to do something for her, but I dared not offer her money.

Abruptly, she made a gesture of adieu and drew away rapidly.

It was as if a veil fell and life suddenly seemed to me to be infinitely sad.

I followed her with my eyes along the boulevard, and I suddenly had the sensation that that encounter had taken its place in the chain of causes and events, and that Irma Pascaud, without my being able to know how, was about to become involved with my life again.

The human soul is so made that the leveling of days effaces the most profound anxieties. Laurence and Eveline became the two poles of my preoccupations again. A month went by. Monsieur de Saint-Aygulf departed with his daughters for the property he had bought the year before in the Midi, facing Saint-Tropez. I rented a small house not far away, surrounded by pines. Michel Kotzebue was installed in a large hotel nearby, and a few of the faithful members if the group of Essenes had joined him there. Their collective presence was to permit him to realize mystical experiments that he wanted to attempt, and of which he kept the secret.

Personally, those experiments left me indifferent. I no longer cared about anything but the two sisters. When I had tried to raise the matter of the pact with Kotzebue he had changed the subject; I had not talked to him about it again since the evening when I had witnessed his terror and that terror had been communicated to me, with all the more force because it had no apparent cause.

A marble moonlight was immobilized on the silent hills whose unfurling was visible from the terrace where we were sitting. The landscape was one of those of which one says admiringly: "One might things it were a stage-set in a theater." Monsieur de Saint-Aygulf's house was some distance from the sea, but its scintillations were visible in the distance through the tangle of branches, like specks of gold moving over the waters.

To the left, the property was only separated from the road by a few clumps of mimosas. A little further on, above it, there was a convent with high walls, with a quadrilateral of cypresses and a bizarre Arab loggia above an iron portal.

In front of us, in the garden, detached eucalyptus leaves were falling with a mysterious regularity, like silvery drops of rain. The garden was profound and compact, heavy with vegetal aromas and terrestrial essences. The paths were narrow, forming vaults, and could only be distinguished by the patches of laurier-roses bordering them.

To the right, an immense avenue of centenarian eucalypti descended toward the highway and toward the sea. Those trees were so straight and so parallel that they were reminiscent of a cortege of old men in procession. In the course of my walks with Laurence I had nicknamed them "the Essenes" in order to show the young woman my lack of respect for those sages.

Eveline was to perform an Orphic dance like one that was danced, it appears, in the celebration of the Eleusinian mysteries by a female myste. It would have been puerile to enquire how that ancient dance had been transmitted to a Levantine dance-teacher who had been working with Mademoiselle de Saint-Aygulf for two years. Kotzebue had met that dance-teacher in the course of his voyage to the Orient, and guaranteed the Orphic character of his teaching.

That evening was the first time that Eveline was to dance before an audience. There were only friends and guests present, but in spite of that, Eveline had been nervous and emotional all day. I had come in the afternoon and had talked to her for quite a long time about her dance and the conception she had of it.

That conversation had irritated me slightly. I found Eveline's tone pretentious when she talked about beauty in general and the moralizing influence that beauty ought to have. I knew that she had a perfect consciousness of her own beauty. Her mother had flattered her excessively, as much out of love as to humiliate Laurence. While we talked, Laurence was working on a slight modification to the costume that her sister would wear that evening. She had no jealousy. She gave the impression of living in another, more vulgar domain, in which one sewed and one was unaware of sacred dances, and was satisfied with that.

Among other things, Eveline said: "To be pure, absolutely pure: that's the supreme ideal. It seems to me that every morning, there's a tissue of desires and needs over me, a material robe that it's necessary to remove. And it always has to be begun again."

My gaze met that of Laurence, who smiled slightly, in a manner that seemed to say: *Fortunately, I'm only a poor impure girl...*

Eveline also said: "The movement of the body when it's in rapport with the movement of the soul can, in certain cases, communicate the exaltation of the spirit that is the end-point of purity. The priests of the ancient mysteries knew that. That's what I'm trying to render."

"Oh," I said, "no one is sure whether or not the sacred dances at Eleusis might have been, on the contrary, a vulgar representation of physical amour."

I said that in order to shock her. I wanted to make her blush. But she looked at me with her immobile and icy eyes, with sadness, as one might look at someone who is drowning, and it is impossible to save.

When she stood up thereafter, as I saw the movement of her legs beneath her summer dress, and the kind of noble lightness in her gait, I was astonished that she could, with a soul so deprived of matter, emit so much sensuality with her body.

And again I said to myself: *Which of the two?*

The Levantine dance-teacher began to clap his hands to announce to the guests dispersed in the garden that Eveline was about to dance. They emerged gradually from the shadows and came to sit down in front of the terrace. They were all crackpots animated by an ardent faith in the marvelous, and that faith, in spite of contradictory beliefs and different religions, bound them together in a credulous and always astonished fraternity.

I overheard Madame Labatut, who was saying, while simpering: "I'm sure of it. It's my spirit guide who told me so."

She had an extravagant hat and frills, and she was huffing and laughing. She was the matriarch of occultism. She was a member of all the groups and all the societies, provided that they were secret. She carried a large notebook under her arm in which she wrote down instructive remarks heard during conversations and phrases that she loved to quote, reading them out in a loud voice. The beautiful citations in her notebook alternated with addresses, for she willingly made marriages, or even simple unions. She sowed discord joyfully by spreading, under the seal of secrecy, a thousand items of gossip that she did not hesitate to attribute to her spirit guides.

Beside her there was a professor of philosophy, a graduate of the university, who repeated frequently: "A little science distances God, a lot brings him closer." There was also a pale young man, with a gold chain around his ankle, whose principal concern was to uncover it from beneath his silk sock by tugging his trousers negligently, and two young Swedish women who smiled while holding hands and whose astonishingly round heads were reminiscent of two marvelous apples suspended from a single branch.

A little further away I saw Madame Vigerie make a sign to young Charlie to come and sit beside her one the armchair into which she had just allowed her thin and quivering body to fall. She was peering ahead of her with myopic and passionate eyes. Everything interested her. She told herself that she was in search of new sensations; her secret ideal was to be a *femme fatale*. She had lovers, but only under the title of experience; amour left her hostile and unassuaged. The intoxication of ether, turning tables and the adoration of a naked adolescent in a chamber hung in violet were vaguely confused in her mind. And she dreamed about black masses, celebrations with the perfumes of incense, and all the unknown pleasures of which she had read depictions in novels.

Mademoiselle Longève, small and rotund, was placed to one side and took a few steps back if anyone came toward her. That was because she attributed to herself a fluidic power so active at certain hours that anyone approaching her might be inconvenienced by it. She was good, and did not want the projection of her fluid to cause the slightest damage.

It was the man we had nicknamed "Poor Jacques" who was the last to arrive. He was barefoot, and clad in a frayed costume devoid of a shirt. He was reputed to have given everything he possessed to the poor. Two years before he had become a Buddhist, had quit Paris and had taken up residence by the sea shore, a few kilometers away. He had built himself a wooden cabin in the midst of the pines and lived there as an anchorite; he had tamed a grass snake and a mole, from which he claimed to receive touching marks of affection. He was very young, but the naivety of his features gave him an infantile appearance. His dominant characteristic was modesty. He would have liked to have been formless in order to efface himself. Michel Kotzebue had told him that by means of magic, once could do that, but he did not believe him, and strove to walk without making any sound, drawing away if anyone looked at him for too long. He had not dared to refuse the room that Monsieur de Saint-Aygulf had offered him, but either because the judged himself unworthy of it or because the open air was indispensable to him, he went to sleep outside, near a cypress behind the convent.

I had stood up in order to join him, but I met the gaze of Laurence, who was coming out of the house after having helped her sister to get dressed. She came to sit down beside me. Eveline was already advancing to dance, amid an admiring murmur and a rustle of wicker chairs on the gravel.

She came down the three steps of the perron without seeing anyone, as if her eyes were fixed on the interior of her soul, and, stepping lightly, she reached an Oriental carpet under a centenarian fig-tree. A dragonfly, like a floating emerald, emerged from the shadow of the fig-tree and seemed to be giving a signal. An orchestra disposed behind a clump of bushes began to play. I noticed local people stopping on the road behind the park in order to watch. Their naïve or stupid faces were covered with the bewilderment that music gives simple souls.

Although still motionless, Eveline was already dancing. Beneath her transparent veils, an unsuspectable beauty was ornamented by the moon. A quiver ran through her, a delicate vibration, which was the harmonious thought by which she was possessed, and which she communicated by degrees to her body. That thought animated her form, lifted her small breasts, descended along her hips all the way to her feet, which were shod in sandals so brightly silver that they had the appearance of two fragments of supple and silent crystal.

Eveline's dance suddenly enabled me to understand the relationship between the human form and the mind. I glimpsed a dolor behind the harmony of the lines. The young woman put her hands together, raising her arms, and in that gesture there was the entire poem of the human soul avid to escape the bonds of desire, to attain another, purer world.

Her body, vibrant with the life of all the muscles that dancing provides, was visible beneath the taut silk of her veil, but neither the impetus of the hands not the undulation of the midriff, nor the perfect curve of the legs, evoked a sensual image. There was a spiritual principle in her that was reminiscent of a rising flame, some unknown offering to the heaven. The human form, at its most accomplished, had been subjugated to the aims of the spirit, and had become beauty in motion.

Sometimes, Eveline's head tilted back and I saw the moonlight flowing in her bright eyes, being absorbed and lost there, like precious water in a sapphire well. At other times she beat the air with her immaterial hands, and I felt that those almost transparent hands were not made for caresses, but for the gift of an invisible treasure that she seemed to be drawing negligently from the gilded atmosphere.

When the final note of the music resonated, the world around the young woman seemed struck with immobility. The members of the audience looked at one another in astonishment, all having the sentiment of having witnessed a spectacle of extraordinary quality. They seemed surprised to have been plunged into such an elevated reverie.

The noise of a fountain that the orchestra had prevented from being heard became perceptible again in the silence. Fresh, odorous gusts were coming from the nearby basin through the mimosas and the rosemary. Eveline was already going back into the house.

Then, not far from me, there was a frightful cry, a kind of gasp in which there was both rage and despair. The cry caused me to stand up. I had a clear sensation that it affected everyone's nerves as painfully as mine. I turned round and saw that it had been uttered by an old man.

He was thin and quite tall. He wore the kind of moustache that might have made one think that he was a former cavalry officer. I did not recognize him as one of Monsieur de Saint-Aygulf's guests. I thought that he was a stroller that hazard had brought on to the road and who had stopped when the orchestra began to play.

He was clutching his cane in his right hand, and with the left he was separating the branches of the hedge that cloistered the garden, as if he were going to launch himself forward. He was staring at Eveline, who was crossing the terrace; his face expressed anger, and also an inexplicable disgust.

But I did not have to run forward to bar his path. He appeared to change his mind and collect himself. I even surprised in his face the pinch of the lips that expresses reflection after a stupidity that one has just committed. He shrugged his shoulders in order to turn his own anger to derision, and then he strode away in the direction of the sea.

"Who cried out? What's happened?" people were asking to the right and left; but the thin old man's movement had been so rapid that I thought at first that I was the only one who had seen it. Then I perceived that Kotzebue had also witnessed the scene.

I was about to ask him what his opinion on that subject was when I observed that he was not in his normal state. I thought at first that he was prey to a kind of exaltation caused by Eveline's dance, but far from it: he was afraid, a panic fear that had almost made him flee.

I approached him and questioned him. "Did you see that bizarre individual? Do you know him?"

At first, he did not reply. He was gazing in the direction in which the man had disappeared. He seemed fearful that he might come back; his terror was so great that it communicated a sort of overexcitement, of painful anxiety, to me.

I persisted, wanting to know who the old man was. Then Kotzebue took a few steps with me in the garden— but he turned round frequently, looking in every direction, and I could not help doing the same myself.

The moon was now low on the horizon. It had changed color as it traversed the sky, becoming increasingly brighter, as if it wanted to dissolve in the calm blue of the night. Its rays, which came obliquely through the trees, had something supernatural about them.

"I don't know him," Kotzebue said, finally, "but I know who he is. He once tried to enter into communication with me. He's a very learned man. He lives in the big house that one can see on the right, behind a row of cypresses, when one goes in the direction of Saint-Pons."

He attempted to talk about something else. He had recovered from his terror, but I was too disappointed not to interrogate him again.

"To what can you attribute that cry and that sudden anger?"

Kotzebue reflected. He gave the impression of deciding to speak.

"I don't know, exactly. He was probably passing by chance. There are certain natures that are impressed by ugliness to the point of suffering. In the same way, there are people who cannot bear the sight of beauty. It has happened to me, before certain spectacles, to hesitate between knowing whether I ought to hate and destroy or fall to my knees and admire. There are men who have deliberately chosen one path. Don't you remember something Lévy said, once? Lévy had already understood it, but I didn't believe it then."

I had started at the name of Lévy. I asked what remark he meant.

"Lévy claimed that there are around us, without our suspecting it, great invisible combats between good and evil forces. Certain men turn their will toward good, but others, with the same ardor, develop in a different direction. Study and wisdom can lead equally to one solution or the other. There will thus be evil conspiracies, men associated in order consciously to do evil. Lévy often repeated that to me, and I have perceived that he saw many things clearly."

We were heading back toward the house. Kotzebue quit me. A few people were shaking Monsieur de Saint-Aygulf's hand. Automobiles were slowly descending between the two rows of eucalypti.

I left on foot. The little house that I had rented was less than ten minutes' walk in the direction of Saint-Pons. I kept to the middle of the road and looked attentively to the right and the left at the borders of cacti, vines and pines, motionless in the increasingly oblique moonlight.

Someone was ahead of me, and turned right. I took a few more rapid steps in order to see who it was. I uttered a sigh of relief on recognizing the silhouette of Poor Jacques. He was going back to a tree in open country propitious to his innocent slumber. Even alone and in the shadow his march was timid. He pushed aside the branches delicately, as if he were afraid of brutalizing them.

And I was astonished, if there really were the combats between forces of which Lévy had spoken, that good was not always vanquished and had not disappeared from the world a long time ago.

I have often wondered whether it was at that exact moment that the transformation that took place among the members of the Essene group began.

I have always had a tendency to attribute natural events to occult causes, and that tendency has only become more pronounced. I dare not affirm, therefore, that Monsieur Althon, the man with the physique of a former cavalry officer, had anything to do with what followed. I cannot say so in a certain fashion. If I question myself frankly, I respond that I don't believe it—and yet, a voice in the utmost depths of my beings affirms that he was the cause of everything.

This was the precursory sign.

On the hill that overlooks the bay of Saint-Tropez, among the pines and the vines, there was a convent, which was a convent for repentant prostitutes. A benefactress had once endowed it in order that the most miserable of women could be gathered there. They lived there without ever going out, submissive, it was said, to a rigorous discipline that made the convent resemble a prison. The edifice was an ancient building, never replastered, cracked by the sun and labored by time, like the faded inmates that it sheltered.

Every morning a maidservant of the nuns emerged from the convent and went down a steep path as far as the road, in order to wait there for the grocer's automobile and to receive provisions therefrom. In order to do that she went past my door. It was always the same servant, a creature of indeterminate age known in the neighborhood as "Marie with the long neck," who was by turns a doorkeeper, maid-of-all-work and a gardener, and seemed to be somewhat fallen into senility.

From my garden I saw her pass by almost every day. She interested me because of her abnormally long neck, and her mask of plaster dappled with red streaks, which she had conserved from her former profession as a whore. Although devoid of make-up and having become a peasant woman again, she bore the stigmata of the past, but they were covered by the purity that idiocy gives to certain faces.

That morning, as usual, she began to laugh in the distance a soon as she saw me, but when she came closer she stopped, and gazed respectfully at my forehead and the space surrounding my head, as if I had an aureole. Then she bent her knees, sketched the gesture of prostrating herself before me, and departed at a run. I stood there, uncertain as to whether I ought to be proud, ashamed, or not attach any importance to the action of a madwoman. But is there any action on earth, any image glimpsed, any sign, no matter how small, that is not a revelation, by virtue of unknown correspondences, of things to come?

I remained obsessed by the wan face and the flexion of the knees of Marie with the long neck, and it was almost mechanically that, in the course of the afternoon, I put *Uncle Tom's Cabin* under my arm and went to Monsieur de Saint-Aygulf's house.

Laurence hardly ever read. It was necessary, for her to pick up a book, that she was racked by ennui. The day before she had made the remark that all those who find reading redoubtable make: "I have nothing to read at the moment."

I had just discovered Mrs. Beecher Stowe's novel in a cupboard. I had said to myself: "That's exactly the kind of literature that would suit Laurence. There was a little intellectual scorn on my part in that opinion.

When I gave the book to Laurence I said: "Here's a novel that impassioned our grandmothers and has impassioned me." I was lying, for I had never managed to read it all the way through. I did not know the extent to which it was going to interest Laurence, and to have a great influence on her.

Perhaps, in the events that followed, there was no magic, Lucifer played no role therein, and only *Uncle Tom's Cabin* acted upon Laurence's mind. There would then only be a responsibility for the tenant prior to me who had forgotten the book at the back of a cupboard. Perhaps a superior will veiled the tenant's memory at the moment of his departure in order that the book that had a role to play would be left behind and could produce the events whose succession will soon be seen. Perhaps it is necessary to take the responsibility all the way back to Mrs. Beecher Stowe herself. But who will ever explain the mystery of causes and events?

All the Essenes had gathered, at the instigation of Kotzebue, and they were ready to follow him into the terrain covered with pines and vines situated behind the house. They formed a vague cortege under his direction and that of Monsieur de Saint-Aygulf.

This was the reason for it:

Two years before, on the advice of Kotzebue and by his intermediation, Monsieur de Saint-Aygulf had bought all the land situated at the extremity of the Bay of Saint-Tropez. I have not ascertained whether Kotzebue, in pushing him to make that purchase, had an objective of a marvelous character in view or whether he wanted to collect a large commission. Perhaps he was both sincere and interested.

In the course of his voyage to the Orient, he recounted, he had searched in Palestine and Syria for traces of the ancient Essenes. In order to do that he had stayed in various monasteries, notably that of Baruth, built on the remains of an ancient maritime fortress of the Templars. There he had rummaged in a library buried under dust and neglected by the ignorant monks. He had discovered forgotten manuscripts and obtained knowledge of lost secrets.

Simon Magus, the ancient grandmaster of the Gnostics, had been an Essene. He had spent several years in the monastery of Baruth, on his return from his voyage along the Mediterranean coast, which had taken him as far as Spain and Morocco. The goal of that sage had been to purify the barbaric people of the Occident, to spread among them the true divine wisdom. He employed for that a method of his own, which was also practiced by Apollonius of Tyana. He magnetized objects powerfully, made talismans of them impregnated with a great spiritual force, and buried them in certain places chosen by him. Those talismans could act across the centuries. They ought to remind future humans of their true destiny. When evil forces were on the point of triumphing, when the love of matter covered the earth, they would be the reserve of spirit, and the task was incumbent upon the Essenes of finding them and utilizing them for good.

The Essenes had been dispersed for centuries, and their tradition had been lost, as well as the secrets of Simon Magus, but Kotzebue had been able to reconstitute their sacred group; it had been given to him, in the library of Baruth, to follow the bearer of talismans step by step in his voyage around the Mediterranean.

A tempest had thrown Simon on to one of the Lérin islands facing Cannes. From there he had regained the mainland and had marched along the seas shore on the

Roman road hollowed out in the mountain-sides that is now the Corniche. He had stopped in the villa of a rich patrician named Lavinius, who had been the procurator of Judea and was a former initiate into the mysteries. In those days the Côte d'Azur had been full of flourishing villas and everything seemed to promise that it would eventually become one of the centers of Mediterranean civilization. It was in the earth of Lavinius' garden, the earth that conserves the force of magnetized objects, that Simon Magus hid one of his talismans, in order to fecundate the future.

Kotzebue had been able to determine the location of Lavinius' gardens by means of searching the archives of the Mairie of Fréjus. They were facing Saint-Tropez, and Monsieur de' Saint-Aygulf had bought, on his indications, the domain that extended along the slopes of Les Maures and was prolonged by vast pine forests.

Searches had thus far been vain, but now the Essenes were united. Several among them had gifts of clairvoyance and it was the beginning of September, when, by virtue of an unknown astrological law, that gift arrived at its apogee. Kotzebue was counting on the unusual intuition of a sensitive, by means of the passage of a subtle current, for the discovery of the talisman. His conviction was so certain that he was carrying a spade over his shoulder, in order to begin digging without losing a moment in the place that would be indicated to him. A chant of his composition, a kind of litany that concluded with the cry "Alleluia!" would dispose the Essenes toward clairvoyance.

They set forth cheerfully. An indisputable faith animated them, and before the gravity of visages, the profundity of gazes and the palpitation of hands extended toward the earth in order to collect the spiritual essences susceptible of being disengaged therefrom. I was ashamed to be dominated by the sentiment of ridicule and the cavils of my reason.

Exactly what was known about Simon Magus? Renan said that he was a thaumaturge who had elaborated a Samaritan counterfeit of the work of Jesus Christ. A professor at the University of Strasbourg denied his existence in an absolute fashion. It required a complete faith in Kotzebue, and belief in the monastery of Baruth and its mysterious library, to think that after two thousand years a talisman charged with sublime powers was buried in that sunlit ground.

And what about the pact? I was revived in my memory in a gripping fashion. Could the man who was to render to the world the doctrine of the perfect Essenes possibly have signed a Luciferian pact in his blood, even without attaching any importance to it?

I considered Eveline's face. It was radiant with the purity of which she made her ideal. She was walking with her eyes lowered, and her delight in participating in such a research was so great that she did not give the impression of placing her feet on the ground on which she trod. Was it the effect of the malediction that I had assumed, was it because of a demonic force multiplied by my curiosity, that I measured while walking the distance between her knee and the curve of her hip, and posed myself the problem of the dimension of her breasts, while imagining Eveline naked?

I attempted to evade that thought, but on the contrary, I only made the obsession more precise, to the extent that I would not have seen her more naked, simpler and more perfectly human if she had been walking beside me without the vain adornment of her dress.

The search had lasted for a long time; we were now descending the sunken road along the road that served as the border of the convent. The sun was about to set.

"Alleluia!" sang the Essenes, in voices that fatigue was beginning to weaken.

Eveline looked in my direction, as if she had sensed my thoughts weighing upon her.

And suddenly, a clamor rose up behind the wall of the convent.

"Alleluia!" howled voice with a hoarse accent of fury and folly.

I turned in the direction from which the sound was coming, and I saw once again the head, the same head that an imagination of reverie had lent for an instant to Eveline, but it was now haggard, hateful and, at the extremity of its mobile neck, it was moving along the wall of the convent. Marie with the long neck must have been running through the convent garden, shouting as she ran, and her head gave the impression of not belonging to anybody. The terrifying, extra-human *alleluia* that she was clamoring, expressed by means of the strangeness of its syllables a horrible dementia, and it was followed by imprecations, and obscene words with precise meanings.

The Essenes stopped, suddenly filled with fear. Under the impact of the words, Eveline was like a statue.

Other voices responded in the convent. Appeals were heard, and scandalized exclamations mingled with hysterical howls. First, a very white hand appeared above the wall; then everyone realized that a person of small stature was climbing on to something with difficulty, in order to appear and express herself decently.

From the frizzed and desolate face of a rotund nun these words fell slowly: "My God, I beg you, please excuse her. It's a crisis. She's subject to crises. It's necessary to forgive her. She's an excellent person apart from her crises."

The apparition vanished; there was no longer anything but the sound of doors closing on someone who was struggling, and words of an incomprehensible vulgarity dying away in the distance, in the silence of courtyards, between the whiteness of edifices.

I went down the path with long strides. I was almost running. Thus, the same chant that elevated the spirit on one side of the wall lowered it on the other. What vocal inflexions, in which Eveline's voice was mingled, in reaching that miserable creature, had caused to rise up again in the obscurity of her soul a dormant bed of ugliness and ordure? And her genuflection that morning! The sign that she had distinguished on my forehead! Had she not saluted in me a sort of priest of lubricity, a kind of demonic saint?

Did Eveline and Laurence love me in the secrecy of their hearts? Did I play any role in their veritable life, the one that unrolls beyond the senses, which the facial features do not express, and which is the sole life of the human being? How would I ever know? The possession of the body signifies nothing, for a woman can abandon herself with savage cries of pleasure and hysterical laughter and yet reserve the gift of herself. The scorn that she affects has no more significance. So stupid is the instruction that is given to young women regarding their so-called duties that they sometimes lower their eyes modestly, and draw away like offended priestesses, when they have a desire to fall into arms and receive caresses.

Nothing of what happened is a proof in one direction or the other. I do not know whether I was loved by Eveline or by Laurence. I do not know whether I am rich or poor. For what one is able to receive of amour along one's route is, in sum, the only wealth that one preserves when one arrives at the place where the road turns.

I got up that morning feeling so well, however, with ideas so clear, my blood circulating so harmoniously, that I had the sentiment of being loved not only by the two sisters, but also by all the women I knew, and perhaps also by those I did not know, and whom a secret intuition was to push toward me.

Nothing is more agreeable than such a perception of the amour that is floating around you. The opinion I had of myself was greatly fortified by it; all of life appeared to me to be singularly beautiful. I was born under a good star. Everything was smiling upon me. I ought not to occupy myself with nonsensical ideas, and take advantage of what life offered me with its untiring generosity.

The sky was milder than usual. There was a light wind that was stirring the pines; I went down toward the sea at a rapid pace.

The first silhouette that struck my eyes was that of Laurence. I perceived her from behind in conversation with Kotzebue, along the shingle. They both seemed to be arguing with vivacity; I thought I saw Kotzebue show Laurence a letter. The morning was not far advanced; it was probable that Kotzebue had already quit his hotel and crossed the few hundred meters that separated it from that part of the beach, that he had a rendezvous with Laurence. But my benevolence for all things was so great that I reassured myself on that subject by persuading myself that only an insignificant motive had provoked that rendezvous.

As events generally harmonize with fortune states of the soul, I saw Kotzebue quit Laurence, and noticed in him the lassitude that one experiences in quitting someone to whose ill-humor one has been subjected. He went up toward the road and drew away. I found myself face to face with Laurence on the narrow strip of sand that serves as a beach on that part of the coast.

Laurence had just finished *Uncle Tom's Cabin*, and it was only possible for her to talk about that. Reading it had uplifted her. But she looked at it from a strange point of view. It was her own history that she had read in the history of the negroes of America. She established an unusual relationship between certain classes of women and slaves.

"Would you believe," she said to me in an aggressive fashion, "that here in France, money or social position creates barriers among us as insurmountable as those which exist over there between blacks and whites?"

"Indeed," said, complaisantly, in order to avoid any argument. And I put my arm gently around her waist.

"One doesn't receive lashes of the whip, one isn't chained up two by two, but the greatest tortures are not caused by blows. When I was a child, there was no greater joy for me than drawing no matter what, with a pencil and pieces of paper, and anything I found."

I made a movement of surprise, which I manifested by a slight pressure on her arm.

"Oh," Laurence went on, "Don't think that I'm claiming ever to have had the slightest shadow of any talent. I'm not even sure of having possessed the dispositions for drawing that one observes in so many children, and which disappear as they grow older. But in sum, I see as the happiest days of my life those when I could, in all liberty, invent landscapes, people, or even completely incomprehensible scenes, and reproduce them as I liked. I didn't eat every day. I was sitting on the floor in a room in a furnished hotel, in which the bed wasn't made until the end of the day, because my mother got up late, and there was a great happiness that came to me from the disorder and uncertainty of life."

We had quit the edge of the sea and were nimbly going up a little path on the hillside. In the harmony that I found in the world, Laurence's confidences had their place; they had been made neither too early nor too late, but exactly at the right time.

"My mother once made me a gift of a box of paints—a very modest box, but in which there were several brushes. Nothing thereafter ever gave me a conception of luxury and abundance as high as the number of those brushes. I daubed without stopping for several days. I had begun a large picture on a large piece of Ingres paper that had been given to me in surplus. I had painted a large face with a white beard, with big red eyes, which gave me an impression of infinite sadness and which frightened me, its creator. It was a portrait of God. When I think about it, that image represented God as well as the pedantic speeches I heard on his subject."

I was about to say something general about God, but Laurence slipped on some pine needles. I felt her arm hand cling on to my wrist to prevent herself from falling. At the same time, she started laughing, showing her teeth, and I respired her breath. It was impossible for me to say anything about God.

"I don't know why I loved that portrait. I had kept it. When, to my misfortune"—Laurence emphasized the word *misfortune*—"it was decided that I was to live with my father, in making an inventory of my wretched effects, Madame de Saint-Aygulf found it and tore it up, in spite of my pleas. Yes, she destroyed, while smiling, the conception that I had of God. That was my first great chagrin, but many others were reserved for me.

"I'm getting to the comparison I made just now. Slaves are no more unfortunate than I was. Among us, too, fiancés are separated from fiancées, mothers from children, and the masters are as pitiless. I believe, in any case, that no greater hatred exists than that of the strong for the weak, especially when the strong believe that they represent justice, good and virtue. Madame de Saint-Aygulf had understood immediately that the little girl who had been separated from the only person who loved her had no other consolation than drawing.

"I did, in fact, draw faces to which I tried to give the resemblance of my mother, No one, evidently, could know that, because evidently, as portraits, they weren't very accurate. I suspect, however, that that Madame de Saint-Aygulf had divined it. She could simply have prevented me from drawing, but no. She let me sketch my designs, making a semblance of to seeing me or having a sudden tolerance. And when I had finished some image, a formless figure in which my imagination recognized the adored features, then only did she take it off me and rent my heart by saying: 'That child is incorrigible!' or 'That's what comes of having a bad example before one's eyes for years!' A bad example! When I remember the hotel, sticky with damp, the putrid staircase, the numbered rooms like prisoners' cells, the shady men without collars, the girls with their trailing clogs, and I compare all that with what my subsequent life was, with rich parents who didn't love me, I find in the bad example a heart-rending beauty about which I can't think without weeping."

We had descended a little valley and climbed up another slope, and we had arrived at a house abandoned after a fire that had consumed several pine woods a few years previously, Nothing remained but the skeleton of the house and a few trees spared by the whim of the fire, From the place where we were, we could see clumps of cork-oaks around us, a cypress posted on a hilltop, and vines hanging on to the stones. In the distance, the sea made a blue circle. The September light was soft and gilded.

I told Laurence that she was loved more than she thought, firstly by her parents, and perhaps other people. I emphasized the last words.

But she shrugged her shoulders. She knew, she told me, what was what on that subject. Behind the honorable décor of the family, unsuspected hatreds hid, and also indifferences even more redoubtable. Madame de Saint-

Aygulf, until the eve of her death, had applied herself to making her suffer. Doubtless she had understood that the sole happiness of a child without a mother, which was susceptible of raising her in her own eyes, was the possibility of expressing herself by drawing a caricature of the ideal. Madame de Saint-Aygulf had never weakened once; she had always forbidden her to draw what she called monstrosities, the product of an immoral imagination. Laurence thought that if she were not dead now, she would have hurled herself upon her before leaving, she would have bitten her, she would have raised up her flat hair with blows of her fist.

"You said 'before leaving,'" I said. "What do you mean by that?"

We were sitting on the stone bench of the house and I was measuring with an interior satisfaction how confidences bring people closer together, even without them being aware of it, especially if the voice that is making them is speaking in limpid air before a beautiful landscape.

"Do you believe, by chance," said Laurence, "that I can stay any longer under the icy guardianship of my father? Look, there's a tale told to children about a little swan gone astray among ducks and brought up with their vulgar mores. I've often thought that one might write about me a tale of a vile duck raised among swans. It would depict the duck as sad because of its excessively garish plumage, excessively clear pools of water alongside excessively flowery parks. And one day, it would open its heavy wings in order to rediscover the natal marsh where good and ugly ducks live, where the mud is warm."

I protested against such a comparison, but Laurence shook her head. She was looking straight ahead.

The time has come, I said to myself, internally.

"Eveline despises me, and it's really not her fault. She's always heard it said that her beauty is so great, that she has an ideal so perfect, that she is so perfect in every respect. And of all that is familiar to her intelligence, I understand so little! As for my father, perhaps he'd experience a certain satisfaction of seeing me married, to no matter whom. The essential thing would be to be rid of me. But in the course of so many scenes he's told me so often that I would turn out badly, that deep down, he wouldn't be sorry to see his predictions realized. I represent 'the errors of his youth,' which have unfortunately grown up, just as Eveline represents the best of him. He has such a desire to efface all trace of sin from his existence, that merely to give him satisfaction, I've often been tempted go off with the first man to come along."

I had drawn nearer to Laurence; she was speaking beside my face. She knew, like all women, even those who have less experience, what minute the man who is next to her will choose to take her in his arms. She did not draw away from me. The words "the first man to come along" were still on her lips when I kissed her, and the savor of the kiss was spoiled by them. Those words remained between us. It seemed to me that it would be the first man who came along, who would deceive her, later, with the words that are always the same and draw their power, I believe, from their banality.

And my deceit was double. I was also deceiving myself. For my bitterness in being the first to come along was simulated. I knew that ulterior remorse would give way to a serene tranquility because of those words. I knew that I would say to myself later, in weighing the pros and cons with some confidant:

"If it hadn't been me it would have been someone else. She told me so herself."

When we quit the abandoned house and I darted a last glance at the charred walls, I found that it gave an impression of sadness greater than half an hour before. In spite of the plans made, the promises exchanged, I had the sentiment of an incomplete victory.

I look around to see whether there might be any sign, a face traced on a tree or in the sky, which would have given all that a Luciferian significance—but no; nature, which is full of speech and images when one asks nothing of her, is determinedly mute when one interrogates her.

I have difficulty analyzing what happened within me during that epoch. The memory of the evening spent with Lévy and the pact concluded had given me thereafter a sort of anxiety. That anxiety was replaced by delight. That was not clear within me. I dared not admit it to myself. I said to myself:

The month of September has a singularly favorable influence in the Midi. I've never had such a plenitude of the body and mind. I've read, I don't know where, that the vegetal effluvia that emerge from the trees accord by sympathy with the people who respire them, and augment their vitality. I'm benefiting from the force distributed by the pines and the eucalyptus, and my soul is growing because of their subtle virtue.

But I gradually sensed that my satisfaction with life had another cause. A protection extended over me. It was sufficient for me to formulate wishes for them to be realized. When I looked at myself in a mirror, I found myself abnormally young. It seemed to me that certain wrinkles to either side of the mouth that had afflicted me by their depth a few months earlier had now almost disappeared. It was true that my hair was graying at the temples, but how abundant it still was! How forcefully it emerged from my head! I was not far from believing that it was multiplying under the action of a new sap. In any case, there was a youth in my soul, perhaps more joyful than that of the twentieth year.

And after all, what if the pact had some reality? I had until now only considered it in its most puerile aspect. When one has been raised in the Catholic religion, the idea of the Devil, the spirit of evil, is inseparable from pitchforks, horns and eternal flames, but those are images for the use of old women and little children. It was possible that I had concluded a pact with an unknown force capable of giving me during my life whatever it pleased me to request. What I had to bring it in exchange remained vague. Was it my soul? I wasn't sure of the immortality of the soul. Wisdom commanded me not to think about the part that I brought to the bargain. It instructed me to profit from the favorable turn that events had taken in my regard. To profit from it, it was necessary to desire, to possess, to enjoy. Yes, that must be the secret. It was necessary to desire as much as possible. The more I desired, the more would be given to me.

I recalled that in my research on pacts I had learned what had happened to a certain Abbé Duncanius.[4] He had encountered a nondescript little lame man in a sunken road and in exchange for his soul—or, rather, the promise of his soul—he had received a book, a simple book, in mediocre binding, the ancient narrator specified. That book was a treatise on architecture. Now, Abbé Duncanius, who was old, had nourished since his youth the dream of building. He had been prevented from doing so by his ignorance. Thanks to the book, he edified convents churches and abbeys. His entire country was covered with them, and became an expanse of architectures of every sort. And in the middle of them was a tower so high that the Devil was unable to go to seek him there. In any case, those stories of pacts always finished like that. The man who had sold himself did not

---

[4] Jacques Collin de Plancy, in whose *Dictionnaire infernal* Magre probably found the legend of Duncanius of Liebenthal, attributes its coinage to the German writers Heinrich Zschokke (1771-1848), presumably following an earlier attribution in the *Musée des Familles* in 1833.

keep his word, and found a ruse to cheat the Devil. It was necessary to comprehend the tower of Abbé Duncanius in a symbolic fashion. I too, by a sublime leap of my thought, would succeed in launching myself so high toward the heavens that the angel of evil would not be able to do anything against me. But before then, I would have built innumerable monuments to pleasure and I would have lived in them.

I was soon at the point of saying to myself: *I'm protected by Lucifer*, and congratulating myself on that protection.

I knew that Kotzebue drank, but I had never seen him drink as much as on that day. I also knew that he didn't like me, but I never saw his hostility in my regard burst forth so liberally.

I had met him at about six o'clock on the road not far from his hotel; his face had expressed by a grimace that encountering me did not give him pleasure. Then he had changed his mind and he said to me familiarly:

"Come and have a cocktail at the hotel bar."

I had followed him. At first he talked to me with gravity about Essenes, the importance of the group, Simon Magus and the mission of which he believed himself to be the heir. I understood that that was only the prelude to other matters. He asked me whether I knew the story of Helen and Simon. I knew it and told him that many people attributed a mythical character to it. Helen would have been a representation of the moon and Simon Magus would have symbolized the sun.

He burst out laughing with an excessively exaggerated scorn, in order not to hide his evident intention to vex me, and he ordered a second cocktail for himself and for me.

Helen had really existed. The woman whom Simon Magus called "the divine thought of God" had been found by him in a brothel in Tyre.[5] She was incomparably beautiful and offered herself innocently to the mariners of the port. In order for the divine thought to penetrate into the hearts of man, it was necessary that it be symbolized by a woman, and that the woman in question deliver herself to them. Simon Magus had understood that. In the course of sacred agapes he sometimes offered his disciples the body of Helen for an amorous communion that elevated the spirit. He, Kotzebue, who had taken up the tradition of Simon, had to do the same. He had to find Helen. He was no longer occupied with anything but that.

Then he changed the subject. He started talking to me about Monsieur Althon, the man with the white moustache who had uttered the strange cry of anger on seeing Eveline dance. He told me that he had renewed acquaintance with him. He was an eminent individual. He possessed one of the finest libraries he knew. Essene thought was familiar to him and he was of the same opinion on the subject of Helen.

I asked Kotzebue whether he could explain Monsieur Althon's strange attitude the other evening.

"I can't explain it," said Kotzevue, embarrassed. "An unimportant eccentricity. A superior mind like that

---

[5] The notion that Helen, the consort of Simon Magus, was a prostitute from Tyre, following a long series of previous incarnations of the original female principle, Ennoia, which had included Helen of Troy, appears to have been originated by the Christian apologist Irenaeus in his refutation of Gnosticism, written circa 180 A.D. Magre elaborates the myth somewhat to suit his own text.

of Monsieur Althon has an idea of purity much higher than that one might acquire in watching Eveline dance."

It was only after the third cocktail that Kotzebue finally arrived at the subject about which he was burning to talk to me. He did so with an appearance of pleasantry both coarse and amicable. There was a silence between us.

"Take care. You're poaching on my preserves. Oh, don't play the innocent. I saw you the other morning, and again yesterday. But I prefer to warn you. The place is taken."

My heart began to beat faster; I sensed my eyes widening involuntarily, but I replied that I had no idea what he meant.

He tapped me on the shoulder, crying: "Joker!" and laughed noisily. "Why not be frank. Anyway, I have priority. Do you remember when I met you at about midnight about two months ago, in a café in the Place Blanche?"

"So what?"

He hesitated. His mouth was thick, and he expressed himself with a kind of rage.

"She and I had dined together. She had been able to escape and I was to spend the night with her. You understand? There's no need for me to tell you any more."

Every time in my life that I have heard an utterly blatant lie, an absolutely unworthy assertion, I have remained mute with astonishment. I have been deprived by nature of the rapidity of reaction, the gift of the riposte. A veil suddenly covers me and I remain silent, in an attitude that might bear the name of cowardice. It is only afterwards, when it is too late, that brilliant and vengeful comments arrive, and I see the fashion in which I should he reacted.

I trembled. I could only articulate, in a low voice: "That's not true! You're a liar!"

Kotzebue's face expressed amazement. He looked to the right and the left in order to see whether anyone had heard such disrespectful words addressed to such an important man. The bar was empty but the barman, behind his counter, had momentarily stooped the back-and-forth movement of his arms agitating the cocktail-shaker.

We looked at one another in silence.

"It's characteristic of the man who is possessed by evil not to be able to tolerate the truth." Then he changed his mind. "In any case, I haven't pronounced any name. You don't even know who I was talking about. You'd be very embarrassed to say."

I wondered whether I ought to allow that hypocrisy to triumph or to protest and confound him. But at that moment I had a sensation of cold, as if at the passage of a breath of air, which could not have come from the open door but from the ambience itself. My back was turned to the corridor of the hotel that opened on to the bar, and at the same moment I heard footsteps behind me. There was nothing extraordinary about that. Doubtless the scene that had just taken place had overexcited my nerves. I evaluated anxiously the resonance of the approaching footsteps.

The barman had come forward, bearing new cocktails. He smiled in a special fashion to make it understood that he considered the words he had overheard as a joke.

Monsieur Althon was before me. Kotzebue introduced us and invited him to sit down with a hint of respect. I was surprised to hear on Monsieur Althon's part a slight foreign accent, perhaps Russian, which clashed singularly with his entirely French appearance of a former colonel. I saw immediately that for him, I was an utterly insignificant person.

Kotzebue, however, lavished eulogies on my account. I was one of those, he said, before whom one could expose the Essene doctrine in all its purity with chances of being understood. He seemed to have completely forgotten the incident that had occurred a few minutes before.

Monsieur Althon continued to gaze at me as at someone to whom a doctrine in all its purity is absolutely prohibited. His scorn was so undisguised and I was so beside myself that I deliberated as to whether I ought to ask him for an explanation or slap him. I did nothing.

Monsieur Althon was very calm. He had ordered a Vichy water. He watched us drink.

I learned from the conversation that he too was informed regarding the voyages of Simon Magus along that part of the coast. Like Kotzebue, he believed in the virtue of rites and ceremonies. He was a partisan of restoring the magical agapes instituted by Simon. Those who, know, he said, might derive an immense advantage from them, augment their being in an indefinite fashion. So much the worse if it were at the expense of others, for the essential thing is to magnify one's own personality." He added: "I mean to divinize it."

While speaking, he always gave the impression of knowing more than he allowed to appear.

As if he suddenly thought about a previous conversation, and was awaiting a response, he exclaimed: "Well, have you finally found Helen? The Divine Ennoia?"

But then Kotzebue got up abruptly, pretending not to have heard.

"Would you like to get some air?" he said.

As Monsieur Althon was about to repeat his question he made a sign to him to keep quiet, with a movement of the head in my direction.

Outside, it was very mild. Night was falling. The hills covered with pines were already in shadow, while the sea, receiving the setting sun like a host, was still illuminated. The little town of Saint-Tropez, on the other side of the bay, had never seemed to me so mysteriously white. It gave me the impression of a city of Ys that was Arabic, a port where some ancient ship might enter by virtue of some Oriental enchantment.

The pure air brought me, with the memory of the evening when I had followed Laurence, the certainty of Kotzebue's lie. I breathed in deeply.

My two companions marched close by, exchanging a few words in low voices. They had an understanding. They were united by a recent sympathy. At one moment, Monsieur Althon even took Kotzebue familiarly by the arm.

I felt a need for immediate amity. I almost asked them to consider me as one of their own, to allow me to participate in their projects. I was on the point of assuring them that I really was capable of penetrating the pure doctrine.

There was a little path to the right that led to Monsieur Althon's house. We stopped and he held out his hand to me, saying *au revoir* with a ceremonious courtesy. He added that he was putting his library at my disposal, He had some curious books. Doubtless I must have a lack of books in the Midi.

He did not smile on saying that to me, but I sensed an unexpressed smile under the mask of the face, and that he was thinking that a stupid individual of my species had not the slightest need of books.

And he drew away with Kotzebue.

The road was straight ahead of me. A man who was passing by with a long staff over his shoulder lit the only gas lamp in the region. The house, whose windows were illuminated, formed a confused mass through the trees. I glimpsed in another direction the line of centenarian eucalypti. I had the impression of malaise that the apprehension of an imminent danger causes, but I did not know whether the danger was within me or exterior to me, hidden in the house, ready to surge forth between the two rows of eucalypti.

It had been a long time since Marie with the long neck had gone back up to the convent and the grocer's automobile had drawn away along the road. The winged air of the morning gave way to a heavy heat. I met Poor Jacques on the road.

He was walking rapidly. I noticed the abundance of his hair, which was damp because he had emerged from a bath. I was also struck by the impetus of his march, the haste that he seemed to be in.

He held out his hand to me with the joyful air that any action gives, even the slightest.

"Since I've met you," he said, "I'll ask you to give my apologies to Monsieur de Saint-Aygulf. I'm leaving, and I don't anticipate coming back."

"Don't go," I said to him. "Stay another few days, and even come along this evening..."

He made a swift negative gesture with his hand.

"I only came to shake your hand and those of a few friends, but I've found them so changed. Perhaps it's me, though, who has become an entirely savage man by virtue of living in solitude. I must confess that I miss that solitude. Then again, there are so many things that I no longer understand."

I asked him, rather foolishly, whether he didn't get bored all alone in the middle of the pines, beside the sea.

He started to laugh.

"How would that be possible? I don't have time. I go to bathe. I cook. I have a little field that I cultivate. Then too, I have friends that are very demanding: a family of snakes and a mole for whom I travel six kilometers a day in order to be able to offer him a saucer of milk."

His gaze became thoughtful. An anxiety passed through it.

"I wonder how disappointed it must be not to have seen me for several days and to be deprived of milk."

He extended his hand, and I understood that he wanted to say something else, but could not find the words. "And are you staying for long? Don't you think it would be better...?"

I retained his hand in mine, in order for him to finish his thought.

"Go on."

He seemed to make a decision.

"I'm going above all because of the mole, which must be waiting for me and unhappy about my absence. But I think I would have left anyway. There's something here I can't explain: an influence, a charm... How can I put it, exactly? The air is less pure. I feel that I have to go."

I wanted to retain him again, to make him speak, but he was in haste to draw away. He resumed his cheerfulness, raised a finger toward the sky and said to me, as he left:

"What does it matter, anyway? The sun purifies everything."

He went quickly. His garment floated around his body like wings. The dust of the road lifted up by his bare feet made a sort of nimbus and fall back in the light.

And I thought to myself: *Poor Jacques has become a poor peasant.*

Monsieur de Saint-Aygulf drew me into the garden to talk to me about the ceremony that was to take place that evening. He was proud of participating in it, proud that it was taking place on land that belonged to him. He pointed with his hand to a group of trees that dominated a hill.

"It's there," he said. "Monsieur Althon will bring a Swedenborgian lady and also a disciple of Vintras. Our group will end up uniting in a single sheaf all the spiritualist groups. That's Kotzebue's secret desire."

He leaned toward me, and in a low voice, for he aspired to give everything he said a confidential character, he added: "Kotzebue really is a great man, isn't he? People will only find out later the role that he will have played in the development of the spirit. I continually have information on his subject that comes from my guides."

I knew that before devoting himself to communication with the spirits, Monsieur de Saint-Aygulf's life had been orientated toward money and the most vulgar desire for women. I had had many examples of his ferocious egotism and his limited respect for the rules of society. It was difficult for me to believe that his guides, leaning over human beings in order to direct them, would have chosen that old man among all of them to be their spokesman. I murmured the confused words of approval that I owed to the father of Eveline and Laurence.

But he took me by the arm in a familiar fashion. He had to talk to me about another subject. His daughter Laurence was very anxious and had been for a long time. He had done so much for her! His venerated wife, whose name he could not pronounce without emotion, had also sacrificed herself for a child who had always returned evil for good. A great problem, that of children, and what a mystery was that of heredity!

He had just had very grave scenes with his daughter. Had she not taken it into her head to want to return to Paris? She had gone so far as to threaten to go without authorization if he did not take her back. And just at the moment when such fine things were happening here, of such an elevated moral order! And what were these stories of negroes with which she had been breaking his head for days? Eveline could not do anything with her sister. No one had any influence over her. She was a rebel. Perhaps his saintly wife had been right when she predicted that Laurence would turn out badly. He was conscious of having done all his duty. Oh, the ideal thing would be to marry her off as soon as possible, but there too it was necessary to reach an understanding. Sacrifices have a limit. He held to what everyone knows—he did not say, of course, "what I know"—and he hastened to add that he was speaking in a general fashion and because that came into the conversation.

He had done all he could for Laurence. She would have almost nothing on marrying. It was just that everyone imagined that he was richer than he was. The duty of a man who has a role to play is not to dispossess himself for his children. He had read *King Lear* and that reading had impressed him. Thank God that his daughter Eveline had decided not to marry!

"You understand me, don't you?" he said, by way of conclusion.

I responded ingenuously that I understood him perfectly, and he shook my hand more forcefully than usual.

When I came to Monsieur Saint-Aygulf's house after dinner, Laurence had already retired to her room. I had the impression that the atmosphere retained traces of a recent argument, but as several other people arrived at the same time as me, I was unable to analyze that impression.

Monsieur de Saint-Aygulf and Eveline were ready to leave.

"It's only half an hour's walk," someone said

I saw that several lanterns had been prepared; I learned that Kotzebue, who had dined at Monsieur Althon's house, was to have preceded us with the latter.

On a hill, facing the sea, in the midst of trees, in the heart of nature, it had been decided that a sort of mystical mass would be celebrated. The ritual had been prepared a long time ago by Kotzebue. He believed firmly in the power of ceremonies and he had resolved, in accord with Monsieur Althon, to celebrate it by moonlight, on the ground that retained the influence of their master Simon.

Several winding roads headed toward the hill to which we were going. Those zigzags were rather steep and our group—there were about fifteen of us—was strung out along the hillside. The night was clear and warm, and a storm not very far away charged the air with electricity. Sometimes one of those bearing a lantern stopped and swung it, as a sign to the laggards to hurry up. A red glow was visible on the other side of the hill, which had to be leading Monsieur Althon's group.

The atmosphere poured a strange overexcitement into the nerves. Not all the conversations had the meditative tone that had been agreed. Madame Vigerie, who was joking and leaning on young Charlie's arm, sometimes uttered a burst of laughter whose musical quality took on an unexpected value and fell into the silence like a metallic cascade. The two young Swedish women were holding one another so tightly as they walked that they seemed to belong to a single form. The Levantine dance-teacher stuck tightly to Mademoiselle Longève. As if obedient to a law, everyone was proceeding in couples.

I was following the zigzags alongside Eveline, but we only exchanged a few words. She had put on a shawl, but had taken it off again and was carrying it over her arm. The fabric of her dress was light and allowed the ease of her body to be seen. The moonlight falling on the milky whiteness of her neck and arms and the human breath that came from her gave me the sentiment of advancing beside a warm and living statue.

As the road turned, Eveline moved aside a mimosa branch that extended in front of her. I was right beside her, and we saw at the same time two forms stationary a few paces away from us. It was Madame Vigerie and her companion. She had fainted in his arms and her head was tipped back beneath his. She was sucking the young man's lips, savoring a kiss whose sensuality seemed all the greater because it was furtive and hasty.

That lasted a few seconds. The sigh they uttered as they unlaced was followed by a laugh of pleasure.

I had grasped Eveline's arm and I squeezed it with a pressure that increased for as long as the embrace I had before my eyes lasted. Still holding the mimosa branch she had moved aside with her right hand. Eveline leaned toward me. The moon illuminated the bright oval of her face and I stared into her eyes. They were profound, blue and indefinite. I could not divine their expression. There was an interrogation, perhaps an anguish. The light of purity that I was accustomed to see there was mingled with a slightly anxious element. My face drew nearer to hers, not by virtue of a definite determination on my part, but by the attraction exercised by the profundity of the gaze, which seemed to hide, very far away, the solution to an enigma of the soul.

Eveline doubtless thought that I was trying to kiss her lips. She pulled her arm away from my hand with an abrupt gesture and the movement of the head of someone collecting herself. The mimosa branch struck me in the face like a slap. At the same time, while she went on ahead of me, I heard a little insulting laugh, and I saw her looking at me over her shoulder, measuring the distance that separated us, as if she were afraid that I might throw myself upon her and as if that action were the most repugnant one that her brain could conceive. I wanted to follow her, but, nimbler than me, she outdistanced me, and I saw her almost running, desirous of escaping my presence.

I continued climbing, alone, invaded by a strange sentiment of muted anger.

The paths died away among clumps of pines and cork-oaks, wild cacti and abandoned vine ceps. A lantern was placed on the ground to guide the new arrivals; a little further on there were others hanging on the cypresses. I saw that the cypresses were seven in number and that, planted in a circular fashion, they designed vaguely the form of a crescent.

The bushes were full of whispers; even though they could not be numerous, I had the sensation of being surrounded by an agitated and mysterious crowd.

I recognized the Russian accent of Monsieur Althon; I perceived him next to Kotzebue and a tall, pale woman who had a necklace of large pearls around her neck and whose haughty beauty impressed me. I thought that she must be the Swedenborgian. I overheard phrases that I knew, but which took on a new value in Kotzebue's mouth because of the landscape and the night.

"Collect the power of the moon...! The spirit of Helen will descend...but don't neglect the flesh..... Perhaps you'll be conducted toward the spirit by a supernatural frisson of a physical nature and the torture of enjoyment..."

I saw silhouettes in the shadows that were adopting poses of adoration. A nocturnal bird frightened by the noise flew away with a heavy wing-beat. One of the Swedes, separated momentarily from her friend, extended her tapering hands toward her and, in seizing her, almost caused her to fall against her. It seemed to me that a breath came from the distant forests that surrounded us, as grandiose as religion, and as terrible as fear.

I did not have time to be astonished. The ceremony had commenced. Kotzebue, standing in the middle of the circle of cypresses, pronounced a ritual invocation. I could not make out what he was saying at first, but I measured his sincerity by the tremor of his voice, its contained emotion. A few words carried as far as me:

"Thought of God! Sister of the Word! By the fire of amour nature is renewed. O you, who have descended into the flesh...you who are Helen..."

Behind the cypresses, women's voices intoned a litany. The voices were not very numerous; there cannot have been more than three women singing. It was not, in any case, a chant but a slightly modulated prayer.

"We are three and we are one... The three are only one... I am exiled from the Pleroma... Let us commune with you, O Sophia Achamoth...!"[6]

And suddenly, I felt alone. I found myself in a solitude whose perfection filled me with an exalted delight. Alone on the summit of a mountain, with the sea blue-tinted in the distance before me, among the motionless

---

[6] Sophia [wisdom] is the principle whose fall into the world is represented in Gnosticism as Ennoia, incarnated, according to the myth of Simon and Helen, in the latter; one of the alleged schools of Gnosticism divides Sophia into two, of which one aspect—the one associated with Ennoia—is Sophia Achamoth

brothers that were oaks, fig-trees and pines! I was the central point of the world, its cause and its end, and I enjoyed the comprehension of it for the first time.

"Let us commune with you, O Sophia Achamoth!" repeated voices that came from nowhere.

That communion was accomplished. There was a great cloud that made a design in the sky and threatened to cover the moon, but I directed my will at it and steered it to the right. I was myself the contours of the cloud, the very essence of the cloud. At my feet I saw the mass of the hotel with its illuminated windows and the steeples of its lightning-conductors. I was the rooms of the hotel, the automobile circling around in arriving at its perron, I was the manager in the smoking jacket, and I could have read all the thoughts inscribed in his brain. The consciousness of that magnification of my being procured me a joy as serene as my clairvoyance, as immense as my pride.

"O Ennoia, divine spirit in the body of Helen...!"

There was a quiver around me of a life so unlimited that I experienced a need to make contact with it. In the same way that on awakening after certain dreams one touches one's body in order to make sure that one is really oneself, I wanted to touch the wood of a tree trunk, the terrestrial matter that was beneath me. I fell to my knees and I extended my hands forward, with the consequence that I was on all fours in an animal posture. But that did not embarrass me, for astonishing faculties were revealed within me.

I was nyctalopic.[7] There was no more darkness. I distinguished the cicadas sleeping on the trunks of the pines, even those a great distance away. I saw the suckers with which they were absorbing the resin, their short antennae, their hyaline wings, their faceted triangular eyes. I enjoyed the peace of their slumber. At the same time I enjoyed the movement of the night-birds, the nocturnal activity of all the sylvan creatures. After having carried a thousand wisps of straw into the anthill, I rested with the thousands of ants. A nocturnal voyager, I accompanied the rabbits along the vineyards, and wallowed in muddy potholes with the badgers. I loved them all because they were part of me and they permitted me to grow. For I grew incessantly with the life of animals, I raised myself in the branches of trees and the flight of birds, and it was the moon, the dead planet, that was my goal.

"Helen, Ennoia," repeated whispering voices, "penetrate the substance of our flesh with your kiss!"

I had the notion that my immeasurably increased body was made of a putrescence vivified by the lunar light, but I was glad of that, and that artificial life filled me, provided that it was always multiplied. And on four feet, like the animals, I waited for the promised kiss of that Helen, to be burned by her mouth, inundated by her sap, transported by her ardor.

My face was turned in the direction of the sea and I received the kiss. There is no sensation, in dream or in reality that is experienced such as one had imagined it. No carnal lip brushed me, and yet a warm, damp and

---

[7] The word *nyctalopique* [nyctalopic] which ought to refer to night-blindness, is sometimes used in French to signify the opposite--i.e., an ability to see in the dark.

simultaneously sad kiss was deposited on my mouth. In the semi consciousness that subsisted within me, I identified the lips that gave me that kiss with those of Laurence and with those of Eveline simultaneously, the lips that I had had and those that had drawn away from me with disgust.

Ennoia, immaterial ideal beauty that I incarnated in two young women, had you emerged from the night and the moon, by virtue of the magic of incantations, in order to touch me with the ember of desire?

The cloud that I had previously steered in its course, abandoned to itself, returned to cover the moon. Obscurity returned me to myself.

A stone bruised my right hand. I was curved by my bestial posture. The lanterns were lifted from the cypresses. I heard stifled sighs. I saw recumbent forms. A naked breast emerged from a ripped corsage and a hand caressed it. It was rosy, marbled, larger than nature, as if charged with a milky putrescence. It made me think of a kind of unhealthy beast that an excessively forceful caress might cause to burst.

I took a few steps. All the living beings had dissolved, had disappeared. The hill seemed deserted.

A panic took possession of me. I started running, I went downhill at hazard. I bumped into trees. Dogs barked. I went alongside a farm of whose existence I was unaware at that location, and which seemed to me to have sprung up by magic. I finally reached the road and went on to the sea, for I needed to contemplate the unlimited water. Thank God! The excessively mysterious whiteness of Saint-Tropez was imperceptible.

Never had the waves and the night seemed so menacing. There was in nature the same aspect of mystery as in the human soul. What vanity to pore over that shadow and interrogate it! And I remembered the words of I no longer remember what ancient author:

They will adventure over the sea of darkness in order to discover the unknown there, and they will never come back...

I made a sign to the driver to stop and I got out of the vehicle.

"I don't think we'll have to wait for long," I said, to reassure him. But he belonged to the species of men of the Midi for whom the notion of time does not count, and who find it as well to be in one place as another. He made a broad gesture to signify that nothing has importance.

I looked at my watch. It was midnight. As the headlights made a large circle of light on the road I had him switch them off and I started pacing up and down. Laurence could not be long delayed.

"Ha ha!" I said to myself, internally. "It's an elopement." And I savored the romantic character that the action takes on, if one gives it the name of elopement rather than that of departure. I strove to expel from my mind the thought of the annoyances that might crop up. I knew that all the agreeable hours of life, those that one takes pleasure in retracing later in telling the embellished story, were always spoiled at the time by petty preoccupations.

My conscience was tranquil. Laurence had not said that she loved me. I had enough confidence in myself to believe that it was only a lack of impetus, and that amour would come later if it had not already come. There had not been any question of marriage between us. Laurence had set aside swiftly, several times, the vague allusions that I had been able to make on that subject. She had declared frankly that it was for her merely a narrower form of the slavery of young women. I was delivering her from her present slavery and permitting her to quit a family by whom she was not loved and whom she did not love.

I did not make myself any reproach. In any case, I knew that my fortune was sufficiently large to compensate generously what Laurence might lose from the material viewpoint in leaving her father. That subject had not been raised between us, and I wondered whether Laurence, absorbed by considerations of slavery and liberty, had even thought about it for a single instant. The sequence of events made me think not. People sometimes act neither out of amour nor personal interest, but by virtue of an obscure movement of their nature, which they would be quite incapable of defining themselves.

As Laurence did not arrive I decided to advance toward the house in such a fashion as to see whether or not her bedroom window was illuminated. Suddenly, however, in the depths of the night, there was the sound of a little bell and a moving light coming from the road turned right and drew away along the sunken road.

To my great surprise I saw a choirboy swinging a lantern with one hand and holding a cross in the other. He was preceding a priest. I distinguished the arched, willfully solemn back of the latter, and the whiteness of his surplice. His elbows were tight against the body and he was carrying an object veiled by a cloth in both hands.

"The Holy Sacrament!" I murmured.

The priest was heading toward the convent, to which he had doubtless been called by someone who was about to die. He was moving rapidly, and I ran to follow him.

Nothing could have filled me with more ease that that encounter. It was an occult advertisement, a favorable sign. I marched behind the symbolic representation of God. The act that I was accomplishing participated in a kind of benediction. I had examined it from every angle. I did not consider it as reprehensible, according to my personal morality. But not only was it not reprehensible, it was good, in the elevated sense of the word, it was divine since the Holy Sacrament was preceding me at the moment when I was about to accomplish it. I believed for a second, in my delight, that I glimpsed beneath the inclined mimosas, as if no priest were carrying it and no veil hid it, the radiant circle of the pyx with golden leaves, gliding on its own to show me the way.

The contradiction between my absolute lack of Catholic faith and that intervention in my favor tried to traverse my mind, but I rejected it immediately.

I stopped at the place where the road approached the house. A window was illuminated. It was that of the room that Laurence shared with her sister. During the first part of their sojourn they had each had their own room, but when Monsieur de Saint-Aygulf's guests had been filled the house Laurence had been obliged to abandon hers and share her sister's.

The day before, when she and I had calculated the difficulties we would have to overcome in order to leave without being disturbed, the question of the shared bedroom had been considered as the sole cause of possible hitches. In order to leave, Laurence had to wait until her sister was asleep. Ordinarily, without having exchanged any words, they each read on their own side. Laurence had become drowsy first and insisted that the electric light be switched off. For two or three evenings *Uncle Tom's Cabin* had caused a truce in that argument. Eveline, who was reading at that moment Saint Teresa's *Interior Castle*, had take advantage of it to mock her sister for the mediocrity of her reading. But *Uncle Tom's Cabin* was concluded. Laurence had promised to simulate fatigue that evening and oblige her sister to interrupt

The Interior Castle. She counted on getting up in the dark, dressing silently and being able to leave the room without awakening Eveline, who would only perceive her departure the next day.

The illuminated window was thus a bad omen. Either Eveline was still reading and it was necessary to wait longer, or she had woken up at the sound Laurence had made, and an argument had ensued. Laurence had foreseen the possibility and counted on being able to override any protest on her sister's part.

The shutters of the window were partly open, and several times I thought I saw shadows passing over the panes. I concluded that the second hypothesis was the correct one. I examined without joy what might happened if Eveline, indignant, went to wake Monsieur de Saint-Aygulf, and if he launched himself on Laurence's tracks just as she was joining me in the garden.

From the place where I was, I could see the entrance door; Laurence could not get out without my being aware of it. I knew that the door in question was not locked, in order to permit the guests to go in and out as they pleased.

"The entrance door doesn't make any noise when it closes," Laurence had told me, while listing the facilities that she would have in leaving without her nocturnal departure being noticed.

My nervousness became so great that it was impossible for me to wait any longer without doing something, even something insensate. I parted the branches of the hedge that separated the little road from the garden, at the exact spot where Monsieur Althon had nearly launched himself through a few days before. I took a few steps on a gravel path, which creaked as I approached the perron. Only then did I think of my imprudence. The night was warm and someone, afflicted by insomnia, might have gone out to sit down on a bench or wander in the garden. A domestic who had spent the evening in the vicinity might come back. I listened anxiously, but I did not hear any noise.

Then I opened the door, which was indeed silent. It opened into a vast hallway full of darkness. I had no fixed idea and I certainly would not have gone any further had I not heard whispering, words spoken in a low voice and something that might resemble the noise of a struggle between two individuals. I remembered that I only had to go around a table to reach the bottom of the staircase that was at the back of the hallway and led up to the first floor. The noise was coming from the corridor that divided the first floor in two and on to which the bedrooms opened.

I learned all the details of the scene later from Laurence.

Laurence, as she had planned, had made a semblance of going to sleep early. Her sister had renounced *The Interior Castle* without any difficulty and had gone to sleep. Laurence had then got dressed silently; she already had her hand on the doorknob when Eveline leapt out of bed in her night-dress. Doubtless the priest carrying the Holy Sacrament and his choirboy had exchanged a few words as they went past the house and the unusual noise had woken her up.

She exclaimed: "What's that?" She turned on the electric light and was amazed to see her sister upright, ready to leave. Laurence had put on an automobile jacket and was holding a small bag in her hand, which did not permit any pretext of taking a walk in the garden. In any case, Eveline had understood immediately. One might have thought that she had had a presentiment.

Her first words were: "You shan't go."

Laurence was surprised at first by her energy, for she thought that her sister would be only too glad to be rid of her. But not at all. She had been mistaken about Eveline's sentiments. However, her resistance did not seem to come from a sincere love, but from a rigorous notion of duty.

Laurence did not deny that she was leaving for good, and an argument ensued.

"It resulted from that," Laurence told me, "that I was a monster of ingratitude, that I had cut Madame de Saint-Aygulf's life short, that my conduct was the cause of my father's unhappiness. I provoked all the men, it appears. My sister, who took so much care to avoid talking to me, took advantage of the opportunity to tell me in a few minutes everything that she had had in her heart for years. I scarcely replied in order not to prolong the scene, and everything she said confirmed me in my resolution to leave, because I understood even more how my father and my sister had always considered me as a being far inferior to them, an instinctive beast whose deviations it was necessary to fear."

Laurence thought that I was waiting. She opened the bedroom door in order to go. She knew that Eveline would be stopped by the fear of an outcry, an immediate scandal.

"I'm going to tell our father," the latter had said.

She had really decided to do nothing about it, but abruptly, she had been gripped by a resolution. She had seized her sister bodily and tried to make her go back into the bedroom, doubtless with the intention of locking the door. They had started to struggle silently, exchanging insults in low voices, face to face.

That was the noise I heard in the dark hallway where I was. Then, holding the banister, I began to climb the stairs. I stopped when I discovered the length of the corridor. It was illuminated by a night-light, and a bright light coming from the sisters' bedroom launched an oblique projection, as in the theater, over the character in the process of playing the drama.

Astonishment nailed me to the spot. Was struck me was the impressive beauty of Eveline. Her night-dress, stuck to her body, was transparent. Her hair, which she had never wanted to cut, fell in ashy sheaves over her bare shoulders. She gave the impression of a sort of angel struggling hand to hand with a woman in an automobile costume, in a picture by some modern painter. Only the stony hardness of her face contradicted her angelic estate.

Neither of the two sisters could see me. I heard Eveline say: "You're a worthy daughter of your mother."

And Laurence whispered a few words that included my name, and she added: "It's because you're jealous! Admit it!"

Both of them remained immobile, as if to give the poison of the words time to envenom the wounds inflicted.

Their grip relaxed. The last blows had been struck. That hardness of Eveline's features gave way to an expression of disgust for the baseness of soul that such a hypothesis supposed. And as she released Laurence, her night-dress, whose epaulettes had broken in the struggle, suddenly slid along her body and she found herself completely naked.

For a second I had the vision of that perfect body, which I had so often delighted in imagining, in the license of dreams.

But Laurence was already going past me at a run.

I followed her and I caught up with her on the perron. She feared being too late and no longer finding me on the road. She started to run through the garden with me. How fast she went! How urgently she wanted to be far away!

A suavity came from the odor of the trees, the clarity of the sky and a light breeze in the foliage. I sensed my companion's momentum, that she was animated by a wild intoxication of liberty. We had launched ourselves into the pathway between the old eucalypti, which was the shortest route to reach the auto.

"The Essenes," Laurence told me, laughing. She said it in a loud voice, in a tone of bravado. She had a desire to shout it.

I had never sensed so clearly the relationship between the eucalypti with the pale trunks and the acetic old men in procession. I was impressed by it. I saw Laurence, beside me, looking to the right and left, as if she were scanning impotent enemies attacked to the ground by roots. She must have been thinking about many tedious evenings, meals without wine, and the humiliations that she owed them. And she laughed in escaping them. But I had the sensation that the ancient ascetics were marching in two parallel lines toward wisdom, and was afflicted by seeing myself traveling so rapidly toward a goal so different from theirs.

I uttered a sigh of relief when we reached the road. The auto was still there. The driver was asleep. I woke him up, and we set forth.

When Laurence huddled against me, I felt something hard in the pocket of her coat; I asked her what it was.

"*Uncle Tom's Cabin*," she replied.

The driver sounded his horn loudly. We went past the choirboy and the priest holding the Holy Sacrament, who were coming back. They had both stopped to let us pass and the vehicle brushed the cross that the choirboy was holding tilted forward.

Did that further encounter have a hidden meaning? I had marched behind God a little while before. Now I had obliged him to stop, to receive the dust that I was raising and I was overtaking him. What symbolism did that conceal? Assuredly none. I did not believe in God, at least in that religious form. I leaned forward to tell the driver to go as fast as he could, and I took Laurence in my arms.

I would have liked to think of her when my lips encountered hers. I did not even imagine the possibility of not thinking about her. But the image of Eveline naked, such as I had just perceived her under the looseness of her ash-blonde hair, presented itself before me with an imperious clarity. In the shadow, I could not distinguish Laurence's features, or her eyes; I saw, as if they were against my face, the features hardened by anger and the blue eyes full of profundity, of Eveline.

Jealous, Laurence had said to her sister, and Eveline had received that word like an insult, which wounded her and was simultaneously revelatory. Why not? Had I not for a long time observed in myself a bizarre power, a faculty of attraction external to myself. Who could tell whether Eveline's scorn in my regard might be simulated? And the night-dress had fallen at the same moment, as if the forces that rule coincidence had wanted her body to be laid bare when her soul was laid bare for the first time.

I counted on reaching during the night a small hotel beyond Toulon, to which I had telegraphed that morning.

I had promised myself a great pleasure in that arrival at first light, with Laurence, in the middle of the palm-trees that surrounded the threshold. We could be there at about five o'clock. The sun would be about to rise. I imagined the sleeping porter who would open up to us and to whom I would say: "It's me who sent a telegram to reserve a room overlooking the sea."

I saw the banal drawing-room, the narrow staircase, the corridor with shoes outside the doors and a room with an enormous bed, whose windows I would open in order to respire the ineffable odor of algae and youth that a beach exhales at sunrise.

But the expectation of such things, which ought to have been delectable, was spoiled for me. I had Laurence in my arms, fully dressed, and I could see Eveline, naked. The speed of the automobile contributed by its vertigo to trouble the notion I had of reality. We went past villas with their pleasant gardens, we traversed villages and pine woods. Sometimes, a minuscule bay where a boat was asleep on a little sand, stood out to our left. I embraced the two sisters at the same time; and sometimes preceding me, sometimes following me, dominating the wooded hills or floating over the sea, there was a Holy Sacrament of dream, whose significance was incomprehensible.

And that was the epoch of my life when the blindfold I had over my eyes thickened, to the point where I was like a blind man—even worse, for a blind man has developed his tactile qualities, he distinguishes the difference between objects, even the most significant, in a surprising fashion, by touching them. But I, not content with not seeing, palpated the most divine substance with my hands and remained ignorant of its quality.

Now that everything appears different to me, I excuse the error of others by measuring mine. I am not scornful, as before, of people who exercise the functions of judges, who handle money in banks, those who make huge profits in great industries by making poorly paid men toil—all those who sustain the rickety and counterfeit edifice of society. They deceive themselves as I deceived myself. They believe in an illusion and if by chance they touch reality, it is with a hand so coarse that they cannot discern anything of its delicate grain.

Glory to the apparition of light that permits one to gaze at life not from the outside but as if one were placed in its very heart. It does not come, as many expect, in the manner of a revelation. It comes slowly, it comes belatedly, and only when one had traversed great darkness. It comes from a constant interrogation, from the comparison of actions with one another, from the observation of causes and effects. No luminous star hangs over the door of the person who receives it. The lover of the marvelous is initially deceived by the simplicity of the phenomenon, but he soon perceives that the phenomenon is rare, although simple. He searches for someone who has experienced it like himself, in order to be able to talk about it and be understood. He does not encounter the person for whom he is searching. He feels alone.

Glory to the power of life that isolates a man in the midst of his fellows, in order that he might be transformed!

We had been living together in Paris for a month, and Laurence had not begun to address me as *tu*. After numerous trials she had finally given up.

"It's not because you intimidate me," she told me, "and it's not because you're older than me. It seems to me"—she searched for her words and discovered herself while speaking—"that I only have the faculty of being familiar with poor people."

That was true. But poor people inspired more than familiarity in Laurence; they gave birth in her to a spontaneous affection. I only noticed that at length. Lack of money was a bizarre entitlement by which one almost certainly gained Laurence's heart. In every new person she met, she only considered the external signs of poverty, and if she did not perceive those signs, a certain distance resulted.

As she and I had thought, Monsieur de Saint-Aygulf made no attempt to retrieve his daughter. The latter had, in any case, reached the age of majority a few months before. He had, on the contrary, written to her to signify a kind of malediction upon her. It was Kotzebue who seemed to have been most afflicted by Laurence's departure. A young man named Lucien Duperré, who had spent the summer with him in the Midi, had come to see me without any apparent motive, but in reality to transmit his words to me and in order to be able to give him a few details about my life with Laurence.

"It's necessary to acquit my commission," he said to me, with embarrassment.

I would have preferred not to hear anything.

"Speak," I said, however, smiling indifferently.

"He said precisely this: 'Tell him that I know the hidden reason for what he had done. His action is the direct consequence of a signature he gave more than fifteen years ago. I consider him as doomed.'"

I relied that Kotzebue's opinion left me indifferent. The young man departed rapidly and Laurence declared that she had a horror of young men who wore a gold chain around their ankles and dressed like fashionable engravings.

I was obliged to renounce seeing almost all my friends, who were also Monsieur de Saint-Aygulf's. Laurence and I would henceforth neglect the spirits, the Essenes, and the members of all the groups who accord, in principle, more importance to the future life than real life.

"Finally! Not to see lunatics any longer! What a relief!" she cried.

I renewed acquaintances with former comrades of whom I had lost sight somewhat. I invited them to dinner, I made them unexpected politenesses in order to attract them. They were people like anyone else, with cars and mistresses, who frequented music-halls and were not preoccupied with any philosophy. To my great surprise, Laurence welcomed them coldly. She found the women too stupidly infatuated with their jewelry and clothes, and she felt even more distant from the men. I searched for the reason and thought I discerned it eventually in Laurence's touchstone for judging people by their fortune.

One evening, when I was going home at about seven o'clock, I ran into a fellow name Falou, whom I had once known in the Latin Quarter and had met several times since, in a tobacconist's shop in the Rue Jouffroy. He was a Bohemian who lived on expedients. He was in the process of buying a few loose caporal cigarettes, which is not an indication of wealth. He hid them precipitately from my sight. I was struck by his expression, more wretched than usual, and something odd in his attitude.

He had never interested me, but I had lost the greater part of my relationships and I wanted to create new ones in order to distract Laurence.

"Come to dinner with me," I said. "I'm having a few friends round."

I understood, by the dignity with which he refused, that he was not certain of dining that evening. He excused himself for not having the time to put on his dinner jacket, but I ended up dragging him along.

Laurence was smiling but distant, and during the first part of the evening she did not seem to notice Falou. He was the last to remain. The conversation died away sadly. He was about to get up to take his leave when Laurence's attitude to him suddenly changed. She began to consider him with a visible sympathy and insisted on him staying a while longer, in spite of the bleak character of his speech. I could not find any other explanation for that action than this:

The taciturn Falou was sitting facing Laurence and me and had his legs crossed. The warmth of the dinner, without brightened is sad visage, had communicated a certain abandonment to him and a forgetfulness of the prudence necessary to a poor man. He had allowed the sole of a boot to show in which a hole traced a large design. I surprised Laurence's gaze posed on that hole and I was initially ashamed on my friend's behalf, knowing the pitiless severity of young women in that order of ideas, but the result I feared was not produced and it was the opposite that occurred.

"He's very nice," Laurence said to me when he had gone. And when she learned that Falou was a poor devil, cultivated but weak and incapable of earning a living, who had no situation, no resources and no family, I saw a glint in her eyes and she declared, to the scorn of all plausibility, that Falou was the most agreeable of my friends and that it was necessary to invite him frequently.

I rediscovered that love of poverty in the slightest details of Laurence's existence. I had wanted, on arriving in Paris, to give my bachelor apartment, which was vast but a trifle old-fashioned, a more modern appearance. She had opposed it, finding everything very good as it was.

My house was kept by a correct old woman, whom Laurence found too correct. The service was provided by a valet de chambre who concealed his timidity beneath an obsequious self-importance. Laurence could not look at him without shrugging her shoulders.

I hired a chambermaid for her, but she seemed too well-trained and she declared that she definitely did not need anyone. All her sympathy went to a nameless creature, a maidservant who came to tidy the bedrooms in the morning. With a red nose and clogs, she was such an extraordinary symbol of poverty that one was initially tempted to believe that she did not belong to quotidian reality but was about to play a role in some fairy tale. Laurence was able to have conversations with that dream-like figure. She gave her presents. She called her

"Madame Honorine" with a hint of respect. I was uncertain as to whether she might take her as a confidant.

I established a link between the anomaly of her tastes and the nocturnal walk around the Place Blanche of which I had been the witness one evening. I had not renounced finding out why, exactly, she had gone to visit Kotzebue in the middle of the night, after having prowled around several cafés. I did not want to tell her, of course, that I had followed her. I proceeded by means of allusions. I accused her jokingly of having flirted with Kotzebue, but she reported the conversations she had had with him with an unsimulated frankness. I had noticed that although she sometimes passed certain evenings in silence, she never employed lies.

"Flirting," she said to me, laughing. "The word is inappropriate for him. He certainly had a hidden agenda in my regard, but he never dared manifest it clearly. He gave me the impression of not having the habit of talking to women. I watched him sometimes from the corner of my eye because I thought he was one of those men who throw themselves on you abruptly and try to tip you over without explanations. Perhaps, with me, he never had a sufficiently favorable opportunity. I think that only one presented itself for him, and he let it pass because I was on my guard. He must have tried magnetism and other similar things, but I'm not a subject, like my sister. A thick layer of matter envelops me. Every time he talked to me, in the Midi, he talked about a certain Helen, whom he also called Ennoia. I didn't understand at first whether she was an imaginary being or one of his female relatives. He said to me that I had an admirable role to play in incarnating Helen. But of what did that consist? I told him that I didn't know anything about all those stories, but he replied that that was perfect, and a Helen who didn't understand anything was better. He made me laugh a good deal, but all the same, I was a little afraid of him."

I returned to the attack several times, but in vain.

One evening, when several friends had come to find us in order to dine at a restaurant, someone proposed that we go to Alberte's. Alberte was the proprietress of an establishment that was half-café and half night-club, which was mostly frequented by regulars and was one of those that Laurence had examined on the evening when I had followed her. She did not manifest any emotion at the time, but as soon as the lights of the Place Blanche shone around us in the taxi that was carrying us, I understood by a straightening of her body and a palpitation of her nostrils that Laurence had an inexplicable connection with that particular point of the city, the vulgar Place Blanche.

During dinner Laurence considered everything around us, the counter of the bar, the kitchen door, and the walls, on which a few humorous pictures were hanging, as if it were a particularly interesting place enjoying a historical celebrity.

The usual waiters, random clients and the women that came in and went out after conspiratorial conversations with the proprietress were full of attraction for her. She never took her eyes off them. Inattentive to our conversation, she lived the life of the bar amorously. Alberte, with her puffy face, her eyes like a benevolent fox and her hands heavy with fake rings, appeared to her to have an imposing dignity.

"She must be a charming woman," she said, several times. And when she left she exchanged a long smile with her.

It was too late to go to the theater and someone suggested that we have a drink somewhere. Laurence accepted joyfully and immediately proposed the Brasserie Romano—which she had seen in passing, she said, and appeared to be very curious.

No distinctive originality characterizes the Brasserie Romano. I had the sensation that the prostitutes hooked there with more impudence than elsewhere. Calm and clean-shaven men were playing cards in a corner. A provincial couple had wandered in.

Laurence was entirely happy. The wines and liqueurs of the dinner gave her a certain animation, but I distinguished an intoxication in her that had another provenance. She was drunk on the ambiance that emerges from the streets of Montmartre, which is reflected in the tinsel of the cafés, and flows with the alcohol one drinks there. The dreary orchestras were only there to provoke embraces. Couples were only dancing or sitting around tables in a provisional fashion; they were soon going to slip into hotel rooms. One sensed that the rouge hastily plastered on lips was soon about to be cracked by the labor of kisses. The women who were seen passing by with vague eyes and a cigarette in their fingers had just undressed and dressed again and were about to recommence. All the houses in the surrounding area were hotels. Bargains were made behind all the counters, over all the marble tables. And there was something bleak, a venal breath, a total absence of joy that propagated a desire for spineless abandonment, caresses beneath dubious sheets.

That night we got home late, after wandering from one nightspot to another, and Laurence had not only not perceived the sinister similitude of all those places but declared that she had found a delectable variety therein.

From that day on it was necessary to renounce dining in apartments or going to the theater. There was no pleasure for Laurence except in second-rate taverns, she only breathed easily in their opaque smoke. I could not do otherwise than give in to her, for every evening, she was like a child deprived of the only plaything that amused her. She fell into a mute reverie, and seemed ready to weep, but as soon as I said: "What if we were to go and get something in Montmartre?" her eyes brightened and she became cheerful and animated. A kind of fever even took possession of her.

She seemed to love everything that commenced in the vicinity of the Place Clichy and ended in the Square d'Anvers. The Place Blanche was like a supernatural star whose light magnetized her.

When, we traversed it I saw her gaze pose on the luminous posters, the newsvendors and the policeman on duty with an affectionate tenderness. And there was then an untiring curiosity in her, which made her consider the faces of all the women with an attention and an amour, the cause of which I thought I had finally discovered.

Reflecting on the questions that Laurence had asked me about the existence of hookers and bar whores, the interest that those women inspired in her and her bizarre passion to be in their midst, a terrible word came to my mind: the word *possession*.

Laurence was possessed. An occult, magical force was attracting her toward the most inferior forms of life. All the aspects of poverty were seductive to her. She loved the poor, not out of charity, but because society had rejected them and they presented the image of terrestrial damnation.

It was neither hazard nor my caprice, and it was not even common sensual affinities, that had drawn me to

Laurence. There was a more powerful bond between us. We were united by a similar love of evil. Forces from below were appealing to us both. They had marked us with I know not what sign to descend simultaneously from degeneration to degeneration.

I thought that I perceived that I had become less intelligent, that I only read rarely, that I was not longer seeking to instruct myself, Laurence had the effect on me of an animal, uniquely animated by base preoccupations, and I was suffering from the influence that she had on me.

I did not discern the part of love that there was in her preference for the poor, in the voluntary choice she made of the unfortunate for the gift of her sympathy. I attributed her penchants to an innate taste for vile things and I feared, above all, imitating her. I tried to react. I imposed on her the presence of certain comrades chosen from among the most stupid, who did not interest me at all, but who might, by the prestige of their important positions and their conventional social life, orientate Laurence in a different direction.

That resulted in arguments, of which I took advantage to make long speeches about the best way of living, the necessity of frequenting people belonging to one's own milieu, and of an irreproachable morality.

Laurence then became resigned and indifferent. She shook her head, and she made general remarks such as: "We're very different. We've made an experiment and it hasn't succeeded. Perhaps we were both mistaken."

Or her gaze ran over me from head to foot, she seemed to be considering a stranger, a being of another race than herself, and was astonished to have been able to remain with him for so long.

"You see," she said to me once, "wisdom is to live with people of one's family." And as I made a gesture of astonishment, she added: "But the problem is discovering that family."

I asked her what she meant, exactly. She explained to me that families were not always composed of those who had the same blood, but of very various individuals, and which formed and dispersed by virtue of a law whose mechanism escaped her.

I began to grasp that she had a secret desire to leave me. Various indications made me think momentarily that she had made that decision. She asked me several times what a modest apartment on the Butte would cost. She stopped once to consider a tiny restaurant in the Avenue de Clichy and she said: "How amusing it would be to come here and eat all alone."

I replied bitterly that I was not a tyrant and that I would not prevent her from accomplishing that dream if that pleased her. I added that she would be disgusted by one or two experiments and would not have any desire to recommence.

But she started laughing as if it were a matter of a joke and contented herself with saying: "Who knows?"

In any case, my fears were temporary. I had too great a confidence in myself to think that Laurence might leave me.

And gradually, by virtue of the charm that enigmas have, I was attracted by the one that Laurence's heart concealed. It was in the evening particularly that the idea of possession took hold of me. That possession was common to us, but it was exteriorized more in Laurence and I acquired the habit of observing her without appearing to do so, in order to discover what road the evil was taking in order to develop, what symptoms it displayed, and with what voice it appealed.

Christmas arrived, and as much to satisfy my curiosity as to please Laurence, I decided to celebrate it in the establishment of the charming Alberte, alongside the blessed Place Blanche, which we could contemplate through the windows all night if we pleased. In order that no cloud could cast a shadow over that marvelous evening I invited the sad Falou—Laurence's elect, because of his holed boots and his ill humor of ashamed poverty—to accompany us.

It was decided that before sitting down in the heart of the star with seven irregular branches that forms the Place Blanche, we would spend an hour at the Bal Wagram, the picturesqueness of which Falou had praised and Laurence wanted to discover. I only report that visit because it was there that the voices began to resound and because the human caricatures began to design the seductive faces of evil.

The boulevards were host to an immense crowd agitated by the jubilation of nourishment. Automobiles were emerging everywhere. The food-shops were sparkling sumptuously. Families were advancing with that satisfied slowness that the certainty of imminent feasting gives. The necks of bottles emerged from the pockets of overcoats.

I was struck by the stature of the municipal guardsmen on the threshold of the Bal Wagram. They were larger than natural, as disproportionate as certain baroque cartoons I had seen at an exhibition of Humorists. They seemed the grotesque guardians of an infernal hullabaloo. The toilets were advertised to the public by enormous luminous letters, as if they were the centerpiece of the establishment, its radiant heart, and a hand painted on the wall designated their entrance as well, in order that they could not pass unperceived even by the most myopic or distracted eyes.

Laurence penetrated first into a vast hall full of dancers and I admired the delicacy of the pastel that her white neck had in the frisson of her fur.

We sat down at a table in the crowd. The air was stifling and transported an odor of human seat. On a placard in front of the orchestra the word *Java* was written.

"I can't stand it; I'm taking my coat off," said Laurence, her face illuminated by joy.

She stood up and appeared in her pink dress, with a scant neckline. I nearly uttered a cry. It seemed to me that she was entirely naked, and as she darted a circular glance around her, a silence fell, and was propagated to the limit of the hall as all eyes her fixed on her young body. I saw sweaty faces grimacing, and such an expression of bestiality appeared therein that I nearly launched myself in front of Laurence in order to protect her from those animal creatures, who were getting ready to pounce on her. That only lasted for a second, during which I had time to be astonished by Falou's indifference.

The din of the orchestra burst forth, the crowd shifted in order to dance. Laurence sat down again placidly. Her coat had fallen behind her on to her chair, and her pink dress covered her normally from the birth of her breasts to her knees.

I recapitulated what I had drunk that evening: a cocktail before dinner, a glass of liqueur afterwards. I could not be drunk without being aware of it. I drank a gulp of the alcohol I had just ordered and sought to discover whether there was anything in the faces surrounding me to justify what I thought I had seen.

Nearby, an elegant mulatto, his eyes fixed on a cherry liqueur, was sunk in a somber reverie. Two blonde women were rotating together, narrowly entwined. A man of about fifty, with a horseshoe beard, was dancing pleasantly with a female dwarf. He must have been the driving force of a group, and his reputation as a comedian was doubtless well established, for each of his gestures provoked burst of laughter from several people at a table. A woman with drooping cheeks was guffawing, and one sensed that the dwarf was pleased to have such a joyful companion. Further away, a solitary dandy was following chambermaids in their Sunday clothes with a fatal gaze. And there were marine infantrymen, sportive gnomes, blasé chauffeurs: a humanity for whom all notion of beauty seemed abolished and who had no regret in consequence.

And suddenly, I had the impression again that Laurence was the focal point of the room's attention. The dandy's eyes had abandoned the chambermaids and were fixed on her. The mulatto alongside me had emerged from his reverie. The quinquagenarian comedian was multiplying his farces for Laurence, and his horseshoe beard gave me the impression of a goat's beard. Further away, an individual as pink as a pig was licking his lips with a significant expression, and a tall young man with spectacles and a birdlike neck was extending it as if he wanted to attain a point between Laurence's breasts. There was no doubt that she was the center of desire of all those inferior creatures, enveloped by an obscene conspiracy.

And she knew it. She was radiant under the effluence of those desires. As was her habit, she was gazing untiringly at faces, following the expressions and movements as if she were seeking to recognize one of those beasts among all the beasts. She was full of ease. Leaning back in her chair, she had crossed her legs immodestly and she was not occupied, as all women with short dresses are, in pulling her skirt up over her knees.

Possessed! I thought. *That crowd is awaiting its signal. It's suddenly going to launch forward, howling, snatch that thin pink dress away, and the modern Sabbat to which I have brought her myself will be unleashed.*

For I was at the Sabbat. The secret feasts of the Middle Ages, which were celebrated on the heath, were nothing else. Those whom life deprives of joy experience at certain times the desire for a collective celebration in which all appetites are satisfied. Thus, all these poor lovers of their own pleasures were getting ready to eat and drink to excess in order then to mingle together. Instead of bestriding a broomstick, the worshipers of the Devil had come on foot or in a taxi, but that was the only difference. Lucifer could not be far away; he was about to emerge from those toilets that had been illuminated so magnificently for that, and we would all kiss his backside, in accordance with the age-old ritual.

Lucifer did not appear and Laurence did not tear off her clothes in order to offer herself to him. She was content to uncover her legs, to smile, and sometimes to raise her head as if to listen to a voice that was calling to her. She repeated that movement so often that I began to lend an ear myself.

The flux had become more numerous. Cries and laughter mingled with the din of instruments, and I thought I could perceive behind those noises a low-pitched voice that was coming from everywhere and pronouncing Laurence's name and mine by turns. I touched Falou's shoulder lightly with my fingertip and said to him: "Can't you hear anything?"

He looked at me in an idiotic fashion and he replied: "Yes, there's a great deal of noise."

There were sometimes sudden silences, and then the voice fell silent; but then it resumed again, confusedly, and I heard distinct words that were addressed to me:

"The sole verity is material enjoyment. You are not sure of anything but the reality of your body and the faculty it has of giving you pleasure by way of the senses. Look at the varied spectacle of things. Eat and drink for the plenitude of the digestion. Take advantage of the facility of women to lie down beside them and swoon over the satin of their skin. Everything that is desirable is around you. I am the unique God and you are respiring me in the air imbued with tobacco. It is my laughter that is on the painted curve of lips. I stretch myself out with the limbs of your mistress, I shiver in the silk of dresses and the curl of hair, I whirl with the music, I shine with the electric lamps, I am the color of eyes, the odor of armpits, the warmth of breasts, what you call beauty; I am matter."

I made a sign to Laurence that I wanted to leave. She resisted at first, but Falou made the remark that if we arrived too late Alberte might not keep the table that we had reserved. That convinced her, and I drew her outside.

In recapitulating the events of that memorable evening, I can still see a taxi glass that I pulled down precipitately in spite of the cold and the protests of my friends. I can also still see in a barley-sugar shop on the Boulevard de Clichy a Japanese man in an operetta costume who is turning a metallic handle with one hand and raising a jar of magical candy in the other.

Alberte's bar is full of the music of an orchestra hired for the occasion. The cloth of our table makes me think of an altar-cloth. I sit down and I look over my shoulder to see if the Japanese man has followed me. I turn my head in order not to see Drevet, a café bohemian of a species inferior to Falou's, whom the latter despises and calls a bohemian. He is a former painter, whom alcohol now prevents from painting. Laurence makes him signs of amity, because Drevet, naturally, has all her sympathies.

Groups with illuminated faces, men in suits, and women in low-cut dresses are coming in and going out incessantly, and I almost have vertigo. One wave of that human tide deposits on a high stool, like a piece of wreckage, a tall thin creature, slightly stooped. It is a woman who is still young, with a nose that is too long. Alberte lavishes consolations upon her.

We ask the cause of her chagrin. She has no special chagrin. She is the tall Loulou, who has no luck, and to whom inexorable life continues to be contrary. Alone among all the women in Paris and perhaps in the world, she has no invitation for the evening of revels.

"That can happen," says Alberte, without conviction, for she knows that it can only happen to the tall Loulou, marked since birth with eternal bad luck.

But Laurence cannot tolerate such an injustice. She gets up with a surge of amour that I have never seen and before I can stop her, she invites the tall Loulou to supper. In vain, Falou protests by means of signs, for he is superstitious and understands in its profound extent what the term "bad luck" can mean. The tall Loulou refuses, timidly, but Laurence is ready to get down on her knees before her and she forces her to sit down with us. I can see under the table that Falou is holding his index finger and little finger extended. Everything that surrounds me takes on a symbolic meaning for me, and I have the sentiment that an event of an occult order is about to occur.

However, I'm calm, and I think: *What folly! Always that taste for baseness! What would my friends think if they saw me at table with a hooker like that?*

Falou leans forward to whisper in my ear: "Something bad is going to happen to us this evening."

But Alberte comes to pour the champagne personally, in spite of the difficulty she has in moving. I had only seen her upper body until then, and her obesity fills me with astonishment.

Thus, what is hidden is revealed, I say to myself.

The orchestra is making so much noise that one can see mouths articulating phrases without being able to hear any sound. Dancers are trying to sketch steps on tables. An odor of food mingles with the perfume of women and regular gusts of fresh air that come from the door, opening and closing incessantly. I still expect to see the Japanese man appear with his jar of barley sugar.

I have no idea how long we stay there. I drink everything that is poured into my glass, but my mind remains lucid enough to notice Laurence's anxiety and the manner, even stranger than usual, in which she looks around.

Her attitude in my regard seems modified. Two or three times she takes my hand with a gesture that is not habitual to her, but I don't respond to the gesture and I disengage myself every time rather swiftly, because I'm exasperated with the amity that she is showing to the tall Loulou and the knowing glances that she is exchanging with the painter Drevet.

That exasperation is attenuated, however, and things around me take on a character of unreality. My head is spinning slightly.

At a given moment and although Laurence has not manifested any sign of it, I'm certain that she has just heard someone calling to her. The voice had no human tone and did not come from anywhere. It's the one I heard at the Bal Wagram. And at the same time, I'm gripped by a power of immobility and indifference, as if, instead of being an actor in the scene I'm seeing, I became a simple witness.

Then I hear a heart-rending cry, like that of someone having his throat cut. Is it the occult event I'm expecting. Is the Japanese man in the room? No. A few paces away a man in a suit is standing, waving his arms, with a knife in his hand and a great bloodstain on his shirt-front, in the place of the heart. But his cries are false. I understand. A glass of red wine has spilled on him, and in order to amuse the audience he has made a semblance of striking himself and is staggering, mimicking the throes of death. He's an old party animal with waxed moustaches and his friends are howling with joy around him. A drunken young woman simulates the preparation of a dressing with her folded napkin.

The door opens and I turn my head away. Someone has just entered, no matter who, an anonymous being with a bowler hat. In the frame of the doorway I have the vision of a few poor people, a beggar, a flower-seller with a little girl and other silhouettes even less distinct.

The man in the suit is agitating on one side like a caricature of assassinated stupidity, on the other, the creatures of the street immobilize, taking on a dream-like quality, and astonishment gives their faces the suave purity that one sees in certain paintings.

What happens then? I have never really understood. Is the voice real? Does it come from the street, does it emit vibrations like all terrestrial sounds or does it only resonate in the depths of the heart? Have the paupers in the street suddenly started intoning a hymn of misery? Is it the voice that I imagine to be that of evil?

Laurence squeezes my arm; she had heard. But perhaps for her it is a voice that is coming from further away, coming from the maternal entrails that bore her and is reminding her that girls are vowed to the same servitude as their mothers. Perhaps there is no voice at all and Laurence has already made her resolution a long time ago.

A soft kiss brushes my temples, at the place where my hair is beginning to go gray...

I have the sentiment of a dress going away, a little of my youth that is being taken away from me...

I sit there without budging, my head in my hands...

Much later, I perceive that Laurence is no longer there. I'm not astonished, but I stay and wait for her for an indeterminate time, while knowing that she isn't coming back. The tall Loulou has disappeared too.

I finally get up. The expression on Falou's face is completely stupid.

"Laurence left first," he says, simply.

And Alberte, without any hidden agenda, with the perfect ingenuousness of which her slack face is capable, adds: "Your lady has preceded you."

I nod my head. I let her believe that I'm tranquil, that I'll find Laurence a home. I'm certain that I won't find her there, that I won't see her the next day, or the following days, or ever again.

Outside, I perceive the Japanese man, who had just closed his shop. He has put an overcoat over is costume and plunged a felt hat over his head. But he still has red slippers of a bizarre form. There is nothing mysterious about him. He walks slowly. He seems poor and sad. Laurence would like him.

I think: *How quickly one becomes attached, without suspecting it.*

And Falou say to me: "That's curious! Nothing bad happened to us."

There is a hint of regret in his voice.

We pass through the Place Clichy. I raise my eyes. The sky is extraordinarily clear and I'm surprised by the different colors of the stars. I remark to my companion that it is perhaps the first time that I've noticed the beauty of the stars of Paris. And I add: "One only looks at the stars in the country."

He replies that he never looks at them, either in Paris or in the country.

He finally quits me. There are no taxis. Then I start running as fast as I can.

Oh, if I could only find Laurence asleep in our bedroom.

The key makes a noise in the lock. I call out: "Laurence!" in a low voice at first, and then in a loud voice, unrecognizable in its tone.

But no, I knew it. There's no one there.

It is futile to describe the regrets that I experienced and how, according to my habit, I recapitulated a thousand times the events that had occurred in the last few months, representing to myself what I ought to have done in some circumstance or other, imagining the exact phrases that I ought to have pronounced on such a day, at such an hour, I let myself fall into an extreme depression. Everything was my fault and I alone knew the extent of that fault. I had not loved Laurence enough to retain her. She would not have left if she had been afraid of causing me a profound and true dolor. I had only experienced desire for her. Who can tell whether even that desire might have been insufficient? I relived every minute I had spent with Laurence since the first kiss in the dining room, since the first embrace in a bedroom with the odor of stuffiness and seaweed until the last nights in Paris, and I eventually convinced myself that I had not loved her at all.

Face to face with myself, I was obliged to confess that every time I had taken her in my arms my imaginative power had, by an involuntary transposition, put in her place the image of her sister. I had begun in the automobile carrying me along the road to Toulon, at the moment when I had just overtaken the Holy Sacrament, and perhaps the initial cause of the evil was in the encounter between the Catholic God and the possessed individual that I was. I had continued. I had never ceased to imagine Eveline when I held her sister against me and many a time, face to face, I had closed my eyes in order to see her better, with her name on my lips.

I had not articulated the syllables of that name, but who can tell whether Laurence had not heard them all the same.

I had the confirmation that I was not mistaken when, two days after her departure, I received a letter from Laurence.

She told me rather briefly not to worry about her. She had wanted to live as she pleased. She did not merit the interest—she did not say the love—that I had taken in her. She apologized for the abruptness of her abandonment and any pain that it might have caused.

The sentence in her letter that struck me most forcefully was: *In any case, I've divined that you were thinking incessantly about my sister, and I don't hold it against you.*

She did not give me her address. I could not send on her things or come to her aid. It was a great relief for me to recall that, a few days before, I had given her a rather large sum for a purchase of dresses that had then been postponed, which had still been in the bag she was carrying on Christmas Eve.

Dismal days passed. I went one evening to question Alberte. She had not seen Laurence again. She assured me of that several times, with vivacity, and even extended her head, swearing on her mother's head, which I had not asked her to do. While making that oath she was squeezing a lemon that she was about to peel in order o make a cocktail, and the fruit suddenly appeared to me as the symbol of a gilded lie. Then she paid no further heed to me, while nevertheless watching me from the corner of her eye, and I thought I discerned in her willful indifference the intention of discouraging me from coming back. The painter Drevet, who was slumped on a banquette in front of a drink, did not salute me, and even took care to avoid my gaze.

I made long stations in the neighboring cafés, but they were futile. Then I took the decision not to go out again and I started reading books in my library. I studied religions. I read everything I could relating to the Essenes, the Gnostics and the various sects that had perpetuated their beliefs. I also read everything I could relating to possession, demons and the relationships between demons and humans. I saw that, according to the priests who had treated the subject, those relationships were narrow and multiple.

But I only read with half my mind. The other half was elsewhere than the books, concentrated in the sense of hearing, avoid to hear whether the doorbell might ring. Sometimes, it did ring. It was the electrician, or the plumber, or someone making a mistake.

I then enunciated, for myself: "I'm not expecting anyone."

In reality, I was incessantly expectant. But was it really Laurence that I was expecting?

It was a Sunday, at about five o'clock. The part of my being occupied in listening, unknown to the other, to the noises of the house, perceived the brief, timid ring of someone who will not ring a second time if no one responds to the first. I had given everyone leave that day, and I was in pajamas, in a darker mood than usual. I had decided not to see anyone. However, I pursed my lips and at a slow pace, I went to open the door myself.

On the threshold, in the demi-obscurity of the landing, stood Eveline. I cannot say that I was surprised to see her. No, I was expecting her. It was her for whom I was waiting. It was, therefore, natural that she had come. We stood there for a minute, however, considering one another.

In the end I said: "Come in."

And she simply came in.

I stammered an apology for my costume, for the obscurity of the antechamber, where one risked bumping into an umbrella-stand, and I took her into the studio.

She darted a glance around the room curiously, and the calmness of that gaze made me think that she was not expecting to see a door open. She knew, then, that Laurence had left me. She did not speak until after that rapid inspection.

The step that she had taken was very painful, and I ought to understand that. She had thought, however, that it was her duty to make it—unknown to her father, of course.

She spoke in a determinedly grave and severe tone.

"I've come on Sunday because I thought that you wouldn't go out on that day."

She repeated that insignificant and evidently unnecessary phrase twice.

She had changed. The blue-tinted ash-gray of her eyes was more profound. Her features were more mobile and animated by a kind of life that had not been there before. She appeared to me to be more beautiful and less distant, and I had the bizarre sensation that she had returned from a voyage after a season on a distant planet. It was very warm in my studio and, without thinking about it, she unfastened her fur coat. She was wearing a white dress, simple and straight. I saw the scene in the corridor again and I turned my eyes away, inviting her to sit down. She remained standing.

She did not want to reproach me. She had not come for that. Everyone had to settle their own conscience. I had to know, undoubtedly, that everyone had judged my conduct severely, perhaps too severely. She alone knew the part of the responsibility that her sister Laurence had. She alone knew how far her coquetry went, and even the

145

word coquetry was too weak. Her mother had often predicted what was bound to happen. Yes, I had excuses. But in the end, there was an age-difference between Laurence and me that ought to have made me reflect.

In saying that she had a glint of triumph in her eyes, and the creases of her mouth expressed a delicious and pure cruelty.

It was not the first time she had made an allusion to my age. That had always been very disagreeable to me. I made an evasive gesture. I got ready to respond that Laurence was of age and that she had not found my age disproportionate with hers, but she stopped me.

"No matter! That isn't the question. I believe that if Laurence hadn't left with you she would have left with the first man who came along."

The first to come along! That was the expression that Laurence had used herself, in front of the abandoned house, when the project of flight had been formed between us.

"What has pushed me to come to see you," Eveline went on, fixing me with her immense eyes, "is the anxiety that my sister now inspires in me. Do you know what has become of her? Do you know her existence?"

I replied that I had received a letter from her and that I had done everything possible to find her, but I had not succeeded in doing so.

"Anyway, what's the point? Laurence left me voluntarily. She knew what she was doing. I consider that everyone is free to dispose of themselves."

Perhaps my voice had a hint of melancholy in saying that. As if she were abruptly interested in the element of chagrin that she believed she discerned, Eveline sat down, invited me with a gesture to sit down facing her, leaned forward and said: "And have you suffered from being abandoned? Are you still suffering now? For you loved her, didn't you?"

I did not reply.

"You loved her?" she repeated.

I made her the observation in my turn that that was not the question and that if I were suffering, it was the punishment for my sin, if there was one."

Well," said Eveline, "personally, I've had news of my sister. Oh, indirectly, for she doesn't love me enough to write to me. Friends have encountered her and they came to warn me about the existence she's leading. But I'm hesitant; I don't want to deal you too painful a blow."

The same immaterial cruelty that I had already seen in her face refined her features, and put a mist into her eyes. Then, firmly, articulating her words so that none would be lost, but nevertheless speaking rapidly, for all executions are rapid. She said:

"Laurence is leading an abominable life. She has been seen with people who belong to the utmost depths of society. It seems that she had attained the ultimate degree of depravity. Personally, I had foreseen everything that has happened and I'm not afflicted by what my sister might do. But it's because of my father. It's necessary, so far as it's possible, that he doesn't know. It's necessary to ask Laurence not to show herself, to offer her money, if necessary, for that. You ought to have at least an idea of the people with whom she might be living. Perhaps—almost certainly, in fact—she knew them with you? It's absolutely necessary to try to find her."

I affirmed once again to Eveline that I did not have the slightest idea what had become of Laurence.

147

"At any rate, I don't believe that I'm qualified to give her lessons in morality."

The vibrations of my voice had a great importance that evening. In the manner in which I pronounced those words there was an intention of indifference that astonished me, and produced an effect as great as the previous melancholy.

Eveline stood up. She was like an archer who has launched an arrow and has just perceived that the target has been traversed completely. She took a few steps around the room without losing sight of me. How nervous she was, and how different from how I had known her. What was that movement of her ignorant loins, in which there was almost a hint of sensuality?

She affected to be looking with interest at the books that covered the walls.

"What of the Essenes?" I said. "Were other nocturnal masses celebrated out there after my departure?"

She turned around abruptly and her voice became lower in order to reply. Dusk had now invaded the room.

"Oh, the masses," she said. "Yes, there are going to be ceremonies, but here in Paris. It appears the masses can have an extraordinary magical power if they're accomplished in accordance with the original rites. They once served to attract spiritual forces to humans. Monsieur Althon and Kotzebue have discovered the ancient ceremonial."

Eveline had pronounced those names with respect, almost with dread.

"Do you see much of Monsieur Althon?"

She turned her head away. "No. But...I once went to his house with Kotzebue, precisely because of the masses. Everything has changed among the Essenes since Monsieur Althon has joined us."

As I could scarcely distinguish Eveline's face in the half-light, I thought it a good idea to switch on the electricity. A lamp lit up. There was an anxiety in the young woman's face. She almost made a gesture of hiding it with her hand.

"Why put the light on?" she said. "The twilight is very pleasant. We can still take advantage if it for a few more minutes."

I switched the lamp off. Then Eveline said, with vivacity: "I don't know why I'm talking to you about the masses. You mentioned them to me first, and then I let myself go, but I beg you not to say anything to anyone. If Kotzebue knew that I had even made an allusion to them..."

"I thought that everyone was admitted to the masses. I witnessed one myself in the Midi..."

"Oh, it's no longer the same thing. Henceforth there will only be a small number of initiates who are allowed to take part in them."

"But why?"

Eveline uttered a singular laugh, whose resonance made me feel uneasy, a laugh that clashed with her nature, and I saw her blue eyes fixed in an upward direction, as if she were seeing imaginary forms of an unexpected character.

"Physical beauty has an action on the development of the soul. The pleasure of the body also, it seems. There is a secret in amour that was lost for ages, and which Simon Magus rediscovered. Of course, neither Monsieur Althon or Kotzebue must know that I've mentioned that secret to you. But you're perhaps aware of the role that Helen played."

I wanted to dissipate the sentiment of embarrassment that I experienced and I said: "It's completely dark now."

I switched on the light.

Then I went to the window that overlooked the street and drew the curtains. As I did so, my gaze chanced to plunge down to the sidewalk opposite. I perceived Kotzebue pacing back and forth in an impatient fashion, in the attitude of a man who is waiting.

My first thought was that he had accompanied Eveline, that there was an understanding between that two of them and that I was a dupe—I did not know of what, but of something.

The curtain fell back. I turned around. But Eveline did not seem to be in any hurry to leave. She had not given a succinct character to her words, as one does when one knows that someone is outside the door and is waiting for you. Kotzebue had not come with her, but he had doubtless followed her without her knowledge. It was to her that he destined the role of Helen in the cult of which he intended to be the high priest and whose rites were only secret because of their equivocal character. I remembered in a second the projects that he had once exposed to me, to which I had listened with admiration, but which he had disdained to develop because he did not judge me capable of understanding them.

I also remembered the moments I had spent in the Rue Ballu outside his door, measuring his jealousy by mine, and I savored a sort of revenge in that just reversal of things.

No, Eveline had no hatred. The shade of the lamp that I had just illuminated was made of Chinese silk with crimson tints. The light that filtered over her gave her a dreamlike appearance. Her abundant hair overflowed beneath the fur of her toque. I thought about the oblique light of the corridor, the circle that the night-dress had formed at her feet.

And suddenly, I had the knowledge of the path that evil follows in the human soul. It gives birth to desire, and desire is creative. I had often dreamed of having Eveline in my home, and she was there, improbable as it might be! I had often dreamed of drawing her to me, of dragging her into my bedroom, and a presentiment told me that if I attempted it at that moment I would only encounter a resistance strong enough to give more value to the success.

I did not have to ask myself how that was possible. I had already observed that, in the course of my life, many women had abandoned themselves to me with facility too great to be explained by ordinary reasons. A power had devolved to me and I did not know from whom I had received it. I had the striking evidence of that power and I understood that it was also exercised independently of me, since an unknown cause had cast Eveline into the state of disturbance in which I now saw her.

I shivered, but I did not think of reacting against the force that seemed to be directing my actions.

"Is it indiscreet to ask to see the letter that Laurence wrote to you?" Eveline said to me, to break the silence and also to recall the purpose of her visit.

"Not at all."

The letter was in a drawer in my bedroom and that bedroom communicated with the studio by a door. I had only to go and fetch it. Instead of that I said: "Come with me. At the same time, you can see the rest of my library. The letter is here in my bedroom."

I had lowered my voice to pronounce the final words, in such a way that Eveline might not have heard them.

She replied, with great simplicity: "Good."

I opened the door and she went in. I recalled at the same time that in all the creations of my mind, after having imagined Eveline in my studio, I had imagined her crossing the threshold of my bedroom. Her feet made no sound on the carpet and the door closed silently behind her.

Everything went similarly. From that moment on I was drawn away by the force of my past imaginations. I was no longer the master of my actions. They were determined by my old desires: my desires, children of evil. I was conscious of that and I said to myself:

No one is free. Every action is the irresistible terminus of a long sequence of causes.

"How warm it is in here," Eveline said to me.

And I replied: "Yes, the heater is open."

The banality of phrases pronounced calmly is always a sign of mental agitation. An ordinary little wind precedes storms.

I took out Laurence's letter and I held it out to Eveline.

"Can you see well enough?" I asked her.

She made an affirmative sign and I leaned over her shoulder as if to reread the letter. A human breath reached me, almost imperceptible, in which no essence of perfume was mingled.

Eveline's shoulders lifted up. She had reached the sentence: *I've divined that you were thinking incessantly about my sister, and I don't hold it against you.*

Eveline turned to me and said: "Really! Is that possible? You thought incessantly about me?"

I was conscious that there was something distraught in her gaze. I ought to have replied to her that indeed, I had been thinking about her, and for a long time. But I was living a scene already dreamed, and those who are dreaming do not talk about desired women; they throw themselves upon them.

I took Eveline in my arms and I pushed her on to the low bed, where we both fund ourselves half-lying down. I experienced then the intoxication of her presence against me, to the point of being entirely overturned. It was as if the inclined position that I had just abruptly adopted had made me fall into another universe, where everything was frivolous sensuality and the delight of realization.

But in that intoxication my intelligence remained active, and weighed the movements, judged the motives with an inconceivable rapidity.

The inaccessible Eveline only defended herself feebly. She scarcely sketched the habitual gestures of modesty. To the distraction of her eyes was added an expression of indescribable fear. As my mouth was upon hers, she turned her head with an abrupt movement, preserving her lips but offering her body.

Why? Whence came that partial consent? Did she want, by virtue of feminine jealousy, to take a revenge on her sister? Ws it not a sort of sacrifice, a holocaust to my desire, by virtue of extravagant ideas by which her mind had been troubled? Yes, that was the pretext, and a will foreign to mine had imposed it on her. I was the plaything of evil, by virtue of a distant convention, and Eveline had come for her fall, and for mine.

It seemed to me that I was lifting the robe of a priestess, placing a hand on a sacred zaimph,[8] offending a chaste goddess in the bounds of her temple. And I rejoiced in the offense, I was penetrated delectably by the profanation of the divine. The dream followed its inexorable march into reality.

I could no longer see Eveline's face, which was turned to the pillow and hidden by the spread of her hair, but I contemplated the perfection of her body. The extension of the legs was so perfect that it was reminiscent of a poem finishing in a cry of hope. In the birth of the breasts, in the movement of the arm folded for a confused defense, there were statuesque graces, the matt texture of marble polished for worshipful admiration. And in its immobility that body evoked, as it had by means of the dance in the middle of pines and mimosas, the surge of the spirit that wants to disengage from matter.

Then there was something like a light within me.

No one is free, I had thought, a few moments before; we are drawn along by our own momentum. I understood that I was free, that I could choose—and for the first time, I saw the mysterious line of demarcation between good and evil.

I had had Laurence; I was about to have Eveline. I had had no remorse in taking Laurence, and even on reflecting on it afterwards, I had approved of myself for having drawn her into life, away from her family, for the joy and the dolor. I was on the point of playing the same

---

[8] The zaimph, or veil of Tanit, was familiar to French readers because of the crucial symbolic role that it plays in Gustave Flaubert's classic *Salammbô* (1862), in a scene of profanation to which this paragraph is a direct reference.

role with Eveline, but I sensed that no bad action could equal in evil the one that I was about to accomplish. For if amour and life were Laurence's law, Eveline had surpassed that goal and had a higher one, more elevated.

Physical love had always inspired disgust in her. No sensuality had awakened in her. She had wanted to devote herself exclusively to the spirit, to neglect material enjoyments for creative chastity. She was like a vestal gone astray in our time.

And I was about to make her regress, to accomplish the greatest crime, one that is unpardonable, one committed against the spirit.

It was because I was veritably accursed, then. Somewhere, in a world very close to ours and yet did not communicate with it, evil beings, with faces in which beauty and ugliness were only one, were rejoicing, alerting one another to the act that I was about to commit. I saw their signs, I understood their language, and I was astonished to resemble them, to have the same duality, to be so beautiful and so ugly at the same time.

But no, there was still time; the act had not been accomplished, and by a deliberate determination, I renounced its accomplishment.

I disengaged the arm with which I was pressing Eveline's breasts and I allowed her to fall back gently next to me, like the splendid burden of human responsibility.

I brushed her golden temple with my lips, and rendered her the light kiss that her sister had posed on mine when quitting me.

She turned, like someone wounded on a battlefield astonished at not being finished off by the enemy, but I understood that, in her perfect ignorance, she thought that perhaps there was no reason to be astonished.

As I murmured a few incomprehensible words, which included the word *pardon*, the clock on the mantelpiece chimed seven.

Eveline uttered a cry. She got dressed, putting on her dress in haste. I tried to talk to her, to explain to her that she ought not to see Kotzebue or Monsieur Althon any longer. Those names put an expression of terror in her physiognomy, but she gave the impression of not grasping the meaning of what I said. As I persisted, she made a sign to me to speak more quietly, and appeared to fear that someone might overhear me—not someone who was listening behind the door, but who might have been everywhere, in the ambience of the atmosphere.

At that time, the valet de chambre should have returned. I rang, and I sent him to find a taxi. He came back almost immediately. Eveline was already in the antechamber.

I would have liked to see her again, to put her on guard, to make her understand the danger that I sensed around her and which I could not specify precisely. I dared not ask her to come back and I sensed that she did not want to. There was no bitterness in the limpid blue of her eyes, but only anxiety and disorder.

She went down the stairs very rapidly and I heard the door of the taxi close.

I went back to the studio and I lifted the curtain. I perceived Kotzebue's silhouette. He was motionless, uncertain of what he ought to do. In the same attitude as me, once, in the Rue Ballu, when I had seen Laurence draw away, he watched Eveline's vehicle disappear. He departed in the same direction, and I almost ran out in order to catch up with him.

He disappeared into the shadow, but cannot have gone very far.

I had let the curtain fall back and I stared at the carpet. It was full of familiar and absurd faces that I knew well, but their expression appeared to me to be transformed. Those faces were threatening, like those of redoubtable enemies with whom I had just entered into battle. I had disobeyed Lucifer. Somewhere, in the sanctuary of my soul, a lamp had been lit of which I had to defend the flame. But was there enough courage in me?

The doorbell rang. I went to open the door myself, thinking that Eveline might have come back. I saw Kotzebue on the landing, I had never noticed his tall stature, his thick neck and his square jaw so clearly.

"I have to talk to you," he said.

And I replied: "Me too."

I sensed when he had come in that we were both prey to an extraordinary excitement.

"If I've offended you in any way," I said, "I'm ready to give you an honest explanation."

He contented himself with sniggering.

"It's you who first reminded me of the pact we once signed, and enabled me to glimpse its scope. At first I didn't take what you said seriously. I refused to believe in the gravity of what had only been childishness. But I've thought about it. Events have brought me proofs. Perhaps I'm only afflicted by a sickness of the imagination, I'm sure that you're afflicted by the same sickness as me. In any case, you know something. You've studied the questions that are preoccupying me. You know what forces we were once able, unknown to ourselves, to put into action. You can deliver me from an obsession..."

I perceived that I was addressing him as *tu* for the first time in fifteen years, so haunted was I by the idea of our equality in the pact.

Kotzebue was not thinking of picking up that change of tone. He had not ceased sniggering while I was speaking. At the same time, he was considering my pajamas, my unkempt hair, and my distraught features. As the bedroom door was still open, he took two or three steps that permitted him to see the disordered bed. He must have found in that sight an answer to the questions that had motivated his visit, and his physiognomy expressed the phrase: *Now I know!*

He remained silent, his head bowed.

"Well?"

"It's too late. You've taken the left-hand path, from which one cannot turn back, It will be too comfortable, in any case. Haven't you received what you asked for? Haven't you seen your desires granted? You've been a perfect instrument of Lucifer, without suspecting it. But he knew it, and he guided you. Now you'd like to get away from him. It's vain to try. He's the companion that one never quits, who accompanies you not only in the voyage of life but that one makes after death."

"Come on" I cried, "You're not being serious. You're holding a grudge, admit it. You think you have grievances against me, so you want to get your revenge. But you don't believe in the existence of Lucifer either as a person or as an active will! You don't believe in the fallen angel!"

"You're mistaken—I do believe it. There are fallen angels. There was one here just now. And redoubtable, believe me. He will become even more so. Why should there not be a greater one who sent him?"

"But you said it yourself, for a long time the world has been directed by men alone. Above the human there were only forces, only laws. Evil was only the human tendency to egotism."

"I might have been mistaken. Since I've seen you, I've learned things that I didn't know. My ideas on that subject have changed completely."

I was convinced that Kotzebue had only come to see me under the empire of jealousy, to take his revenge on me and torment me, so I only half-believed what he said. I examined his face, where there was a hint of sudden gravity, and I discovered with anguish that he was speaking in all sincerity.

"But then, if you believe in the existence of Lucifer, you've made a pact with him, like me, you're accursed, like me. We're at the same point."

He shook his head, screwing up his eyes and smiling scornfully.

"What tells you that I haven't accepted the pact in all its consequences, and that I'm not very glad of it? You, you're like a wretched moth frightened by the flame of a lamp and bumping into all the window panes. Sooner or later, you'll burn your wings, if you haven't already. In any case, you can renounce flying in the light and the air."

A cold chill ran through my body, at the same time as I was invaded by a nameless terror. Distant memories of childhood reappeared. I recalled a book of tales and an image of the Devil that had frightened me when I was four or five years old. I recalled the stairway to an attic that was the demon's lair in my games. I tried to put on a brave face and started to laugh. My laughter rang false.

"I don't believe a word of what you're saying."

He shrugged his shoulders. "Get away! But you're sweating with fear, and you're right. You're afraid, and you don't know why. What would you be like if you knew! You're a miserable ignoramus. You're one of the countless naïve individuals who leave belief in the Evil Spirit to simple folk—imbeciles, as they say. They think themselves very strong, with their science, with their reason. It's them who are the imbeciles. Lucifer exists. I, who once made a pact with him by chance, have searched for him and have found him. There are also those who have searched for and found God. That's their business."

Yes, Kotzebue was speaking sincerely, and my fear increased. I tried in vain not to let him see it, but I sensed my eyes widening and it seemed to me that I was struck with immobility.

"You see, when one belongs as completely as you do to Lucifer"—he was emphasizing his words—"when one has been heaped by his benefits"—he darted and oblique glace at the bedroom—"what good is there in struggling in vain? It's better to be with him frankly, to take advantage of his grandeur, to serve his power."

"Be with him? I don't really understand. You mean that it's better to do evil amorously?"

Kotzebue shrugged his shoulders. "You always come back to good and evil. Yes, if you want, you can call Lucifer evil. That's one of his names, but he has others, and finer ones."

He took a few steps into the bedroom. A street-lamp caused a sad light to filter between the curtains over the window, which illuminated it.

"You say that I've been heaped by his benefits, but I don't see in what respect. My life has been average. I haven't succeeded in what I've attempted. I've attempted painting, and then literature. Where have I ended up? If I had had a protection over me..."

Kotzebue burst out laughing.

"You've had what you desired deep down. You only desired base things—the bodies of women. You're uniquely a being of flesh. Your flesh has been lavishly supplied. That began with Irma Pascaud, remember. She didn't much like you to begin with. Me, I daren't even look at her. I was timid. I placed her so high. Well, you only had to make a sign, and you had her. The woman who has no soul: you were the one who gave her that nickname among our comrades, and everyone adopted it. There was only me who didn't call her that, because I didn't understand. I thought her a very beautiful soul.

But you knew full well that you were right in saying that she had no soul. She had had one, but you must have taken it away from her."

"Me!"

"Yes. For the Luciferian takes from those who have the misfortune to love him their luck, their capacity for happiness, the little patrimony of goodness that constitutes their soul. He dispossesses them, unconsciously. I haven't followed you in life, but I'm certain that if you care to cast a glance backwards you'll see yourself giving your hand to a chain on soulless creatures, all those that you've left on the edge of the road after having stolen their invisible treasure, their modest baggage for eternity."

"That's not true!" I cried.

But I knew very well how much truth there was in what Kotzebue said. I contemplated in the depths of my memory the faces of vanished mistresses, and I heard, as if it were resonating in the room, the voice of a sweet petite blonde woman encountered in a café at midnight, who said to me, a few days later:

"It's you, you alone, who have doomed me!"

I had laughed at the time, for the little woman was known as a professional and did not hide it. But now I thought that her words might perhaps have had a more profound meaning than their apparent significance, which had escaped me before. Yes, perhaps I had doomed her, as she said.

"Then, you're claiming seriously that Lucifer exists, and that there are men who obey his will, render him worship, believe in him."

I had raised my voice. I was speaking in a tone of which I was not the master. Kotzebue's voice appeared to me to be all the lower.

"It was Lévy who was right, the man we mocked so forcefully when he talked to us about certain secret communities in which Lucifer is worshiped, as Jesus Christ is worshiped in monasteries. Those communities are only secret here and now. If you want to see your brothers, our brothers, celebrate public ceremonies to the spirit of evil, go to ancient Assyria, to the slopes of the mountain called Djebel Maklouh, among the Yezidees—which is to say, the devil-worshippers. Go to the Indies, among the black Jews of Cochin, or to the Antilles, with the Voodoo cults. There are infernal cults in northern China, and near Lake Chad in Africa. And I'll tell you something more astonishing that I've seen with my own eyes.

"In the course of my voyage to the Orient, I went to the edge of the Dead Sea in order to contemplate the place where the Essenes once lived, those wise and perfect men in whose midst Jesus was instructed. I believed at that time in that wisdom and perfection. I was hoping for I know not what inspiration, I know not what marvelous encounter. Well, not very far away from the place where Jesus was baptized by John the Baptist, there is a monastery, a monastery without a chapel, whose threshold is not dominated by any cross. There you can see the conscious disciples of Lucifer..."

He stopped, like someone who regrets having said too much.

"But after all, you can't say that brotherhoods of evil men exist who labor voluntarily in the development of evil. That's impossible. If it were true, it would be known, people would talk about it, and they'd succeed in destroying them."

"That's true, and there are people who know about the existence of these brotherhoods, but they don't talk about them and don't think of destroying them, for reasons of prudence, and they're right. Perhaps I'll astonish you too much by telling you that these brotherhoods have numerous affiliates, and astonish you even more by telling you that you're one of them."

I uttered a dry of fury. "You're lying."

But I observed, with despair, that I had already said to myself what he was saying to me.

His little eyes, whose fugitive gaze I had never caught, settled on mine.

"There's no need to shout. Anyway, you understood. Even if you didn't articulate any sound, if you didn't formulate your thought, it will be seen and it will be judged."

"By whom?"

"By them, the masters of the left-hand path who have pushed self-love to the point of becoming divine. They are the ones who direct you and you can no longer escape them. You're their instrument. They have an invisible contact with you. It was them who sent Eveline here, in order that you could bring down a creature who had wanted to rise too high. You've carried out your mission faithfully. You've pushed into your bed that young woman, who might have been the living symbol of the pure spirit, and is henceforth designated to incarnate matter and its pleasure. For they only accord a price to degeneration. Believe me, follow the advice I'm giving you. One can't fight them. It's better to serve them frankly and at least have the advantage. I have no interest in telling you that."

"Then why are you doing it?"

"To spare you torture of certain nocturnal appeals, nightmares of an excessively frightful nature, apparitions that might trouble your reason."

Kotzebue's gaze plunged deep into mine. He dominated me with all of his tall stature. He was about to continue.

I cannot explain, now, the violence that took possession of me. Perhaps I had measured in a second the fear to which the words I had just heard were going to give birth, and the miserable quality of that fear to come was the cause of my anger. Perhaps I was angry with myself for already having thought what Kotzebue had just expressed.

I threw myself upon him and grabbed him by the collar of his coat, crying: "Get out! You're nothing but a wretch!"

To my great surprise, he did not resist. In spite of his weight, I pushed him without difficulty all the way to the antechamber, astonished by my strength. I had the sentiment that his mass was unresistant and that if I shook a little more forcefully, he might suddenly disperse, like one of those great menacing forms that one sees in dreams and that a thought suffices to make vanish.

He had opened the entrance door himself. I handed him his hat. Under the light of the stairway his powerful frame seemed to condense again. He breathed out, collected himself, extended the tip of his index finger toward me like a rapier and said: "You're the wretch! But I forgive you, because of the suffering that is reserved for you."

I slammed the door. I turned round and saw myself in a mirror. I was haggard, and my face was narrower than usual. But was there not another face behind me, considering me?

I went back into the studio and I inspected the bedroom. It seemed to me that someone there had pronounced my name.

The valet de chambre appeared almost immediately.
Was it the noise that had attracted him or had he had a
secret thought? What a singular expression he had! But
how had he entered my service, and how long ago? I
scarcely heard the phrase he proffered, in which there
was mention of dinner being served, but I remarked its
demonic irony.

I made him a sign that he no longer had to watch
over me and I went to get dressed in order to go out,
avoiding looking in mirrors, because it is in the depths of
their infinite distance that the visitors from beyond begin
to march.

I didn't know where I was going. I went down the Rue Ampère, turned the corner, and I saw a little stone church that I didn't know. I passed before it every day in order to go and buy cigarettes at the tobacconist's and get the newspapers from a kiosk nearby, but I had the sensation that it has not been there the day before, that it had just surged abruptly from the pavement of the street. My first thought was that of a miracle of a religious order. I stopped to contemplate it.

How beautiful it was, with that bearded archbishop who, crosier in hand, was standing above its portal, with the heavenward surged of its architecture, the tip of its steeple terminated by a lightning-conductor.

My admiration was spoiled by that lightning-conductor. That divine house ought not to have had any need of any such protection. There was, therefore, an enemy who menaced that church from the direction of the sky and against whom the cross was insufficient.

Suddenly, I said to myself that I might be able to put an end to my torment, escape the threat of nightmares, mysterious voices and orders given by the invisible brothers of evil. Possessions were well known to the Catholic Church. I had at home the works of pious and erudite men who had catalogued the demons and specified the means of triumphing over them. Why not put myself under the protection of the Church? It is true that I had not practiced since childhood, and sincerely believed myself to be an unbeliever; but my mental disarray was so great that I was disposed to believe as I had on the forgotten day of my first communion, if only a little peace could return to me. Then again, in the singular encounter with that church, which I had never seen before, there was an indication of sorts.

Reading a handwritten notice under the porch was already an appeasement. That notice summoned the Children of Mary for imminent dates. It announced the feast of Saint Geneviève and the gathering of the Holy Family.

The Children of Mary! The Holy Family! How far away those groups must be, how different from those of which I had just heard mention, and the existence of which filled me with terror.

I went in, and I was astonished by the number of candles that were burning, and forming a kind of circular procession. There were large ones and small ones, doubtless proportionate to the fortune of those who had said prayers, or the magnitude of their sin. I saw one that was so tiny that I was gripped by pity for the person who had had it burned, thinking that it might be someone accursed, like me, someone very poor, twice accursed.

I was reassured by a large number of dwellings in sculpted wood to the right and the left, which must be the confessionals. I looked at an inscription on the door of one of them: Abbé Durand. At the same moment, an aged man wearing an overcoat, who had his hat in his hand, came toward me. He had begun to blow out the lighted candles, and had interrupted himself in order to consider me when I came in.

"The church is about to close, Monsieur," he said.

I replied that it was absolutely necessary that I see the curé immediately.

He made the gesture of raising his arms to Heaven.

"The curé of Saint-François-de-Sales! But that's impossible. Strictly speaking, it might be possible to see the priest on duty, who is presently Abbé Durand"—he pointed to the little sculpted house next to which we were standing—"but it's too late now. Abbé Durand is having dinner. Come back tomorrow morning at eight o'clock."

The man must only be occupied in a modest ecclesiastical function. I put a silver coin in his hand and begged him to go in search of Abbé Durand.

"Tell him that it's a very grave and very urgent matter."

Abbé Durand was dining in the house next to the church. I saw the man disappear into the depths of the church, near a niche where wax individuals surrounded an Enfant Jesus of the same material.

I imagined the pious family in the bosom of which Abbé Durand must be dining. The tablecloth must resemble an altar cloth. What good sentiments! What a complete absence of malediction!

Abbé Durand arrived a few minutes later. He had a round face charged with benevolence. He made an effort to appear severe and pressed. I divined that he was in haste to resume his interrupted meal.

He asked me immediately whether it was a matter of giving the Sacraments. When I said no, and explained that I wanted to confess, his effort of discontentment increased.

"There are hours for that," he said. But he opened the door on which his name was inscribed and made me a sign to kneel down facing him. At the same time, his face was covered by a mildness that must have been natural to him and filled me with emotion. I nearly got up and left in order not to scandalize such an excellent man.

Abbé Durand was doubtless accustomed to the revelation of the most various sins. When I had warned him in a low voice that what he was about to hear had a particularly terrible and singular character he nodded his head distractedly, as if to say: *Do it quickly, I've heard many others.*

And he invited me to recite a *pater* while he made the sign of the cross. I replied that I had forgotten the exact text of the prayer. That did not appear to astonish him in the slightest. Other sinners must have come, driven by the hope of absolution, who were as ignorant as me.

"Repeat after me," he said—and he recited the *pater* with such great rapidity that I could only mumble unintelligible things in my turn.

"I'm listening, my son," said Abbé Durand, lowering his eyes in the attitude of a listener.

Then I gathered all my courage and I told him, without omitting any detail, the story of the evening once spent with Lévy and Kotzebue. I recounted the conditions in which that pact, forgotten by me, had returned to my memory, how it obsessed me and in what fashion I had arrived at believing that it had influenced all the actions of my life.

At first Abbé Durand tapped the wood of the confessional on which he was leaning several times, as if to tell me to go more rapidly, to skip unimportant matters. Then he stopped, made a backward movement, and I thought that he was about to flee. He looked at me with extreme attention, as one looks at an extraordinary being or a madman. I sensed, without it being expressed in any way, that the abandoned dinner had lost all its importance in his eyes, given the gravity of the case. And there was also some suspicion in him, as if I were susceptible of delivering myself to a sudden extravagance. I affected the simplest and most modest appearance in order to reassure him.

But I sensed hope quitting me. I had told myself vaguely that perhaps, in the presence of the majesty of the church, my story had less importance than I thought, that many people secretly concluded similar pacts and that I was about to be immediately reassured and perhaps delivered by some ecclesiastical prestige—but I was undeceived by the sadness that was painted on Abbé Durand's visage.

While I continued my story the gray-haired individual that had greeted me blew out the circle of candles. He returned from time to time and looked in my direction. I thought that he was in a hurry to see the importunate sinner depart who was preventing him from going home.

When the last ex-voto was extinct, the church was filled with darkness. I had finished, Abbé Durand remained silent and I could not distinguish his features. I raised my eyes. The vault above my head was distant, immense. It seemed to me that I had penetrated into an edifice so vast that I would never be able to get out of it again.

Finally, Abbé Durand spoke. First, he asked me for some information about the Essenes, Kotzebue and me. Then he said: "Your case is very serious, my child, and it far surpasses my feeble competence. It's necessary that I refer you to a superior authority. Between now and then, you must pray, in a constant fashion, even fast in a certain measure, and come to see me again in a few days."

In a few days! It was impossible for me to wait so long. I was there as if in consultation with a physician. I needed a consoling beverage. I asked him whether the superior authority could not be consulted immediately.

The prospect of a sleepless night appeared to me to be too redoubtable.

Abbé Durand shook his head. He reflected. He would like nothing better than to lighten my woes in accordance with his means, but there were hours...there were hierarchies...

"Come and find me here tomorrow morning at nine o'clock. I'll get up early and do what is necessary beforehand. There's no one more qualified than the person you'll see tomorrow."

He stood up, and I did the same.

"But this evening?" I said, with anguish.

"Prayer is the sovereign power against demons."

He remembered that he was dealing with a sinner who did not even know the *pater*, and made me a sign to wait. He went into the sacristy and he came back with a little book.

"You'll find the seven psalms of penitence there, and also the *Pater* and the *Ave Maria*. Say them as many times as you can."

"Is it necessary to think at the same time about what I'm reading?"

That question astonished him. He reflected.

"Read the prayers. That's sufficient."

As I took my leave of him he slipped into my hand a small round object that I thought at first was a sou.

"Put that medallion around your neck this evening. It was given to me once, and it's miraculous."

As I went away with my book of prayers and my medallion it seemed to me that I had returned to the distant time of my first communion. I had been afraid of the Devil then, but the sentiment of my infantile purity rendered me invulnerable. If demons surrounded me, there were also angels to combat them. Now, I had lost all my allies and the enemy was more powerful than ever.

I almost threw the book and the medallion into the street. They could not be of any help to me without the faith that I had lost.

At nine o'clock Abbé Durand was already on the threshold of Saint-François-de-Sales, waiting for me. He had been occupied with me, he said. He had informed the authority competent in a case like mine and we were awaited by an individual highly-placed in the Church.

On the way, Abbé Durand rubbed his hands. His desire to come to my aid was embellished by the satisfaction of playing a role and seeing a great theologian, a master of religious science.

I knew that every bishopric has an exorcist attached, even though exorcism is only carried out very rarely.

It's to the exorcist that we're going, I thought.

I was not mistaken. Père Théodore lived in a small detached house at the back of a courtyard, beyond the Avenue de Maine. We were introduced into a modest drawing room, well kept, into which a hint of Spanish ostentation penetrated in spite of its modesty.

"He's a first rate man," said Abbé Durand, who was intimidated. "A little severe at first sight, but first rate."

The door opened abruptly, in a theatrical fashion. A fulgurant gaze traversed me and I saw a Spanish priest standing before me, examining me. He was Spanish in his teeth, his jaw and his flattened nose. He did not appear to have any flesh or muscle, nothing but bones. I was surprised not to discover, when he spoke, any foreign accent.

He made me an imperceptible sign of the head and he saluted Abbé Durand with a hint of disdainful arrogance.

"I've been fully informed," he exclaimed. "Are you even baptized?"

At a gesture from Abbé Durand he turned to him and murmured: "There are some devotees who are so unconscious."

I was resigned to everything. I replied that I had been brought up in the Catholic religion but that I had ceased to practice it a long time ago.

"How long"

"It was about my twelfth or thirteenth year that I lost the faith."

"You've doubtless been educated in a lycée?"

"Yes, in a lycée."

He showed me redoubtable teeth. I wondered if it was to bite or laugh. He uttered a muted sound, a sort of grunt. He was about to ask me other questions, but he changed his mind.

"It's not worth the trouble of wasting my time if, as is possible..." He touched his forehead with his fingertip.

Then he sat down at a little desk and he wrote a name and address.

"Go see Doctor Tallier on my behalf. You'll find him before noon. I'll telephone him during the day. Come back to see me afterwards—tomorrow, for instance, at the same time."

"Dr. Tallier? But I don't think that's necessary. I'm quite well."

That assurance, however natural, appeared to exasperate him.

"The first condition, at the point you've reached, is obedience, an absolute obedience. If you don't consent to abdicate your pride completely, there's no point in coming back."

The interview was terminated.

Outside, Abbé Durand breathed out like a man relieved of an oppression.

"I'll explain to you," he said as we walked. "Père Théodore's minutes are precious. He's a luminary of theology. The situation he occupies causes him to see many importunate individuals, and also people who—how shall I put it?—do not have their faculties in perfect equilibrium. So he's obliged to defend himself, and as he has a vigorous nature, he sometimes appears abrupt. But he has a heart of gold, and I'm sure that he likes you already, without allowing it to appear. Go see Dr. Tallier. He mainly treats mental illnesses, but it's a matter of a simple formality."

I asked Abbé Durand whether he had any idea of what would happen the following day when I returned to Père Théodore's house.

He hesitated. He did not know, exactly. Ceremonies of exorcism were very rarely carried out any more, but a theologian like Père Théodore knew so many things! I could not be in better hands. He concluded by saying: "Have confidence, and above all, be humble."

I wanted to take Abbé Durand back by taxi, but he insisted on going on foot. He seemed to continue taxis as an unnecessary luxury whose ostentation was rather embarrassing. I left him regretfully. I would have liked to invite him to dinner, but I dared not. While taking account of the absurdity of that idea, I sensed clearly that nothing would have done me as much good as seeing that well-meaning priest eat, who transmitted forgiveness professionally and must heighten the message of God with the color of his human goodness.

The days that followed were the bitterest that I have known; they were those of my veritable possession.

Dr. Tallier recognized that I enjoyed all my faculties and that my cure was not within his competence. Père Théodore had been informed of that when I presented myself at his home. He experienced a horrible satisfaction, betrayed by the noise of his teeth and the gleam in his eye. He made him recount my life story in all its details. While I did so, he interrupted me with exclamations.

"Always the sin of fornication!"

What brought his exasperation to its peak was the story of my religious anxieties and my participation in the Essene sect.

I was a major heretic, an enemy of the Holy Church! How many penitences would be necessary! And even then, he was not certain that they would be sufficient.

"Doesn't God always forgive?" I asked.

His fury redoubled. Had I not heard mention of the unpardonable sin, which leads to eternal damnation? It would be necessary to fast, to pray, to repent.

Behind the house occupied by Père Théodore there was a charming little garden with box-trees and an acacia, and at the back of the little garden there was a door to a little chapel that opened on another street. It was to that unknown chapel that he led me, and prescribed that I should spend several hours there every day.

The chapel was not heated, and I shivered there. It was strangely bare and empty and there was nothing there but a large painted Christ, brand new, with a curly beard and a regular beauty. Blood was dripping from his hands and feet in little droplets that were in bas-relief.

Sometimes the door opened and a kind of lumpen peasant in a monk's robe, who also had a Spanish character about his physiognomy, came to prowl around me with a hostile expression.

"Here, at least," Père Théodore told me, when I left him on the first evening, you'll be sheltered from any demonic manifestation. You'll acquire the habit of coming here as to a refuge, the only one where you won't suffer the afflictions of demons."

Those words seemed horrible to me. So Père Théodore expected me to be coming back for a long time! So he thought that I might be the victim of manifestations of the spirit of evil!

"I thought," I told him, "that my possession was internal, and that the Church rejected the possibility of demonic apparitions?"

I thought that indignation was about to make him leap up and that he would disappear before my eyes. Then he seemed to be gripped by a ferocious joy.

"Always the spirit of personal research, the source of all heresy! Oh, you think! Oh, you examine! You seek to know what the Church thinks instead of praying humbly and imploring your pardon. Wretch, who has sold himself to Lucifer and who hopes that Lucifer will not have the power to appear to him and torment him! Wretched and ignorant! Read Saint Augustine, Saint Thomas, or even Bossuet's *Elévations sur les mystères*."

"And what will I see there?"

"You'll see that they all believed in the interventions of the Evil One in human existence, and you'll no longer wonder whether the danger you're running is real. You're skirting the abyss, and you'll open your eyes to measure its depth. You're going to fall! You've fallen! Every sin gives birth to its punishment at the outset. Satan is a form of the justice of God and if you need to see him in order to make penitence, well, you'll see him, you'll touch him, by night, lying beside you, and you'll respire his odor."

It was from that day on that various inexplicable phenomena were produced around me.

I know that the wood of furniture has a life of its own and that it creaks naturally. Warmth and humidity makes it contract, emitting sounds whose origin is not supernatural. But the creaking of my furniture became so regular and so strange that I had no doubt that it was expressing itself in a strange language at that the words were addressed to me. Fortunately, I did not have the key to that language and I refrained from seeking it. The furniture was silent until I went to bed, but as soon as I drew back my bedclothes and lay down with a hope of sleep it began to speak, and drove away slumber.

I plugged my ears with cotton, but that was not sufficient. I sold an old cupboard and my work-table, which appeared to me to be the organs chosen by the voices to express themselves. The noises diminished at first, but then emerged from the floor-tiles, the walls and above all the doors. I thought I noticed that the doors were noisiest when they were locked, and contended myself with closing them. Then without my being able to attribute the cause to any air current, they moved by themselves, as if pushed by the hand of an invisible visitor.

Mists formed on mirrors and faces were sketched in the mists. I veiled all the mirrors with pieces of cloth. I was obliged to change the pieces of cloth, which were handkerchiefs or pieces of silk because my gaze went to them mechanically and I saw in the designs of the silk the same sketches of faces. I replaced them with monochrome fabrics, but, although they were fixed to the frames with little nails, the fabrics trembled with inexplicable agitations, as if a head placed behind them had pushed them mischievously.

The books on my bookshelves also became a subject of obsession. I was obliged to think about some of them, always the same ones. Sometimes I launched myself abruptly toward one of those that I had sworn not to open again and started riffling through it feverishly in order to nourish myself with the sight of an engraving, dolorously to enjoy an image that frightened me.

First of all there was a work on Tibet with a reproduction of the devils of that country, taken from certain monasteries in the Himalaya. Oh, how much more terrible and infernal was the conception of evil disengaged from them than the one evoked by our rather comical Satans with their cloven hooves and their corkscrew tales. It must have been a damned artist who had created those eyes that only looked into themselves, that mouth devoid of lips, those mute features in which there was no possibility of redemption.

I looked for a long time at the face of the Tibetan devil, until I found a perfect resemblance of my own face therein.

I was also obliged to pick up another ancient folio book of travels in which there were, in all their aspects, the strange stone statues of Easter Island. Vestiges of extinct cults, sculptures carved by a people that had probably worshiped evil, nothing more cruel had been engendered by the human imagination. Those evil gods gazed at the ocean and one sensed that they were sad because, turning their backs to the land, they were nevertheless devoid of hope in the afterlife. I tore them out of the book of travels, scattered them around me, and identified myself with them. Between those accursed brothers, I contemplated on a stone shore an ocean of male-diction.

I made the decision to burn all those books in my fireplace.

But when the creaking paused, when it was impossible for me to yield to the obsession of books, I still had difficulty sleeping because of another image. The memory went back to my childhood. I had seen it in an old publication called *Le Journal Pour Tous*.[9] It represented a recumbent man whose hand overlapped the edge of the bed. He woke up because another hand had gripped his own, and his face expressed the greatest terror. The strange hand was long and pale and belonged to a kind of ghost that the illustrator had scarcely sketched, in order to leave to everyone's imagination the concern of creating its horror.

What prevented me from sleeping was the dread that my hand might accidentally slip out the bedclothes while I slept, and be seized by that formless ghost, never to be released.

When I left home and went to spend several hours at the home of Père Théodore I had the pleasure of going past the church of Saint-François-de-Sales, where I had been welcome benevolently by the well-meaning Abbé Durand. I admired the old stones of the venerable threshold, the harmony of the construction launched toward the heavens.

That small joy was forbidden to me.

---

[9] The periodical to which the narrator is referring is presumably the Sunday weekly that began publication in November 1891 and existed until 1906, although it recycled the title of a mid-nineteenth century periodical. Magre would have been familiar with it while still living with his parents in Toulouse.

As I was going back at dusk and I turned the Rue Brémontier, I saw that the bearded archbishop who was standing motionless above the door on a stone pedestal had been dislodged, or had undergone a strange transformation. He had been replaced by a large ape. That ape was watching for me to pass by, for he agitated his animal jaw when I appeared and brandished in my direction the club that he was holding instead of the Episcopal crosier.

I retraced my steps precipitately and made a detour in order to reach my house.

That persecution of images and forms only increased with the augmentation of the hours of penitence. I spent in Père Théodore's chapel.

I saw him every day. He sometimes prayed beside me. He fixed his inflamed gaze upon me then, and I sensed the divine wrath that enveloped me like a redoubtable cloud. For Père Théodore was only thinking about my chastisement. He saw nothing in me but an enemy of the Church, a heretic who would have been justly burned on a pyre in the Middle Ages. And, perhaps unknowingly, he resuscitated he ancient method of the Inquisitors. He had imprisoned me in the dungeon of fear. He put me on the rack with the questionnaire of confession. Before an ideal cathedral, in the Toledo of his dream, unable to burn me in reality, he burned me mentally with the fire of demons that he stoked up with his irritated speech.

But above all, he hated me. I symbolized in his eyes the sin of fornication. I was the opprobrium and the ugliness before which forgiveness recoils. As my sensitivity increased, I sensed his hatred in a palpable fashion, before even having crossed his threshold. It surrounded, like an aureole, his square cranium planted with black hair; it resonated in the sound of bones that he made as he walked; it emerged like a black current from the tip of his index finger as he turned it toward me. The chapel was so full of that hatred that it was even reflected on the mural of Christ, and altered the banality of his indifferent face.

That morning, when I rang Père Théodore's doorbell, I did not find him in his drawing room, as usual. An old maidservant who was like a lily withered by the sap of her interior purity, told me that he had preceded me to the chapel and that he was waiting for me there.

I passed under the acacia in the middle of the boxtrees in the garden and I noticed that the ground, instead of being hardened by the morning frost, was soft and damp by virtue of the eternal mystery of spring. Against a wall, in a little pot, a geranium was displaying delightedly a variety of shades of orange.

I had scarcely sensed the sweetness that emerged from vegetables when they are happy than I had already opened the door of the chapel. It closed with an unusual sound and I was astonished by the light that illuminated the unknown place into which I penetrated. It was gray, and the vault of the chapel was low, having come down to the extent that I thought I would bump my head on it. Its arches made crushing semicircles and the walls were massive, as if they were formed by an accumulation of cyclopean blocks. The Christ had hunched up his arms and seemed corroded by a subterranean damp. I had just penetrated into a Medieval prison.

In the middle of the chapel, in front of the altar, four candles formed a square at the center of which was a prie-dieu. Père Théodore was holding a large book bound in black, and was scanning it with his gaze. He was nervously handling a metal cross with his left hand. Behind him, the Spanish peasant was standing motionless in an attitude that betrayed an effort of solemnity.

"We're going to proceed today with the deprecatory adjuration," said Père Théodore, authoritatively, and he made me understand with a gesture that my place was behind the prie-dieu, between the four candles.

I ought to have cried out: *At last!* and rejoiced in approaching the desired goal.

I gazed anxiously at Père Théodore and remained still.

An imperious glint passed through his eyes and he designated the prie-dieu to me again. I advanced slowly to the place he had indicated and had the sentiment that a great danger was suspended over my head.

"Perhaps, my child, perhaps I'll be able to give you absolution today."

It was the first time that Père Théodore had called me "my child" and it was the first time that a certain mildness had insinuated itself into his voice.

"Kneel down," he said, in the same tone.

But I remained motionless, standing.

"Kneel down!"

He thought that I had not understood, and with a commanding voice he said: "On your knees!"

I shook my head. I was plunged in uncertainty and astonished by my rebellion. I was still standing, my head raised, and then a light dawned within me.

Forgiveness was not here. It could not be given to me by that man devoid of generosity. I did not know where it was. Perhaps it was outside, in the little garden, with the acacia, the box and the geranium, perhaps it was elsewhere, far away in another country, and perhaps nowhere. Perhaps it was not necessary that it should be given to me, because I had not committed any sin, and was still as innocent—me, the fornicator and the heretic—as a new-born child. Perhaps the desire for forgiveness was sufficient to receive forgiveness. But if I were the prey of the spirit of evil, if the concluded pact linked me to it, no divine functionary had the power to break that bond. No, I did not want to hear the words written in the exorcist's book, the age-old invocations, the formulae of prayer by which souls became slaves. I did not want to forge new chains for myself, to sign a new pact. Faith is not conferred by a ceremony. I only needed love. No holy water, no recited prayer, cold confer that love upon me, the miracle of which did not come from the Church.

I emerged from the area comprised by the four candles and uttered a sigh of relief.

"Decidedly, I give up," I said to Père Théodore, who was considering me with amazement. "I prefer to remain damned."

He uttered a cry and made a gesture to order me to resume my place.

Not knowing how to reach the door decently, I added: "Please excuse me."

But Père Théodore blocked my path. His eyes were blazing. He must, for a moment, have formed the hypothesis of a trick. He rejected it and thought of a case of unusual unconsciousness or a loss of reason, perhaps a manifestation of the Evil One.

He raised his cross, and our gazes met. He had made a sign to the Spanish peasant, who has advanced to lend him reinforcement. And in that sign he had summoned absent Inquisitors, soldiers with halberds, hooded executioners. I was living a scene from the fifteenth century.

I was only thinking about getting out. I had the bizarre sensation that if I had had to struggle against the two men facing me, I would have encountered the same lack of resistance, the same sensation of nothingness, as when I had shaken Kotzebue in my apartment.

I did not have to make the experiment. I don't know whether I passed through Père Théodore or whether he stood aside abruptly in order not to be touched by the accursed one, but I reached the door and found myself in the garden. An extraordinary beauty of colors reigned there, animated by a terrestrial breath.

I traversed the apartment with a single surge and reached the sunlit street. I went at a slow pace as far as the Avenue de Maine, looking at the shops and the merchants who were pushing barrows full of vegetables in front of them. I was not delivered from Lucifer, but I was delivered from God.

I only felt a slight sadness, because it had never been given to me, as I had dreamed in a puerile fashion, to dine with the excellent Abbé Durand.

What to do? Where to go? Peace might be in another dwelling than that of the Catholic God.

I took a taxi, and then commenced an interminable course across Paris. I went to the Rue Vergniaud, where the temple of the Antoinist sect is.[10] The bizarre black bonnet of an adept who seemed to be waiting for me on the threshold caused me to leave again. I went to the vicinity of the Jardin des Plantes, to the house of the Quakers; one could hear the distant roar of lions there, and I thought that a bad augury. The house of the Theosophists in the Square Rapp appeared to me to be too white and too vast, and there were too many magical signs on the façade.

I had lunch in the company of the driver at a vegetarian restaurant adjacent to the house of which a greave in the address, in Bourg-la-Reine, of the last worshiper of the stars, the Sabean priest of the Aquarian Church. The church was closed and the priest absent. But I remembered that the planet Venus plays an important role in the cult of the stars and I remembered at the same time a passage from the prophecies of Isaiah in which the planet Venus is a synonym of Lucifer.

We quit Bourg-la-Reine at top speed in order to reach the slopes of Mont Valérien and the house of the Sufis. We were about to reach the first habitations when I saw a tree whose foliage forms a strangely regular globe that rendered it similar to the tree of good and evil at the foot of which, in primitive paintings, the serpent

---

[10] Antoinism, founded in Belgium in 1910 by Louis-Joseph Antoine, was a doctrine that attempted to fuse Spiritism—the French version of what English-language speaker call Spiritualism—with Catholic doctrine and a belief in reincarnation.

offers the poisoned fruit. I seized the driver's arm, just as we were about to pass under the shadow of the tree and we set off again.

The concierge of the Modernists of Israel resembled one of the Easter Island statues, that of the Martinists a Tibetan devil, and before Christian Science a tall woman with a masculine appearance was pacing who had oblique eyebrows so curiously disposed that she made me think of an Irish Mephistopheles. I fled without looking back.

A cloud abruptly veiled he sun when I arrived at the base of the Spiritualists; I slipped and fell on the stairway of the Swedenborgians, and when I pulled the antique bell-cord of the representative of the Millenarians no sound emerged, by virtue of the effect of a significant prestige. In the bookshop in the Rue Joseph-Dijon, the headquarters of the Divinist sect, I saw in the sparkling window, like an indicative beacon, book entitled *Le Diable à Paris* and I didn't even get out of the taxi.[11] A traffic jam in the Rue de Rennes present me from getting as far as the offices of the Salvation Army, and when I arrived in the Rue Féron in order to speak to the disciples of Zoroaster, a thunderclap rang out, rain began to fall, and I ordered the taxi to turn round.

"Where are we going?" the driver asked me.

---

[11] *Le Diable à Paris* [The Devil in Paris] was the title of a series of satirical texts subtitled *Paris et les parisiens* published by Pierre-Jules Hetzel in the mid-1840s, supplied with material by the leading figures of the Romantic Movement, which might well have been on display in the window of a second-hand bookshop, although its significance here is purely sarcastic.

"Drive at random," I relied, in order to have time to reflect.

We wandered around Paris. Night fell. The rain became heavier. Sometimes the vehicle stopped. It was in front of a sanitarium of a modern bank. The driver had seen me make so many stops before assorted monuments since the morning that he thought he was obeying a fortunate initiative in stopping of his own accord outside anything that might resemble a temple in the dim light. We even made a long pause in front of some scaffolding where a cross-beam in the center of a square of planks had the appearance of a hieroglyphic sign.

And I wondered in the meantime where it might not be better to treat evil with evil. If there were organized Luciferians in Paris, why not seek them out? Why should I not attain that mountain Djebel Makloub where the Yezidees were? Why should I not go to the Antilles, in order to dance by night in the middle of a forest of coconut palms with the Voodoo cultists? Why should I not take the trans-siberian railway and reach the mysterious suburb of Shanghai where the disciples of Zi-Ka were, the sectarians of the San-ho-hoei, in order to aspire with them the juice of the necromantic poppy and worship the jade Dragon with the five golden claws? Would it not be better to discover by the Dead Sea, in the midst of calcareous cliffs, the monastery of the perverse Essenes, in order to profane with them the landscape where Jesus walked, until I had made myself a soul resembling their nothingness?

The taxi was climbing the slopes of Montmartre.

"Where are we going?" said the driver again.

"The Place Blanche," I replied, mechanically.

I saw the driver peering in all directions, looking for a church. I showed him the Brasserie Romano.

And he was disappointed when I paid him, not because of the tip, but because, having considered me all day as a kind of saint uniquely in quest of religious edifices, he saw me becomes again a vulgar customer of an ill-famed brasserie.

There was a confused mass alongside the table where I had sat down. That mass rose up at regular intervals and I perceived that it was formed by the junction of a human back and a curbed head. I was in the process of examining it curiously when I saw the head straighten up and a face appear.

Over that face, of which I could only see the profile, tears were running. I retained a cry of surprise, for I thought I recognized Laurence—but a Laurence so transformed and aged that I could not add faith to the testimony of my eyes. Was it possible that in such a short time, her slim form could have thickened, that bags could have weighed down her eyelids, that her hair could have changed color?

That Laurence with a double chin turned toward me, and I recognized Irma Pascaud.

Thus one can stay for months, I thought, without remarking something that leapt immediately to the eyes: Laurence resembled Irma Pascaud.

A halting conversation began, and for the sake of politeness I asked Irma why she was weeping. I remembered that in her youth she had also had crises of chagrin, but she did not reply to me when I asked her the cause. I hoped internally that she was going to keep the same discretion, for, hypnotized by my obsession, I was only interested in myself.

But she talked. At first it was in incoherent and general phrases.

"There's no justice! There's nothing to hope for from anyone, and if one wants to do something good, one might as well go and throw oneself in the Seine right away."

I said "No, no," gently and I made a sign to Irma that I was ordering a port for her.

"There's no more reason for me to hide it," she said, "And why did I hide it anyway? Do you remember the time when I loved you, when we were young, in the Latin Quarter?" She had a bitter smile, and she went on, swiftly: "No, you don't remember it. Me neither, or hardly. You said, to make fun of me, that I had no soul. You were right. I didn't have one anymore. I didn't have one anymore because it had been taken from me."

I made a movement of alarm. Irma Pascaud reassured me.

"You had nothing to do with it. It was the men, all the men. There's a law that makes sure that one's punished when one tries to do something good. You weren't much occupied with me then, but you might have noticed that I had a secret. I was hiding something that made me weep when I was all alone. I remember that you asked me questions and I kept silent. You didn't insist, anyway. When I knew you, I had a daughter that I loved more than anything. I had no soul but she, that girl, was my soul. And I loved her all the more because I wasn't absolutely sure that her father was really her father. I could have confessed that to you, couldn't I? There are men who don't ever want to believe that they're the father and others, on the contrary, whose self-esteem...well, the one I told believed it, He was already at least forty at that time. His name was Saint-Aygulf."

I didn't make any movement because I had glimpsed the truth while Irma Pascaud was speaking.

"You know her, you've been in her home, according to what I've been told, you've seen my daughter. The world seems very great, and yet it's exactly as if it wasn't, in that some people find one another incessantly. I never talked about Laurence before, but you can't imagine how much I loved her. I loved her so much that I consented to be separated from her forever, and never see her again.

"Her father came to find me, after years. He had remorse. He wanted to take his daughter with him, not because he loved her, but because of certain moral principles that people of his kind have. He would bring her up, he said to me, and make her a rich young woman, whom he could marry suitably, on condition that I would renounce her completely, that I never made any effort to find her. I don't know what someone else would have done in my place. I asked myself the question. You know how I lived. Hotel rooms, cheap eating-places, Bohemia...

"That was the way my daughter was going to live, since she would grow up with the sole example of her mother's infatuations before her. I imagined her whole life, a model for painters, a girl-mother at the hospital, and the sweat of poverty that she was bound to shed. So I accepted—and it's incredible, I even accepted joyfully, because I thought it was for Laurence's good. And for fifteen years I can say that when I thought about her, and I thought about her every day, I didn't even suffer, because I knew that what I was, she wouldn't be, that she would share in things that I couldn't reach, that she'd be better than me, better educated, that she'd have a soul, she..."

Irma Pascaud's eyes were dry and she was looking straight ahead. I wondered whether I ought to flee or beg her pardon. She resumed speaking, but in a low voice.

Wasn't it you who told me once that happiness isn't the goal of life, but something else? To become more intelligent, to elevate oneself?"

I made a sign that I might indeed have said something analogous.

"Well, what happened isn't anyone else's fault, it's mine, and I've been punished for having believed that a child can be brought up better with money than beside her wretched mother. Laurence lives in Montmartre now, as I've lived here and as I still live here. Perhaps she lives in the same street as me and perhaps tomorrow she'll come to install herself in the same hotel. According to what I've been told, she goes with anyone, just like that, because she'd had enough of her kind of life and her mother's blood was running in her veins. You're doubtless wondering how I know that. It's by chance...while talking...

"One evening, Laurence made confidences to a woman, Henriette, that I've known for a long time. I'd often mentioned by daughter to Henriette. So she made connections. She understood everything. Laurence told her how she had left her father, she even told her with whom, but Henriette didn't remember the name. Well, she left him, not because she didn't love him enough, and not because she loved him too much, but because she wanted to lead the same life as her mother. And she's leading it. It appears that she's been with one, then another. Many people say that it's by vice, for the desire to have men, but I've passed through it, and I know that it isn't that."

Irma fell silent. I interrogated her with my eyes. Her power of explanation must have had a limit, for she sketched two or three phrases and then stopped. Then another thought came to her and she turned toward a clock on the wall.

"Is that the time?" she asked me.

I looked at my watch and confirmed that it was quarter to seven.

"I need to leave you," said Irma, and she hastily pulled on gloves that had an odor of turpentine. But she had something else to say. She raised her head and I saw her features crumpled by an extraordinary expression of joy; the bags of her eyes, the pleats of her mouth and the rice-powder dissolving in streaks suddenly made a kind of ecstatic sun, and Irma Pascaud suddenly had the air of a saint contemplating an apparition of the Virgin.

"You won't believe it," she said, "but Laurence has never ceased to love me. She's always thought about me and she tried to see me. I don't know how Kotzebue had guessed that I was her mother, but he tried to find me. He had seen me in a café in the Place Blanche and he had told her, and it appears that Laurence slipped out of the house when she could to prowl around here, in the hope of meeting me. Eh? All the same, if we'd found ourselves face to face, do you think that the voice of the blood would have caused us to recognize one another?"

I didn't have time to respond, because Irma Pascaud had stood up, and anything I might say no longer had the slightest importance.

"I'll know her at seven o'clock. I'm going to meet Laurence at Lucienne's. She asked for the meeting and I believe that it will be the most beautiful moment of my life."

"Why were you weeping then?"

"Because of what you said once about me. You said that I had no soul. So I thought that I wasn't worthy to embrace my daughter."

I would have liked to drop to my knees to kiss the hem of her dress and beg her pardon a thousand times over.

But she headed for the door and I saw her draw away rapidly,

I walked rapidly. It was raining and I had taken off my hat in order for the rain to refresh my forehead. I was intoxicated, not because of the port I'd drunk but by virtue of an interior alcohol that the flux of my thoughts distilled.

The sound that the shutters over shop windows make as they fall was audible. Automobile horns resounded. People under umbrellas were running. The sky was so low that seemed to be touching the roofs of the houses. I wandered beneath a tenebrous lid that was only illuminated by a single light, that of the love of Irma Pascaud for her daughter. That light had just shone for me, and it was extinct, but I knew that it existed. There was a light that was love.

I went past the widow of a jeweler's shop, and behind the fake diamonds, the Japanese pearls and the streams of imitation pearls, in the middle of electric flames, I perceived Mammon, the Hebrew demon of wealth. He was standing up in a correct jacket and holding up, with the smile of a conjuror, before a young blonde woman, a green emerald like a drop of absinthe or the eye of a corpse. I stuck my face to the window and I perceived the ravishing features of the young woman, which seemed to be decomposed under the effect of desire. A pact similar to mine was about to be concluded there, and I was tempted to run into the shop and force the young woman to listen to my story.

Perhaps I would have done so if, as I stepped back on the sidewalk, I had not collided with an individual with gold-rimmed spectacles and golden rings on his bony fingers. He was thin, his face affected geometric forms, and in the lines of his arms, their relationships with the angles of his legs and feet, there were complicated problems of trigonometry, like those I had been able to solve when I was preparing for my baccalaureate. He was similar to Astaroth, the genius of the science of numbers and measures, such as he is represented in books of demonology.

Behind him, mouth painted and cheekbones powdered with raindrops like scales on the plaster of his forehead, a rose in his buttonhole and his hips swaying, advanced an equivocal young man, who licked his lips on seeing me and in whom I recognized Belial, who had a statue in Sidon and had been adored in Sodom as a god.

I had imprudently stopped at a diabolical crossroads. Lilith, the princess of succubi, who caused new-born children to perish, was traversing it almost nude, in a circle of water droplets, lifting above her head an umbrella so small that it could only be a magical object to capture scattered forces. She penetrated into a restaurant, and through the open door I perceived, in the process of eating, Behemoth with his enormous belly and his elephantine face, the demon of stupidity and continual absorption in nourishment. Near to him was Kamosh, the demon of flattery, and the monstrous Ronwe with her daughters, who drew men into beds where they hissed and changed into serpents. An orchestra began to play and I saw a musician striking a tambourine while winking, in order to indicate to initiates that he was delivering himself to the magical operation of Kamlat, by which sensual enjoyments are multiplied tenfold.

I thought about going away, but there were demons everywhere; they had invaded the earth, they had taken possession of it and they were coupling with the daughters of men as in the first days of the malediction. I saw Abigor, who cherishes uniforms, Andramelech who had peacock plumes because of his pride, the Lamias that adore the particular warmth of the lips of young men and the Lemurs that are believed to be alive but have been dead for a long time.

I saw Leonard, the great negro, and To, the demon of speed, who once ran on foot through the deserts of Arabia and has engendered so many frightful machines in order to traverse the world rapidly. Samiaxas, enveloped in a pelisse, was sniffing the perfume that emerges from women's dresses, seeking to unite with them with the ardor that is reported in the book of Enoch.

White Samael, the messenger of gluttony, was carrying dishes in a basket on his scullion's hat, and black Samael, preparer of philters and poisons, was emerging from a pharmacist's shop where the strange flames of jars had just been extinguished.

Ardarel, the spirit of fire, was blowing into automobile engines. Tallius, the spirit of water, was stretching in the rays of the rain, and the frightful Furlac was crawling on the paving stones, laboring to render the mud living.

And incessantly, in all the houses, under the doors, in the cafés and the squares, pacts were being signed I saw the three candles being lit, the unrolling of virgin parchments, and I sensed around me the impalpable dust of their ashes.

And then a verity appeared to me. I was only accursed in the measure that all humans are. All of them had sold themselves to the spirit of evil, some for money, others out of ambition, others for the pleasure of their flesh. Witchcraft was natural. It functioned in the tribunals, in the rites of marriage, in the transactions of banks. The signature of pacts was at the bottom of all contracts, it was reproduced in the newspapers, it was quoted on the Bourse. All of society was diabolical.

What Lévy had one made me do, everyone did on a daily basis, without knowing it. Mothers, as soon as the first kiss, dedicated their children to Lucifer. Lovers coupled in the infernal manner. Priests, when they lifted the host in a church, were extending to the heavens the symbol of egotism. Humans followed the backward path, and followed it joyfully, having extinguished in themselves even the hope of the divine goal.

The rain was still falling, and my garments were stuck to my body, but the chill I felt was agreeable, because it was like a bath, after a long soiling. I had run all day from temple to temple, everywhere there were people seeking the truth, and I perceived that I had only had to look around to discover it.

To the right and left I saw streets hollowed out profoundly between corridors if stone, and then lose themselves I know not where. A tide of darkness rolled over the houses, descending, increasingly menacing, over the vague palpitations of the street-lights. And I walked, slowly. I was a man like all the rest, neither better nor worse, curbed by dread, lifted up by desire, who had only ever been able to love himself sincerely.

Spring came and was followed by summer. I lived alone. I had dismissed my housekeeper and my valet de chambre, and there had been no other change in my existence. But I knew that if my pact was the resemblance of all of them, I ought, by a striking action, to efface the trace of my signature on Lévy's parchment.

What would that action be? It appeared to me one day, and I believe that I sensed immediately that it alone could relieve my soul of its burden, by shaking the fulcrum on which my life rested. It was necessary to realize it without losing a minute.

I found in a drawer, on an old piece of paper, the address of the housemaid who had been Laurence's confidante and I drafted a pneumatique to her in which I asked her to come to see me without delay. I went to put the pneumatique in the post myself, but I did not have to make a detour to avoid Saint-François-de-Sales. The stone archbishop had long ago resumed his place above the portal of the church.

Then I waited with the same impatience that I had once experienced in other days when I was waiting for a mistress whose arrival was uncertain.

The afternoon was reaching its end when the doorbell rang and I saw Madame Honorine come in.

Her nose was redder than usual. She was wearing, like the uniform of a poor woman, a gray shawl crossed over her bosom, and was holding a net that contained an object of greasy nature wrapped in newspaper.

"I'd just come from doing my shopping," she said, lifting the net, "when I got the..."

The pronunciation of the word stopped her, and as I was searching myself for the beginning of my speech she embarked on recriminations. She knew that the valet de chambre had a grudge against her. She had not been astonished that she hadn't been brought back after Madame had left. First of all, she had been warned that Madame was going to leave. Madame had told her so herself. The valet de chambre thought her too common. She was proud of being of the people. One can wear clogs and be more honest than those who wear shoes.

I hastened to tell her that that was of no importance, and that it was another matter.

"Does Monsieur know that the tariff per hour went up by twenty-five centimes three months ago?"

I indicated to her that I knew that and asked her to sit down. She did not. I perceived then that she was trailing her finger over my table and tracing a primitive design in the accumulated dusk. Her gaze wandered over the furniture, observing the disorder. Through the open door she could see, on the other side of the antechamber, the dining room where the remains of the lunch remained that I had prepared for myself. An obscure professional faculty doubtless permitted her to measure the sum of labor that my apartment, left to abandon, required.

A gleam of pride passed through her dull gaze, at the same time as a desire to for servitude.

People found her when they had need of her. Work had never frightened her. Oh, she knew how difficult it is to procure a housekeeper nowadays.

"No, Honorine," I told her, "I'm not looking for a housekeeper. I thought of you because of the eulogies I've heard in your regard. I know that you're full of merit, that you've been abandoned by your husband, that you've worked all your life to feed your children. I want to make you a gift, or rather a donation."

Honorine's eyes were suddenly most, for no one can ever hear an allusion to the misfortunes they have suffered without being moved by self-pity. But at the last words I pronounced, her face took on a bewildered impassivity.

"I want to quit Paris and lead an entirely different life from the one I've lived thus far. This apartment and all it contains will be useless to me henceforth. I don't want to sell it. I thought of making a donation to the person who, of all those I know, is most worthy of it."

The impassive Honorine remained silent and nodded her head as a sign of approval. In the end, she said: "I don't understand what Monsieur means by a donation."

"I mean that I'm giving you everything in this apartment, and the apartment itself, or which I'll engage myself to pay the rent. The furniture, the carpets, everything that is here is yours. You can sell it or keep it, as you wish."

Honorine started to laugh, as one laughs at an incomprehensible pleasantry.

"Monsieur is joking."

I assured her that there was no joke, that my resolution was serious and irrevocable. She could take away whatever she pleased right away, including the silver cutlery. I cited the tableware because I knew what prestige they exercise over the simple.

Honorine was obstinate in repeating: "Monsieur is joking."

But her face expressed the most vivid anxiety. "People have told me in the neighborhood that since Madame left, Monsieur was...but I'm not a woman to profit from..."

I thought that she was about to point at her forehead with her finger, but she stopped.

I assured her that I had all my common sense and that my resolution was made. But Honorine had also made a resolution not to take advantage of it. If I was not mad she was wounded in a hidden self-esteem, and she repeated: "So there's nothing else to say."

"Well, think about it!"

"I've thought." And she made as if to get up in order to leave the extraordinary world into which I had just caused her to penetrate.

"If Monsieur wants to give me something, I'll take that little medallion in memory of Madame, whom I liked a lot...and Monsieur too."

The medallion that Abbé Durand had given me was resting in the dust, on a cup.

I gave it to her gladly.

I spent the evening marveling and glorifying the sanctity of simple hearts. Laurence was right. I had not been able to distinguish under that coarse envelope the pure gold of disinterest.

It was late. I was about to go to bed when the doorbell rang.

It was Honorine, who had come back. She had an embarrassed but decided attitude.

"Monsieur said to me: think about it. So I've thought about it—or rather, it wasn't me. Me, I think it's necessary not to profit from it...but it's my daughter. My daughter said to me: you have children. There are several of us..."

"Then you accept?"

"Since its Monsieur himself...by the effect of goodness...I accept."

"That's perfect. I maintain what I said. Everything here is yours."

Honorine shook her head. "It appears that, at any rate, it needs a regular paper. And for the rent too..."

"You'll have a deed of donation, and my business agent will take care of the rent. Help me to pack my valise. I'm going to leave right away."

"Why?"

"I'm no longer at home here."

She started to laugh. She had taken on the wily expression of someone who doesn't want to allow herself to be deceived.

She watched me put my underwear in my valise almost with regret, but she changed her mind and insisted generously that I should take more. I was grateful to her, for I knew that she also had sons.

"Monsieur loves books; that will keep him company. Me, I never read."

She stuffed my valise at random with all the books within arm's reach.

"Would you like to spend the night here?" I asked her.

She refused swiftly. She would never have dared. Only when she had the papers.

I gave her the key to the entrance door. She took my valise. The weather outside was fine. I experienced an immense happiness.

I scarcely took the time to deposit my valise in a little roadside inn of which I had noticed the humility the previous year. Hastily, I savored the rustic odor, the lack of comfort and the difficulty of procuring the water indispensable for washing after a long voyage. I asked the jovial landlady, who had a pink double chin and was standing behind a counter, whether an eccentric still lived in the vicinity of Cap Myrte, in a little house of planks facing the sea, which he had built himself.

"Poor Jacques!" the woman exclaimed, her face brightening. "Yes, he's still there, but not for long."

"I didn't know that he was known by his nickname."

"Yes, but it's a nickname that doesn't suit him at all. It's messieurs from Paris who gave it to him. I don't know why."

The woman had stood up and I was able to admire a strong build and a copious figure, the potency of feminine maturity.

I remembered having heard it said once, in a precise fashion, that Poor Jacques had given all that he possessed to the poor before retiring to solitude in order to seek perfection there. His own words had been quoted to me with admiration:

"As long as we have something of our own we are enchained. The first thing that the person who wants to be pure should do is to break the bonds that attach him."

I wanted to consult him about that rupture of bonds. The first step might be easy, but the difficulty of continuing appeared to me to be immense.

Undoubtedly, I thought, *this innkeeper only knows Poor Jacques via rumors.*

I quit her and launched myself on to a by-road that climbed a hill between pines and mimosas.

It was hot and the air was motionless. It was mid-afternoon. Insects were buzzing. I could see the sea in the distance. My enthusiasm for the beauty of a new life augmented while I was walking.

As had been indicated to me, I left the road to take a path between vines. I went down one slope, climbed another, and found myself in front of the little house of planks where the sage had come to shelter a soul henceforth devoid of passions.

Poor Jacques was standing before his door. He was not surprised to see me and he did not manifest any pleasure. I could even have interpreted the crease of his brow as a sign of ill-humor.

I was ashamed of troubling his meditation. I explained the goal of my visit to him. I was tempted to imitate him. I wanted to get rid of the evil that every man bears within him. I knew that the first act of liberation must be to distribute everything one has. I had begun and that commencement had been agreeable to me. But I realized that what had pleased me more was the somewhat theatrical character of my generosity. I did not have the courage to go further. An obscure displacement to the profit of a charity of all the titles constituting my fortune was impossible for me. How had he been able to deprive himself completely?

Poor Jacques stated pacing back and forth. He seemed annoyed by my question. At first he attempted to reply in an evasive fashion.

"Everyone must act according to his conscience and what he does is no one else's concern."

But I was sitting on a rudimentary bench outside his door and I did not seem disposed to go away without an answer.

In the end, with a certain impatience, he said: "To give everything away is impossible. No one has the courage. One gives away one's overcoat and one's furniture easily, but one's fortune, never! In any case, money has been excessively decried. It still needs money even to live as a hermit in a cabin of planks like this one. First of all, it's necessary to pay for the planks. Even if one only eats potatoes and salad, it's necessary to pay for those potatoes and that salad."

"But I thought you lived on the produce of your labor." I pointed to a charred terrain where there seemed to have been the vestige of an abandoned cultivation.

"Nothing that I planted has grown. Everything was burned by the sun or rotted by the rain. I'd have been dead a long time ago if I hadn't had the income that the Crédit Lyonnais sends me regularly."

"So you don't believe a fortune to be incompatible with the life of a sage?"

He started to laugh and looked me in the face. Only then did I perceive that he was fatter, that he was wearing a new suit, and that he was wearing shoes and socks.

"Sagacity? First of all, where is it? It's arbitrary to place it in a cabin of planks near a pine-wood rather than elsewhere. I wonder whether it isn't wiser to live in a house like everyone else, with one's fellows."

I was disappointed. I gazed at the hills that were ranged and prolonged into rocky capes toward the sea swollen with azure. The sun was about to set and the tranquil air seemed to be gently pushing mute amorous thoughts over motionless trees.

"You've set an example however," I said.

Poor Jacques appeared to decide to confess.

"If you'd come tomorrow you wouldn't have found me here. This evening will be the last I spend here, and it will probably seem long to me."

"Why?"

"I've reflected. Nothing makes one reflect as much as interminable hours spent, in winter listening to the rain, and in summer contemplating the sunlight. I've changed my opinion. I find that the company of a mole and a snake are insufficient for a sage."

"And what company would you prefer?"

"That of a woman, of course." He blushed slightly, lowered his eyes, and then raised them toward me proudly. "Why not?" he said. "I've made the acquaintance of someone in the locale...someone who shares my ideas." He paused, shifting the earth with his new shoe.

"Aren't you a Buddhist?"

"The young woman is Catholic, but what does that matter?" He lowered his voice and the pride in his expression was accentuated. "She's a widow, very pretty and the proprietress of a hotel nearby, which doesn't spoil anything."

I thought, shivering, about the stout innkeeper with whom I had exchanged a few words. A great sadness invaded me.

"Do you believe in the Devil?" I said, to change the subject.

Poor Jacques nearly lapsed into anger. He thought that I had divined who his fiancée was and that I was making an insulting connection with the Devil because of the fiery pink color of her cheeks. He looked at me for a long time, saw that I was perfectly innocent, and replied:

"No, I don't believe in him. If I had believed in him, I wouldn't have spent a single night in that cabin. Oh, I understand the temptation of Saint Anthony now. One can't imagine all the voices that emerged from the woods, all appeals that are uttered in the fields by errant creatures. I sometimes sense them stuck to the other side of my door, listening to my respiration. I've even wondered sometimes whether the proximity of Monsieur Althon has something to do with it."

"Monsieur Althon? Why?"

"There's gossip. It's better not to pay any attention to it." He made a broad gesture that signified that life was more beautiful than all those imaginations.

"And the mole and the snake?" I asked

"I went several kilometers on foot to lose them in those woods you see over there, on the horizon. That gave me a great deal of pain. I can't explain how, but those animals had understood everything. The snake hissed, the mole snorted. It was heart-rending. Oh, it's impossible to conciliate everything."

I started walking rapidly. Dusk was falling. I reached the main road and walked straight ahead.

I had been walking for more than an hour and night had fallen completely when I passed a small tavern whose terrace was illuminated by a lantern. I sat down to rest.

I recognized the landscape that was in front of me. On the flanks of the hill, that line off gray walls was the enclosure of the convent of repentant prostitutes. The mass of stone riddled with electric light was the hotel. I distinguished between the branches the roof of the small villa that I had rented the previous year, and on the right

I saw the driveway opening between the eucalypti that led to Monsieur Saint-Aygulf'a dwelling.

Around a table to one side of me, chauffeurs in livery were chatting and laughing with local people. The same words recurred incessantly in their conversation. There was mention of "dingos" and "crackpots" and I was immediately certain that it was a matter of people I knew, and perhaps myself.

Involuntarily, I listened. I understood that a fat taciturn man and a valet de chambre with a face like a weasel were Monsieur Althon's domestics. After confidences in a low voice which made them snigger, the taciturn fat man exclaimed in a loud voice: "D'you want to know what I think? Well, they're simply pigs."

The laughter resumed. A chauffeur told a joke that I didn't hear, but my heart bat faster when the name Saint-Aygulf was pronounced. He had just departed suddenly for Paris, it was said, leaving his daughter all alone, and they were going to take advantage of that this evening.

"They're going to treat themselves. That's why they've given us the evening off."

A peasant with a large moustache, who must have been a gardener, must have had a benevolent reservation relative to Eveline.

"She's like the rest, perhaps worse," said the weasely valet de chambre, with a smile.

Then I heard the peasant say: "They have the right, since they have the means, but why the Devil do they have to mingle stories of religions with it?"

And the taciturn man clamored again: "They're pigs, I tell you."

I got up and left. I was ashamed of having listened, and yet I was glad to know. Curiosity devoured me. Monsieur Althon! Eveline! If there still existed in my imagination beings consecrated to evil and who worshiped Lucifer as others worshiped God, Monsieur Althon must be one of them.

The moon was full and shining with an extraordinary brightness. I had not had anything to eat, my head was empty, and it seemed to me that the moonlight contributed to my intoxication.

But suddenly, I stopped. I had arrived in front of the little path that led to Monsieur Althon's property. A group coming along the road in the opposite direction had just turned and plunged under the trees, with something furtive in their movements.

When I try to remember now what thought impelled me, I'm incapable of retrieving it I didn't believe that I had a role to play, a duty to accomplish. Nor was I avid to witness a scene of collective eroticism, for which that kind of gathering is usually the pretext. I started to walk along the little path behind the group that was preceding me, like some visitor invited by Monsieur Althon.

Having arrived at the house I stopped and instinctively hid in a bush to allow three people coming behind me to go past. I had recognized Madame Vigière's laughter. She was leaning on the arms of two young men that I knew, and while walking she was unbuttoning a large fur coat that enveloped her all the way to her feet. I did not have time to be astonished that she was wearing a fur coat on such a warm evening; the coat opened as she arrived alongside me; she was naked underneath it.

And while the three silhouettes drew away in the moonlight, I was struck by something special in the heavy fashion of walking, the movement of shoulders, a thickness of necks, that I had never noticed before. I remembered the words that I had just heard in the tavern:

They're pigs!

I went into the garden after them. It was formed by thick clumps of bushes, and it seemed to me that the plants composing those clumps belonged to unknown species.

But I was then in a semi-unconscious state and I headed for the house at a tranquil pace. No light appeared therein. It was massive, silent, dead. It had swallowed the visitors by I know not what door, which had closed again silently. I wanted along the façade, futilely, and wondered seriously whether I might do better to call out in a resounding voice, shouting my name. But I told myself, with reason, that Kotzebue, who would undoubtedly be there, would have me thrown out.

I also had the idea of igniting a few pine branches, which I could collect and dispose in front of the door in order to set fire to it. I searched in my pocket for my matches, and that thought amused me to the point that I started laughing all on my own. I renounced the project, however, thinking it wiser to wait in the garden for the arrival of a new guest who would permit me to penetrate by surprise.

I took a path at hazard and walked as far as an open space where I saw the gavel sparkling in the moonlight. I stopped when I distinguished a white form, indecisive and motionless, which was bizarrely suspended in the air. On looking more attentively, I saw above the white form the straight line of a pole.

It was a cross that was in the center of that crossroads, and an immaculate being with bloodstains on the body had been crucified there. I was hypnotized at first by the eyes, which appeared to be staring at me, obstinately fixed and astonishingly empty, like glass eyes.

Of an absolute whiteness, from the extremity of its little pointed ears to its narrow hooves, was the crucified lamb in the presence of which I found myself. In order for the forepaws to be nailed, the legs had been dislocated by pulling them apart. A cord held the neck tight, obliging the head to straighten. The nails were profoundly driven in and had broken the bones. I discovered, on passing my hand over the animal's fur and feeling a slight warmth therein, that the surprising torture had been very recent.

Everyone knows that animals are killed in order to be eaten and no one is indignant at the butchers; but the death of that lamb, that exhibition on a cross and the mysterious ritual character that seemed to me to be attached to that death, filled me with disgust. I darted a glance around, and the garden seemed to have become singularly menacing, heavy with an incomprehensible enigma.

Then I was struck by the resonance of a distant chant. It was a trailing, muffled lament, which came from the ambient space rather than a determined place. I thought at first of someone singing at the top of a tree, through the foliage. The voice died away and was renewed, monotonously, and I soon realized that it must be coming from the terrace on the roof of the house. What was its significance? Was a ceremony commencing at that moment, of which it was the accompaniment? Of what order was that ceremony?

I quit the shadow of the bushes and started making a circuit of the house, my nerves suddenly overexcited by the strange anguish of that chant.

I found myself on the side opposite the façade, in the party of the garden overlooked by the kitchens. I bumped into a rubbish-bin. I tried to open a door but it was locked. On examining a small window attentively, however, I discovered that it was only closed; it yielded to the pressure of my hand. It was broad and not very high. I hesitated momentarily, evoking the hypothesis of a redoubtable and silent dog that might be waiting for me on the other side. Then I introduced myself into Monsieur Althon's house.

Everything that happened thereafter unfurled rapidly, and I have only retained thereof the memory left by things accomplished in a dream.

By the light of a match I saw that I was in the kitchen and that the remains of the servants' meal were still on the table. My first concern was to unlock the door that led to the garden. Then I applied myself to turning soundlessly the handle of a door on the other side of the kitchen. After having devoted a few minutes to that, I found myself in a servants' parlor before another closed door. I employed the same precautions to open it, and another match showed me a silent and deserted drawing room. There were panoplies of arms and Turkish fabrics on the walls. It seemed to me to be furnished with the Oriental bad taste that had presided over many installations fifty years before. I saw men's hats and three or four women's coats on a divan surmounted by an awning of Tunisian veils.

I only took vague account of the poor welcome to which I had to be going. The worst thing that might happen to me was being thrown out brutally, but I had cast aside all self-esteem. I thought that the best thing to do was to be audacious, and I switched on the electric light. In any case, I was weary of turning creaky door-handles slowly.

I went one after another into another drawing room and the dining room. The ground floor was deserted. The gathering must be on the first. I listened, but could not hear anything except the exasperating muffled lament of the cantor who must be on the roof, face turned toward the moon.

At the extremity of the drawing room I saw the staircase leading to the first floor. I climbed it in three bounds and hesitated between several doors. Finally, a voice that I recognized struck my ears. It was Kotzebue's voice. It was emphatic, even though the tone was veiled. He must have been reciting a prayer, but that prayer was in a language whose syllables were striking my ears for the first time.

The door of the room in which Kotzebue was speaking opened by a crack at that moment. A thin middle-aged woman who must have heard my footsteps poked her head through the gap and examined me with a lorgnette in the semi-darkness of the landing. I thought I recognized an enigmatic creature that I had perceived the previous year on the beach, and who had been identified to me as Monsieur Althon's secretary.

"You're late, hurry up," she said, standing aside to let me pass.

I went in and she closed the door quietly behind me.

At first I could not distinguish anything, because the light only came from three lamps disposed in a triangle, and those lamps were on the far side of the room, which was very long. It had to be a kind of studio-cum-drawing-room separated into two parts by columns, which had been cleared of furniture for the occasion. Around me were men and men, many of whom were unknown to me. A few belonged to the group of Essenes, and I saw by the shriveling of their features and the gleam in their eyes what ardor they brought to this worship, so different from their former ideal. The faces were so taut that I could not tell whether the women were pretty. I saw some who were old and haggard. As for the men, it was impossible for me to definite the class to which they belonged. They all had their eyes fixed on the extremity of the room and a curtain that veiled a party of it; they seemed to be waiting for a strangely attractive event.

The curtain was made of dark blue silk, sparkling and moving, on which lunar crescents and silver stars were embroidered. The beauty of the fabric was captivating. It made one think of the sky of an extraterrestrial region, the secret zaimph of the temple of Carthage. A semicircular balustrade was disposed between the columns. All around, the walls were hung with colored fabrics, in which crimson and violet were dominant. In the middle, a divan on a platform gave the impression of playing a preponderant role. It was covered in the same silk as the curtain, but that silk was crumpled and soiled, and even had rips in several places. On a low table reposed a copper vase filled with water, and various metal objects. The nails were visible that held the fabrics to the wall, and the plaster that had fallen. The ensemble had something about it that was fake and improvised, reminiscent of the drawing room of a conjuror or scenery hastily erected in a photographer's studio.

Sitting beside the divan was a curly-haired man with a cynical and cheerful face, who was completely naked. He was so hairy that I thought at first that he was clad in some sort of fur, and I leaned forward to assure myself of his nudity. He must have been short and a trifle deformed, but his bull-like neck and his enormous arms seemed to indicate a professional wrestler. He straightened up, and sometimes darted a sly and surprised glance at the audience. He gave the impression of being embarrassed, astray in an unknown milieu, to which he had been induced to come by paying him, in order to accomplish some bizarre action.

Alongside him was a large cage in which white-plumed birds were stirring. There was an occasional flutter of wings and clicking of beaks, and the naked man then turned toward the birds, at which he stared attentively, in order to put on a brave face.

On the other side of the divan, Kotzebue was standing, intoning the prayer that had immediately struck my ears. I found that he was thin, and that his eyes were smaller than usual. He was wearing a costume that was formed by a sort of dalmatic, half-Byzantine and half-Egyptian. He was reading the prayer from a parchment of elongated form, and as the light was insufficient he sometimes brought it very close to his eyes. The trembling of his hand, the lividity of his face and a hunching of his shoulders betrayed the fear to which he was prey. That fear was visible and material around him; everyone felt it by receiving its radiation, and it was that inexplicable fear that rendered terrible a scene that ought to have been merely grotesque.

I was struck by the resonances of certain words that recurred in Kotzebue's prayer, especially the resonance of one word, a proper noun: Apophis.

Apophis! The syllables of that name floated in my mind for a few seconds, dead and deprived of meaning, but gradually they were animated and colored by the repetition, along with them, of other evocative syllables.

A few years before, at the moment of my initial curiosity about the history of religions, I had studied ancient languages, notably the rudiments of the Coptic language. It was in Coptic that Kotzebue was expressing himself! And I recognized the name of the being to which his prayer was addressed, with a voice simultaneously imploring and terrified. Apophis: the serpent that personifies darkness in the Egyptian *Book of the Dead*; the serpent that is called Nahash in *Genesis*; the very principle of eternal evil! And Kotzebue was invoking it in a tone galvanized by fear, and he was also invoking Astes, the lord of the Amenti; Ouadj, the extinguisher of radiance; Azi, lust; Khem the ithyphallic; Khepra the transformer; and Sokari, who cuts gladioli with which to fan the dead. He was giving the demons the first names by which humans had designated them, in order that his appeal might be more powerful by virtue of the virginity of the primordial names.

I had thought I was assisting at a caricature of the black mass, a base orgy to which the religious dreams of certain sects engender, in which mysticism is confounded with sensuality. But no: I was in the presence of the most ancient cult of evil, whose rite had been perpetuated through the ages, and without understanding it, I gazed at its ridiculous and mysterious accessories.

Suddenly the voice quavering with fear broke. There was a shiver among the audience, who pressed forward to see, and the marvelous azure curtain slid away silently. It only allowed the sight of a bust, and my first impression was one of disappointment. On a black plinth, it was not even a bust, but only a marble head, in the Egyptian style, a head of natural size, with curly hair, a straight nose and regular features. That head was crowned with recently-cut branches of a pepper-bush.

It took me a few seconds of attention to take account of the inexpressible attraction emanated by that visage. Did the attraction come from the indifference of the smile, the perfect harmony of the lines, the love of pleasure concealed by a slight prominence of the chin or the passionate intelligence reflected by the emptiness of the eyes? I could not discern that precisely, but the more I considered that Egyptian head, the more I felt penetrated by a kind of laxity, a desire to continue contemplating the void of that gaze, the fascinating beauty of that face. And at the same time I had the sensation that my ideas were melting, that my personality was in the process of dissolving, that I was ceasing delectably to be myself.

I made a violent effort to react, to recover consciousness of myself, and I perceived that my teeth were chattering and that I was afraid, with a panic fear, a fear that chilled my bones: the same fear that I saw before me, inscribed in Kotzebue's features.

Then a little door that the curtain had uncovered as it slid turned on its hinges, and I felt my heart beat precipitately on seeing Eveline appear. Her loose hair fell over her shoulders. She was naked and I was dazzled by the astonishing harmony that her tottering body emanated. The silhouette of a man was outlined behind her. I understood by the movement of Eveline's shoulders that the man had just aided her to take off a peignoir or a cloak that he was still holding in his hand, and which he dropped near the door. I realized that it was Monsieur Althon.

Eveline's eyes were wandering, and seemed not to be seeing anything. There was a curl of dementia in her lips.

Then Kotzebue approached the cage; he opened the door and his enormous hand took out a bird. He lifted it up in the air, held it toward the divinity with the dead eyes and, murmuring a few words that I could not hear, let it fall.

The bird, stifled by Kotzebue's grip, made a white patch on the azure divan. At a sign from Kotzebue the hairy man had stood up, and Eveline and he found themselves face to face on either side of the divan, like a symbol of good and evil, under the aspect of perfect beauty and victorious ugliness.

The re-enactment of what ancient rite was I about to witness? I knew that, since the commencement of the world, profaners of beauty had celebrated their love of degradation. I saw passing in the disordered vertigo of my ideas the image of the goddess Mylitta of Babylon, that of the Carthaginian Moloch, the secret festivals of Suburra in Rome, the obscene agapes of the Nicolaitans, and the adoration of the demonic goat in the Sabbat of the Middle Ages.

I saw flourishing before me the ultimate branch of the tree of evil. According to its ineluctable law, it was those who had sought good beyond the common law that corruption had attained and who had become the priests of ugliness. Unfortunate Essenes, so full of good intentions in the beginning, they aspired to contemplate the symbolic degeneration of beauty! And I was among them, scarcely more conscious and just as consumed by fear to the marrow of my bones. For fear was curbing heads, causing eyelids to flutter and teeth to chatter.

My gaze strayed momentarily over the backs inclined in front of me.

I was surprised by the abnormal curvature of necks, the movement of faces suddenly changed into snouts. I was at a gathering of beasts, in the midst of pigs in the process of adoring the radiant visage of intelligence turned to evil. I was participating in that festival of retrogression. I was about to see the living representation of it, by the material pollution of a pure body.

It was then that a strange power took possession of me. I do not know whether I uttered a cry, but the room was filled by a sound that emerged from a human throat, which had a resonance simultaneously terrible and insensate. That noise must have augmented the ambient terror at the same time as, by virtue of an interior alchemy whose explanation is impossible, it mutated my own terror into a divine courage.

The impetus that shoved me forward carried me to the extremity of that long room as if there was only a single pace to cross. I had the sensation of people abruptly knocked over to the right and left, groaning, but I did not have the leisure to seek the cause of their fall. I was possessed by a project that I had to realize immediately, and that realization occurred as soon as the project was conceived.

I remember the perfect delight that inundated me when I seized with both hands the great bronze lamp to the right of the azured divan and raised it above my head.

It seemed to me that I was a knight of light, covered in silver armor, and that I was lifting an enchanted sword. With all my strength, I brought that lamp down, which seemed light to me but was made of heavy bronze, on the marble visage, on the evil intelligence, on the Lucifer of distant ages.

The head, collapsing noisily, brought down the second lamp, which went out at the same time as the one I had just broken as I brought it down. As if he had received the blow himself, Monsieur Althon fell to the ground, his arms open, doubtless in order to pick up the fragments of a treasure that must be inestimable to him. Confusedly, I saw Kotzebue, livid and recoiling, shouting: "Wretch!" at me, and extending an arm before his face. With the bronze stump that remained in my hand I struck the naked man who, by virtue of professional instinct, tried to throw himself upon me, and his fall dragged down the third lamp, with the result that the room was plunged into darkness, the opacity of which multiplied the terror therein.

Trembling, Eveline had remained by the door. She had only made one gesture in the midst of the general disorder, that of picking up the peignoir that was at her feet and throwing it over her shoulders. My lucidity redoubled with my delight. I launched myself toward her, seized her by the arm and drew her through the door, which I slammed behind me

I did not know whether there was an exit in that direction and the darkness was profound; it was Eveline who guided me. She reached a stairway that must have been a service stairway and we found ourselves on the ground floor, in the kitchen by which I had come in. The moon illuminated us, but it seemed to me that Eveline did not recognize me. A great tumult reached us from the first floor.

"I'll go with you," I said.

I had scarcely pronounced those words than Eveline had opened the door and run outside.

My astonishment was so great that I let a few seconds go by. When I came out behind her she was already some distance away. I launched myself after her and even called out to her several times. I heard the sound of footfalls from the direction of the garden. And I saw forms fleeing. I was held back by brambles, in the midst of which I became entangled. I finally reached the small side-road that Eveline had taken, but she had disappeared. I started running as fast as I could, I feared that the state of distraction in which she was might push her to some irrational action. I perceived her silhouette under a group of pines, and then a little further on, alongside the wall of the convent. The road she was following led back to her house.

I had succeeded in getting closer to her. I called to her again. I did not know, however, what I wanted to say to her, and if she had retraced her steps perhaps I would have been mute before her. But she did not turn round. I saw her go through the hedge that separated the road from here garden, at the exact spot where Monsieur Althon, a year before, had uttered a cry of hatred on perceiving her, and had doubtless conceived the project that I had just aborted.

She reached the threshold of the door and I heard the battens close loudly.

Then I stopped. I listened. Another door closed inside the house. Everything became silent again. The moon seemed to me to be icier above the landscape, more motionless. In the far distance, the barking of a dog on a farm dragged on with infinite sadness. A eucalyptus leaf spun and came to fall at my feet, like a regret.

And it seemed to me that, for having attempted to save Eveline from evil, beauty was forever lost for me on earth.

How long after the scene I have just recounted was it that I visited the exhibition in Nice? I can't remember.

Around me, a few rare visitors were laughing and pointing at canvases they judged incomprehensible. But scarcely had I entered that I was struck by astonishment before the first picture I contemplated, so much did I sense the profound life of the color and the landscape penetrate to the roots of my being.

It was sunset over abandoned fields. There were feet of sick vines, twisted by old storms and trees deprived of leaves that one sensed to be so poor in sap that they were about to expire. In the foreground, sunk to the knees in muddy furrows, a semi-human creature was making a powerful effort to extract itself from the shifting earth. That creature was not a woman, for the extremity of its limbs extended in roots and even its legs were formed of vegetal tissues. But the body had an animal form, was hairy, and the grossness of the belly gave the impression that it was pregnant. One of its arms was drawing from the redoubtable soil a sort of larva, a phantom of a child, streaming with mud and covered with herbal filaments. But the breasts and shoulders of the creature were human and covered by the softly veiled complexion of feminine flesh. The contour became increasingly delicate as it rose toward the face. And that face covered by a dolorous beauty in which, shining distinctly in the gleam of the eyes, were hope and courage, that face whose temples were radiant with amour, had a perfect resemblance to Laurence.

Over that struggle of the creature enchained to obscure matter, who wanted to become spirit, the painter had caused the supernatural light of a sun the color of blood to fall. A line of sterile hills cut the horizon, but the shade of the sky above the hills was sufficient to make one think that there was a more favored valley further away, with grapes on the vines and flowers on the trees.

I started considering the other paintings. In all of them, there was Laurence's face, and in all of them, under different symbolisms, through multiple subjects, I found the same conception of an extraction from imperious matter that holds humans by the roots, and in all of them there was, evoked by a ray of light, an incomplete horizon or a star in dense might, the sentiment of an ideal landscape that was further away, invisible, inaccessible and yet real, in another world.

Who was the painter who could only imagine an individual with Laurence's gaze? My astonishment increased further. There were paintings in which my personal imaginations had taken substance, to the point that I wondered momentarily whether it was not me that had given birth to that gallery of dreams, during hours of unconsciousness.

I saw a public dance-hall full of animals with an orchestra of negroes charged with carcans and chains. The drinks were represented by incandescent embers, and those who had lifted them to their lips had frightful burns that magnified the design of their mouths. In the center of the dance-floor floated a nebulous aerial form whose head was that of Laurence, and at the extremity of her robe of light trailed a dog with the face of a demon, on which Laurence was casting a gaze full of pity. I recognized the Bal Wagram by the style of the columns that framed the painting and the gigantic door to the toilets toward which the human-animal couples were flooding.

As I was certainly not the author of the painting, I thought that it was me who was represented by the dog with the demonic head, and in considering it further, I found that it was indeed painted in my image with a rigorous exactitude.

Demons often recurred in the canvases of that painter so fraternally close to me. There was one who was kissing Laurence on the lips, but who was weeping so sadly while giving her that kiss that my heart was moved by it, remembering myself. There was a demon of avarice represented by a fat man with a pelisse and a rosette of the Légion d'honneur, who was sprawled on banknotes and had just perceived the vanity of his amour, for his eyes expressed an infinite despair.

One picture showed Laurence lying down and offering herself to the demon of lust. It was a larger canvas than the others, in which the quivering fat flesh, the overflowing bellies the gelatinous torsos and the acned faces of men reddened with abject rictuses of desire. The lower part of Laurence's body, camped on the ravaged bed of a brothel, had an obscene movement, the thrust of a resolute and remorseless offering. But her features were those of a martyr whose flesh is being tortured and who is attaining by the excess of suffering the ecstatic illumination of sanctity.

The painting that struck me the most, because it opened a new door to my meditations, represented a sunken road rising toward a hilltop beyond which one perceived desolate landscapes extending to infinity. The sunken road was strewn with stones, somber and enclosed; the hilltop was desolate, the distant horizon a succession of deserts. A meager Christ, naked and stooped, so thin that one could see his ribs, so stooped that he seemed hunchbacked, was advancing painfully, leaning on the arm and shoulder of a Lucifer equally emaciated and hunchbacked, who was climbing the hill with him. Fatigue was visible in the jutting of the muscles, the droplets of sweat, the bloody feet. An enormous cross weighed upon their common shoulders, and one sensed from the movement of arms and the tension of necks the double effort that each of them was making to assume the heavier part of the burden and liberate his companion slightly. The Christ and the demon were supporting one another like two brothers. They were not looking at the low and heavy sky above them, or the immense extent of the deserts they had to cross. They were turned toward one another, their faces full of pity, and one could see that they were deriving a marvelous comfort from the division of their misery and the sentiment of their reciprocal love.

Who was the painter whose soul contained such an elevated conception of fraternity? I ran to a little glazed compartment in which an employee was standing as wan and fleshless as the Christ and the Lucifer of the painting. But the resemblance stopped at that emaciation. The gaze, behind the spectacles, was vile. With a gesture of scorn that embraced both the painter and the person who was interested in the painter, he handed me a catalogue and I read a name: Drevet.

That name told me nothing at first, but on considering a portrait that was on the catalogue, I seemed to see a face that resembled that portrait in the cloud of ancient memories. That face was slumped next to an empty glass and several cups, in Alberte's bar, and it reflected brutality and hostility in my regard.

Drevet! That was the alcoholic painter, the degenerate Bohemian that I had known in Alberte's bar, and whom Laurence, with her innate liking for the spoiled and the wretched, had immediately found so sympathetic.

Phrases of hers returned to memory.

"I'm sure that he would have a great deal of talent, if he contrived to work, if someone loved him enough to make him work." And when I had asked her how she could have such an idea on that subject, she had replied in a natural tone: "But I recognize immediately those who have a need to be aided by a little happiness. There are so many people who do not realize themselves because of that little bit of happiness that no one has ever given them."

I was at an exhibition of Drevet's works and I saw Laurence idealized in every canvas. And those canvases, perhaps incomprehensible for the public that was looking at them and mocking them, appeared to me to be profound, revelatory and sublime.

Where was Drevet? Where had he painted my own dreams? How had he escaped the nightmares of alcohol and by what astonishing communication did he respond my soul in his visions?

The villainy of the employee's gaze had informed me that I could, with money, obtain what I desired to know concerning Drevet.

I interrogated him, and he spoke, punctuating his discourse with scornful shakes of the head and sniggers of hate.

Drevet was a wretch. He meant "wretch" in the sense of poor, and he stressed that poverty, which seemed to him, a petty employee in an exhibition hall in Nice, was the most withering thing of which one could accuse anyone, the utmost degree of abjection. The pauper was an alcoholic who was no longer drinking for the moment, but would certainly drink again. He was also consumptive. At that point the employee tapped his chest forcefully to emphasize the gravity of the disease and also the joy he felt in announcing Drevet's imminent demise. For there are people who have unmerited strokes of luck, and the alcoholic painter Drevet was one of them. He had found, God knows where, a woman who was willing to go with anyone at all, who was useful to him. She was devoted to him, like a bitch. She admitted him, she made him paint, she found him the subjects of his paintings. Who knew, perhaps it was even her who painted them. She did herself harm in order to sell those daubs. If there was an exhibition it was her who arranged it with the boss. Ha ha! And the art-lovers. They sometimes bought these horrors very dear, because they knew that they could have the woman into the bargain. Ha ha! The painter was very content He was painting now, but he would soon be drinking again. Poor people! Paupers! Wretches!

I asked whether they lived in Nice.

Yes, yes, they had settled here like all the consumptives who came to die. They had a shack in the suburbs...

I made a note of the address and fled,

I took a tram. I searched for a long time for that road bordered by gardeners' houses, in an outlying district staged in the midst of stones, overlooking the sea. The afternoon was reaching its end.

It was a very small, very straight road. On one side there was a file of wooden fences, absolutely similar, with modern houses constructed on the same model, and on the other, waste ground strewn with wild cacti, old newspapers and food-tins. Every fence had a number painted in blue, far too large for the exiguity of the domains whose threshold they decorated. The gardens one perceived were almost all composed of neatly aligned cabbages, over which tomatoes hanging from pickets made red patches. Only the number ten, before which I intended to pass, had a garden devoid of vegetables, where there was nothing but a folding chair and an empty easel. At another time, that landscape, with its crepuscular nostalgia, would have given me a desire to weep, and I would have fled without even reaching the threshold of number ten.

But a little breath of warm tenderness passed through me, similar to the effluvium that emanates from a place where people are happy. I advanced along the road. At a window of the house there was a raised pink curtain. I recognized Irma Pascaud behind the pane, who was sewing. She had a tranquil and mild profile and she was following the movement of her needle with a placid attention. The wooden gate had only been pushed to, as if someone would soon return.

I continued marching straight ahead.

And suddenly I perceived them. But I had no fear of being seen myself, so much were they thinking of each other and occupied by their own presence, Laurence was holding Drevet's arm, and she was squeezing it proudly. He was walking like a man who has just escaped a great danger and was now saved. They were leaning on one another with an attitude similar to that of the Christ and the Lucifer in the painting I had just seen. They were the Christ and the Lucifer, the redeemer and the sinner, and I divined above their heads the cross of life that it would be necessary for them to bear until the end of time.

I was on a hill. I started to descend slowly. The light of the setting sun illuminated me obliquely. Street lamps were lighting up here and there. The landscape that unfurled before my eyes, of stony slopes, a little clump of pines, and three fig-trees in the middle of a field, appeared to me to be clad in a noble and familiar grandeur. The sky over the suburb was a more profound, more limitless blue. The resonance of sounds penetrated further into the heart.

The window of a small grocery at the corner of two streets suddenly lit up. Oh, how pleasant it would have been for me to go in any purchase oil or coffee and carry them lightly toward a house where beloved individuals were waiting for me! Oh, how light the cross would be for the two companions on the sunken road who were sustaining one another!

I perceived that tears were running down my face, but it was all the same to me, I watched internally, with a pious curiosity and a total absence of self-pity, the images of a life unfurl that would never be mine.

No, it was not grief that I experienced but a sudden comprehension of the value off souls and of my own soul, and that discovery was so passionate that it enabled all regret to be effaced.

I had arrived at a crossroads where people were passing by. Shutters closed over a window. I passed children who were going home.

My God, how simple life is, in sum. Everything is clear. The last are really the first. The gift of oneself, to which I gave the name of sin, is the most divine holocaust of amour. Fortunate are those who have understood that it is necessary to extract oneself from the furrow of terrestrial mud and incline toward the beautiful landscape of light that is always further away beyond the mountain, and of the existence of which one is uncertain. My God, you have not extended malediction over anyone, No pact links to evil. Everyone has his task on earth somewhere. It is sufficient to discover it and execute it humbly.

A tram stopped in front of me. I boarded it. The conductor, no doubt struck by the dolor in my expression, asked me where I was going. I replied that it was all the same to me and that I would get off at the terminus.

It was not the talismans of Simon Magus that had attracted me to this point of the globe. I had ceased to believe in their existence. It was not the presence of Eveline. I had been told that she had gone back to Paris. It was not the union of pine, rosemary and mimosa mingling to form a unique perfume whose intimate communion one only encounters on the slopes of the hills facing Saint-Tropez.

An idea had taken possession of me with such force that I had not been able to put off its realization for one day, and I was shivering with impatience in the little train that snaked slowly along the coast, following the detours of gulfs and sometimes stopping as if it were drunk on the sunlight and the sea air.

The commencement of autumn had an ardor hotter than that of summer. I launched myself alongside the peasant house that represents the station at Beauvallon and I almost had a desire to start running when I perceived the gray line of the convent walls and the quadrilaterals formed by the old trees and its interior courtyards.

There lived humble women who had found consolation in the practice of prayers, reclusion and renunciation, but there was one among them so deprived of reason, so inaccessible to the elementary instructions of religion, that she had been judged unworthy of admission among the nuns, and who only fulfilled the functions of porter and maid-of-all-work. Her simplicity had prohibited her from making vows. According to what I had been told, she did not pray, she listened to the mass without comprehension, and she had been seen laughing idiotically when the priest lifted up the host. The unique light of her intelligence only shone brightly enough to permit her to receive the provisions from the hands of the grocer that she carried to the convent along the road where I had once watched her pass by. She also knew how to open the door and close it again, and to dig at the place designated to her. That was all. And I was pleased to think that if there was in that soul no hope of future life, it was at least covered by the calm darkness of ignorance

But I had sometimes recalled the "Alleluia!" sung through the autumnal vines and the crisis of filthy dementia that that song had provoked in the unfortunate Marie with the long neck. The shadow within her was not so peaceful! It had dolorous eddies. The old life of the dives of Marseille still uttered its appeals. Then, a madness took possession of her, and brought her to a degree even lower than the one where she vegetated. Carrying provisions, digging and laughing idiotically at mass, was perhaps the most elevated point that she could reach, and she was not even sure of remaining there, by virtue of occult influences departing from below.

And suddenly, like a light coming from a star hidden by a cloud, I had been attained by a memory. One sunlit morning, that wretch, as she had passed near me, had prostrated herself as if she had seen an aureole round my head. I had not understood then the sanctity that she seemed to attribute to me. I had put that inexplicable veneration down to her madness.

Now, though, I thought I understood. It was a brother she had saluted, a being similar to herself, devoured by an evil of the same nature, but who had taken a few steps further in the possession of life and the consciousness of that evil. And that brother was a saint for her because, she had believed that he would save her.

She expected salvation from me. In what form? I didn't know, exactly. A few infantile words orientated her toward a very simple ideal, an attitude in her regard showed her that she was a poor woman for whom one might have amity. Who can tell? A gesture with the open hand might have sufficed.

But how belated I had been! She had seen the guide on the side of the road. She had prostrated herself and waited. Who could tell whether he had not wearied, whether she had not despaired, whether her soul had not eventually closed to all hope?

How rapidly I walked along the road that led toward the convent! Everything I saw, the placard of a garage, the inclination of the trees, a distant well, took on a meaning symbolic of forgiveness. I wanted to redeem myself in my own eyes. Every man ought to accomplish once in his life a great act of love, freely chosen. It was toward my act of redemption that I was running, but without any fixed intention and without knowing with what words I would render it plausible.

I went past the avenue of eucalypti. They had the air of having acquired with the rusts of autumn a new sum of wisdom. I saw Monsieur Saint-Aygulf's house through the foliage, closed and silent. And as I was about to arrive at the sunken road that rose toward he convent through clumps of mimosas, I heard the little sound of a bell. In the same place where I had encountered him the previous year, a priest was advancing, preceded by a choirboy. With the same gesture as before, he was holding the Holy Sacrament to his breast.

A fat man who was driving a carriage and who overtook me on the road stopped abruptly beside the priest, at the exact moment that the latter was about to turn into the sunken road. They must have known one another. The fat man removed his straw hat respectfully and he asked a question that I did not hear while pointing at the convent.

I heard the last words that the priest spoke: "It's Marie, the one who runs errands, the one they call Marie with the long neck. I've arrived too late. She died suddenly an hour ago."

I saw the fat man make a vague gesture that seemed to signify that that death was the least grave of those that one might fear. He whipped his horse. The choirboy's bell rang out. A shadow coming from somewhere unknown seemed to glide over things. I stood motionless at the corner of the path.

Once in life, a great act of love! How difficult it is! And when one has let the moment pass, it never returns.

Sunlight on quays. But were they those of Marseille, Toulon or somewhere else? I was about to depart, or perhaps I had already departed, and that was happening in a distant land?

I was sitting in a little tavern sheltered by a tattered awning, and the wind was making it flap. I was waiting until six o'clock in order to embark on a steamship, whose funnel was smoking, drinking a beverage that I had raised to the height of my eyes in order to gaze at its color.

I suddenly perceived—for my sensitivity had increased immeasurably—that there was someone not far away who was looking at me and tormenting me with his thought.

I put my glass down and I did indeed see an unknown man who was standing still beside a burden laid on the ground, and who was staring at me with eyes covered by thick eyebrows.

It was a workman, a stevedore. He had no collar and he had torn sandals on his feet. What struck me to begin with was the disproportion that existed between his paltry appearance and the enormity of the burden he had beside him.

I was about to let him see that he was importuning me with his persistence in staring at me when he suddenly decided to approach me. With a familiar, unhurried gesture he picked up a chair and sat down at my table. He was not at all embarrassed. He was even smiling beneath his unkempt graying moustache.

"You don't remember me," he said, "but I recognize you. I'm Lévy."

And as I remained mute with astonishment, he added: "Lévy from the Latin Quarter."

We exchanged the habitual words of recognition. I apologized for not having recognized him immediately.

"You've aged a great deal," he said to me, with satisfaction.

I asked him if he was married and he started laughing as if at the enunciation of something foolish.

"Do you remember the pact?" he said.

I inclined my head to say yes, and he understood by the heaviness of my head that the memory must have played a considerable role in my life.

"Do you want me to tell you what has become of Kotzebue?" I asked, thinking that it would interest him.

"No, it's all the same to me."

"Would you like me to tell you what I...?"

He stopped me, making me understand by the gesture that everything concerning me was indifferent to him.

"Oh, I had a narrow escape that evening," he said. "You too, in fact."

"Why?"

"It wasn't by calculation. I wasn't intelligent enough at that time to dupe Lucifer. Now, it would be a different matter. It was simply by virtue of forgetfulness. The pact, as it was conceived and signed in your room, left us a way out. There's no point in my trying to explain things that you wouldn't understand. Only know that I had forgotten to draw the magic triangle in charcoal."

"So?"

"The pact was valid, for him as for us, but in those conditions the man retains the capacity to escape Lucifer if he wants to, with human will-power, and if he returns what he has received."

I considered Lévy attentively. He was speaking with the same sincerity as before. He was penetrated by his old conviction as to the existence and power of the demon.

"Do you mean that you've regretted the pact and that you've tried to escape its consequences?"

"I admit it," he said, in a loud voice, and his eyes glittered beneath his bushy eyebrows. "I was mistaken. It was when I saw the scant value of what I had requested and obtained that I understood my error."

"You requested something and received it?"

"Yes, and I've returned it."

"What?"

"Intelligence. I was insensate enough to desire to be intelligent when I was twenty."

I murmured to myself: "I too received something and returned it."

He uttered a little scornful laugh, but without ostentation. There was a sincere sadness in that laughter.

"Yes. Lucifer gives honestly what one requests of him. That's rather curious, in fact. Lucifer is honest, whereas God promises a great deal and doesn't keep the promise. Perhaps you've perceived that? Well, by virtue of the honesty of Lucifer, I've been the most intelligent man in the world. But intelligence is evil. It's nothing. It was necessary for me to get rid of that nothing. It took a long time, but I've got there."

"How?"

Lévy pointed at the sack that he had put down on seeing me, from which scrap metal was emerging.

"By physical labor, by effort, by sweat. By getting so close to matter as almost to resemble it. Loading and unloading ships is the ideal profession for a sage."

"And you're happy?"

He shrugged his shoulders and seemed irritated by the question. "You're like everybody else, you think it's happiness that it's necessary to seek."

"What is it necessary to seek, then?"

He made a gesture that seemed to project a flame toward the sky.

"God."

"Where can he be found?"

"In not thinking. In looking into the depths of oneself. He's dormant there. He sometimes wakes up, but rarely. I often ask myself...and just now when I saw you..."

Lévy's voice became lower. He leaned over the table. I understood that he had something to tell me, but that he was hesitant.

"You see that little breakwater that advances into the sea at the extremity of the harbor?"

"Yes."

"Every evening, I go to sit down on that breakwater. I don't move. I wait. Night falls. The sounds of the land die down. Those of the sea become more regular. The sky seems to descend. Then God wakes up, timidly at first. It's difficult to explain. Why is God so timid when Lucifer is so audacious? It's sufficient for the footfall of stroller, or the light of a boat's lantern, to brush the breakwater, for him to disappear. So..."

"So?"

"So, I thought that you might be able to help me. I explained it to you once. It's a secret that only the great masters have known. There have to be three."

I didn't understand. I didn't want to understand.

"Three?"

"Since one can make a pact with Lucifer, and even, in certain cases, break that pact, why shouldn't one with God be equally valid?"

I took a ten franc bill from my pocket and gave it to the waiter, making him a sign to keep the change.

"I learned once the magical power of ceremonies. I know that it's possible to sign a pact with God. Would you like to sign it with me? I know a poor fellow who, in exchange for a little money, will replace Kotzebue advantageously. Oh, this time I'm certain of not forgetting anything!"

I couldn't contain myself. I stood up, seized Lévy by his torn shirt and with my face close to his I cried: "No! No! No more pacts! You don't know what it took to extract my mind from the fear that took possession of it because of you. You've labored, you've sweated, you say? But you've found a consolation of sorts in your solitary madness. You still believe that Lucifer and God are two separate beings and you've extending your arms naively toward one after extending them toward the other. But I've seen them going forth fraternally, bearing the same cross toward a region where, in the end, there's no longer any light or darkness. I prefer to stay here and love them equally, since they're myself."

I seized my valise, made a gesture of adieu and drew way without looking back.

About an hour later, the ship on which I had embarked left port. It went slowly, leaving a circular wake behind it. From the deck I watched the lights of the harbor sparkling over the moving water.

I seemed to recognize to my left the breakwater that Lévy had pointed out to me. There was a human form crouched at its extremity and I thought that it was my

239

friend who was delivering himself to his evening meditation.

Was he seeing God? Was he not, on the contrary, tormented by a return of Lucifer? I watched to see whether there might be a revelatory contour in his silhouette, outlined against the masts of boats, a symbolic figure of the kind that hazard had so often designed for me.

But no, I only saw the reality. There was only a poor man, motionless in the dark.

Author's Note

It was on his return from his voyage to Alexandria and Palestine that I encountered J. N..., the author of the confession that you have just read.

The proprietor of the small hotel where I was staying for the summer, some distance from Aix-le-Provence, told me that an eccentric who had arrived from the Orient had rented a detached property with three rooms on land that belonged to him.

"He's asked not to be disturbed by anyone," he told me, "and he only speaks to the waiter who takes him his meals out there twice a day. I wouldn't be surprised if he had something for which to reproach himself. He seems to me to have chosen that property because it's situated on a hill and he can see at a distance if anyone is heading his way. Does he fear an unexpected visit, or is he a crackpot, of which there are so many?"

Impelled by curiosity, I acquired the habit of strolling every evening along a sunken road framed by trees that headed toward the isolated house. I arrived one day closer to it than usual and I remember that, while walking, I had put my cane over my shoulder and was holding it like a rifle—a gesture without importance whose import I only understood later.

The eccentric of whom I had heard mention emerged abruptly and ran toward me. He appeared to be prey to a rather vivid emotion. From a distance he looked at my cane attentively and shouted: "What do you want with me? Who are you?"

I recognized J. N... immediately, and we shook hands affectionately. We had seen one another quite frequently in Paris, two or three years before and we had one of those inexplicable sympathies for one another that acquire the name of friendship after a while.

He excused the abruptness of his greeting, but without giving an explanation.

"I thought for a moment...," he said. "I thought that decidedly..." And he tapped his forehead with his finger, laughing.

I was less surprised by the change in his features than the profound modifications that seemed to have taken place within his character.

He had pleased me once by his spontaneity and his own manner of being sincere. He had appeared to me to belong to the category of individuals who only accord importance to women and the possibility of conquering them. I had always judged him as vain and even slightly stupid. He had acquired an excessive nervousness and a habit of looking to the right and left as if someone might be watching him.

We encountered one another almost every evening during a long month of September in Provence, alongside olive groves and russet vines, and it was in the course of those walks that he told me the story of the crisis of his existence. I have transcribed that story as faithfully as I could and without adding anything, which explains its disconnection and the absence of certain developments.

"And Eveline?" I asked him.

He made a vague gesture. "The first become the last. I've heard tell that Eveline has pulled herself together, and that she's gone to live in Bretagne with one of her relatives, in order to escape her former environment."

But in spite of the questions that I asked him, and which he evaded, J. N... told me almost nothing about his voyage to Palestine. He had been deeply impressed by the character of certain landscapes on the edge of the Dead Sea. He only evoked them reticently, and with an evident displeasure.

It was only later, on the eve of my departure, that he decided, at my request, to recount an episode of his voyage that I think it as well to report.

"I had resolved to verify what Kotzebue had told me. I knew that he mingled truth and falsehood without being able to recognize them himself, and I thought that in order to be certain about the existence of the monastery where beings powerfully developed in intelligence devote themselves communally to spiritual evil, there was no other means than to go there and see with my own eyes. I remembered the name of the village that Kotzebue had given me. It was situated not far from the place where Galgala was, in the plain of El-Ghor.

"I'll pass over the difficulties of the voyage, the length of the journey on horseback from Jerusalem, a bad night in the abode of the Sheikh of the village. No one knew anything. There was no monastery. I set forth at sunrise with my guide, whom I almost obliged to follow me. I went to the right and left across the plain of El-Ghor, and its blocks of stone posed on top of one another to infinity, and that lasted for hours. In the end, I was exhausted. I remember that I distinguished in the distance the bituminous sheet of the Dead Sea, like a lump of molten lead. The blocks that surrounded me affected geometrical forms and succeeded one another regularly. It seemed to me that a flock of birds in flight was circling above the place where I was.

"Suddenly, I perceived a series of buildings, so flat and low that they were almost confounded with the clayey earth. No tower, no belfry above those juxtaposed roofs, which were barely the height of a man. I urged my horse in that direction and toped, without being able to explain why, some distance from the threshold. I felt the arm of the terrified guide pulling me backwards.

"Then the low square door opened silently; but when it was open, I couldn't see the person who had pulled the battens. and no one appeared on the threshold to greet me.

"The sun was burning overhead and the stones were reflecting a bleak brightness around me. I thought I could distinguish in the distance, in the form of gray mists, the unhealthy emanations that emerge from the mud of the Jordan. It was a little further on that John the Baptist has baptized Jesus, and the convent had been erected there in conformity with the law that dictates that the finest fruit contains a worm, that spiritual effort is immediately undermined by the appeal from below.

"Perhaps I was impressed by my guide's words, or did the extreme heat act upon me? From the empty threshold, from the diamond-shapes formed by the mute buildings, as if crushed against the earth, emanated such an atmosphere of extrahuman solitude that the idea of going through the deserted portal gave me the sensation of a danger compared with which death would be nothing.

"I exerted an effort upon myself. I did not want to have come so far for nothing. I went forward, but only a few paces. From a path that I had not seen, a number of white-clad monks emerged who went toward the monastery. They were monks like any monks, but without rosaries and without crosses embroidered on their robes. They had ordinary faces, which they turned in my direction indifferently: ordinary, but so icy, reflecting such a complete insensibility, that terror gripped me, and I fled as quickly as I could.

"I did not go back, and when my horse stopped on the road that goes along the Jordan, I wondered whether I might have had a dream.

"I know that I was a coward, but no power in the world would make me return to the plain of El-Ghor. One does not break twice the bust of the young man crowned with pepper-leaves."

We were now walking in silence. I accompanied him over the winding paths that ended at his detached house and I reflected on what he had just told me. I also remembered everything that, in his story of the previous says, concerned the brotherhood of evil with which he had tried to enter into a contest. Did it really exist? Had not the evening at Monsieur Althon's been a banal celebration of crackpots in which the rites of a puerile Luciferianism only served to sharpen sensuality? Was not the monastery of El-Ghor a monastery like any other, which only the troubled imagination of its visitor had rendered redoubtable?

I thought that, at any rate, J. N...'s solitary hours must he haunted by apprehensions. If he had chosen that little house on top of a hill, it was surely to be able to keep watch on the comings and goings of those who approached him. I imagined his insomnias, his anguished face against the window pane, the voices he must hear in the sound of the wind.

As I held out my hand to quit him, I took pity on his solitude.

"Don't you find this place very isolated," I began, "given..."

He understood my thinking and smiled.

"You think that I'm afraid of them? A few months ago, that would have been possible, but not now."

I looked at him in surprise. His gaze reflected a tranquil confidence.

"One cannot be afraid of those one loves. That's the secret: to love the bad as much as the good—more, even, for they have more need of it. The coalition of a thousand brotherhoods of the damned can't cast the slightest shadow over the dream of a soul full of love."

The shadows were now filling the country. The trace of the paths had faded way. The lights of the village seemed infinitely distant and lost. A bat passed before us several times, but I understood that for J.N..., the darkness did not contain any menace.

"I thought...," I said, "I thought that you were prey to certain ideas...the very situation of this house led me to think..."

"I'll explain to you what made me choose it. Can you imagine that I've got it into my head, I don't know why, that when I succeed in reaching the point of perfect love, I'll be informed of it by a material sign. I've described to you the painting in which Drevet represented Christ and the angel of evil carrying a cross together and helping one another long a sunken road. When I came here I noticed that the road that we've just climbed resembled the one in the painting. I firmly believe that the sign by which I shall know that my redemption is complete will be the sight of Christ and Lucifer advancing toward me, fraternally, united under their common burden. I've found, very nearly, the appropriate landscape. It only lacks the characters. And can you imagine that, when I saw you appear the other day, with your cane over your shoulder, I wondered for a moment whether that cane might be a cross..."

"But I'm nothing like Christ, or Lucifer," I said.

"You're mistaken. Every man is both of them in turn, and sometimes simultaneously, and it's their intimate union that it's necessary to operate in the depths of our heart."

I quit him after those words. I left the following day, and I have not seen him since.

THE NIGHT OF HASHISH AND OPIUM

The Bad Omens

I lifted the blue gauze that was undulating before my window. A flock of black birds, emerging from the palm trees in the garden, striped the sky slowly, trailing above the scattered masts of the harbor and disappearing to the left in the gilded fleece of the beach.

A bad omen, I thought.

And I established a relationship between the color of the birds and the black color of the opium whose intoxication was to be revealed to me that very evening. The evening of opium was poorly announced!

For I have always believed that a sage providence informs us by a small sign, when we cast our first glance at things, whether the day is to be fortunate or unfortunate.

Scarcely had I lost sight of the birds than a Brahmin beggar that I knew went past on the avenue. He was protecting himself from the sun by extending his fan of areca palm leaves, and sometimes he agitated his rags. He stopped for a second before my door, raised his head and saw me, He squinted frightfully. He made a bizarre grimace, and I immediately drew back, for I was almost naked.

I murmured: "Another bad omen!"

And at the same moment, a tari, a kind of trumpet with a heart-rending tone, which signals mourning, resonated on the landward side, in the Hindu quarter.

I had also seen the Brahmin with the squint lift his fan and grimace in my direction, and I had heard a tari in the distance, firstly on the morning of my marriage, and afterwards on the morning of the day when I had discovered and read the letters addressed to my husband by a certain Juliette Romano—letters that legitimated my divorce.

The heart-rending trumpet evoked for me, with a gripping verity, that decisive day of my life.

I have noticed that, when one has just taken a bath and is not yet dressed, the soul has a tendency to appear naked, like the body. For our true soul only shows itself, even to ourselves, at rare intervals, and preferably in the morning.

In truth, I no longer loved my husband when I found the letters and learned that he was the lover of an adventuress recently installed in Pondicherry. He had almost ruined me. That wasn't of any great importance, but I felt that he was going to destroy my inner fortune, which is made of self-confidence and confidence in life. The fear of that invisible ruination had killed my love. I didn't hold against him a few base actions that I had discovered—one doesn't attach oneself to a man because of elevated sentiments—but I resented the fact that he had only considered me as a legitimate wife, and had not appreciated me as a lover.

I no longer loved him, to be sure, but I suffered nevertheless in knowing that he no longer loved me.

The tari announcing the death dragged on lugubriously that day, as today, and aggravated by pain. I remember the desire for certainty that animated me, my shrill voice calling for Sheik Sultan and my telingas, the fashion in which I traversed the garden and in which I fell into my palanquin, shouting an address. I remember my confrontation with the woman who had been depicted to me as a redoubtable adventuress, a whore capable of anything, expressly created by God to break homes and damn men.

Juliette Romano was a timid individual whose blue eyes had a slightly fleeting gaze, who would have had the appearance of an English schoolmistress full of innocence if a certain something in the milky hue of her neck, and in the solid roundness of her breasts beneath her corsage, had not betrayed a hidden ardor and a capacity for abandonment. After five minutes of conversation she had begged my pardon and confessed everything that I wanted to know. I quit her without having said a wounding word and during the hours that followed I cursed the tari player more ardently, who never ceased to rend my ears for a unknown mourning caused by the timid creature of prey who had just taken my husband from me.

All that was so far away now! In any case, it's only the present that counts. But the present was a flock of black birds rising from the right to the left; it was a Brahmin beggar who had just squinted at my door; it was a trumpet announcing the death of a Hindu in a wretched hut of compressed earth.

It was even more than that, I suddenly remembered. It was one of the good God's creatures that I had inadvertently crushed the day before; it was a chemise that my ayah had presented to me inside-out as I was about to put it on; it was a game of dominos that children were playing at the foot of the statue of Dupleix, each domino of which they had wrapped in paper—which is, as everyone knows, a sign auguring great calamities.

Never had there been as any contrary presages against me, never had I been informed with such certainty of the evil fate that was lying in wait for me.

In the pure light of the morning I saw clearly what it was necessary for me to do. I had to find a pretext to refuse Lord Portman's invitation, and not go to smoke opium at Chillambaram.

Nothing was easier. I only had to write two letters of apology, one to Lord Portman and the other to Comtesse Aurelia, who was to accompany us.

Was there not, in any case, something bizarre about the insistence that Comtesse Aurelia had put into begging me to accept that pleasure party? Comtesse Aurelia had excessively thin lips and an excessively narrow forehead. Her black hair was naturally curly and shone like the plumage of a crow. Were those not the characteristics of an evil influence? She hated me, I was sure of it, because I was twenty and she was thirty-five, perhaps more. Why had she suddenly praised the magnificence of the pagoda of Chillambaram, as she had never previously paid much attention to the ancient monuments of India, and seemed perfectly ignorant of the beauties of architecture—and of beauty in general? Why put on a show of being so passionately desirous to see me dance, as she had made fun of my pretention of learning the ritual dances of the bayaderes before all Pondicherry and all Madras? Why had she depicted to me with so much eloquence, the day before the voluptuousness of smoking opium in a dreamlike décor, when she had told me, a few months before, that she had a horror of the drug and all those who smoked it?

Was there not something bizarre about that gathering at Chillambaram of three men who had all been in love with me and all disappointed in their desires? On what was their so-called friendship based except their common desire to talk about me, to slander me collectively and to affirm after having drunk or smoked that one or other of them would have me sooner or later, now that I was divorced. For those three men were now inseparable. When they were not cruising along the Coromandel coast or hunting in the forests of Trivatore, they were getting drunk together. Lord Portman was an alcohol drinker, the Rajah of Tanjore was an opium smoker and Prince Vanini attained artificial paradises with the pellets of hashish that were fabricated for him by a Bengali physician in Madras.

It was by virtue of living in their company that my husband had been detached from me; it was with them that he had lost a part of my fortune in the gambling dens of Madras. I didn't hold it against them, and I even had the weakness to see them, because there is nothing insensate that one doesn't do to escape ennui.

But was there not something bizarre in the recommendation that Lord Portman had made me not to bring with me either the faithful Sheik Sultan, who always marched at the head of my palanquin-bearers, or my creole chambermaid, who would have been so useful to me for changing costume?

"You'll find all the necessary staff at Chillambaram," he had said. "I promise you a night such as you've never spent."

In saying those words he had run his tongue over his fleshy lips and had made me think of a wild beast about to make a meal of raw flesh.

He had immediately added, as if to reassure me: "You're risking absolutely nothing; Comtesse Aurelia won't quit you."

"What would I be risking?" I had said, immediately, putting an icy innocence in my expression.

"Nothing other than not having experienced hands to take off your dress and put on the costume of the bayadere Cammatatchi."[12]

And he had started to laugh, the distant laughter that is habitual to him, while his eyes were deprived of all human expression, to the point of giving the impression that his spirit was no longer inhabiting his body.

For the evening at Chillambaram had been organized in order to see me dance. I had made the imprudent promise to do so at Comtesse Aurelia's house, one evening when Lucilio Vanini, pill-box in hand, had just described the architectural marvels of Chillambaram and made me ashamed of never having traveled the forty-nine miles that separate the ancient pagoda from Pondicherry. That same evening I had made known to the Rajah of Tanjore that desire to try, once, the effects of opium.

Lord Portman, always prompt to multiply opportunities to see me, had proposed organizing a dinner and a night in the pagoda. He had taken charge of bribing the Brahmins and getting them to empty the space for the entire extent of the vast enclosure of the walls. He took

---

[12] "Cammatatchi, a Dancer," is an oft-reproduced print, still easily available. It is credited to the Orientalist Eugène Burnouf (1801-1852) because it was used as an illustration in one of his books, but he is unlikely to be the artist. The portrait does not show its subject dancing, nor is her costume provocative; the author only seems to have borrowed the name.

charge of having two or three rooms cleaned before the sacred pool and organizing a comfortable smoking-room sheltered from mosquitoes, lizards and snakes. We would have an orchestra and intermediate dancers, but on condition that I animated the artistic feast by dancing in the same costume and in the same place where the celebrated bayadere Cammatatchi had once danced.

I had accepted. Everyone had uttered cries of joy. Lord Portman had added: "We'll be tranquil. I'll bring my panther to guard us." Then, his eyes fixed, he had fallen into a meditation and profound as the void.

And now the day had come for the departure for Chillambaram, and destiny was sending me all kinds of warnings to incite me to postpone that departure.

I got dressed slowly. I took several turns around my room. I was going to write the letters of apology. I would not go to Chillambaram.

I affirmed to myself that what was guiding me was only the imperious notification of destiny, and not the ridiculous bourgeois sentiment that comes from fear of compromising oneself.

I have never been afraid of compromising myself, either in France before my marriage or since my arrival in Pondicherry. I deem that a well-established bad reputation is one of the conditions of happiness. One wears that bad reputation like an armor, the sparkle of which distances you from mediocre and tedious individuals. The darts of calumny slide off it and it permits the conquest of the most redoubtable of the enemies of our pleasure, which is our natural timidity.

I wandered in the garden under my parasol and I was about to go back upstairs to write the letters when I heard the prolonged cry that palanquin-bearers utter when they stop.

Behind the gate I perceived the exceedingly wrinkled face of Comtesse Aurelia.

"Well, are you ready? They've just fired the cannon of the yacht to alert us."

I ran toward the door to declare my resolution.

"No, no, I'm not stopping," said the Comtesse, with a determined volubility. "You know that I don't like to be late. Lord Portman has sent you this little golden box that you must put around your neck. It's a surprise, but it's necessary not to open it until this evening. And some news—perhaps bad news, or good, I don't know. Mir, the Rajah's son, will be with us. His father is bringing him because he asked to see you dance, it seems. But I'm afraid that one spectator more might be too much for your timidity."

She started to laugh, and before I could reply she made a sign to her telingas to start walking.

I remained motionless, considering the Chinese flowers of the silk parasol, which I had lowered. In my left hand I was holding a little gilded box suspended from an antique chain, which Comtesse Aurelia had handed to me though the bars of the gate and which I passed mechanically around my neck. How singular the flowers on the parasol were! In the calyx of each one there was the face of a student at the University of Madras: the face of Mir, the Rajah's son; Mir with the impenetrable eyes; twenty years old, like me, perhaps nineteen, whom I identified mentally with the Rama of the Hindu poems, and to whom I gave that name when I thought about him.

I started running through the garden. "Sheik Sultan!" I shouted.

Then I reflected that there was to need to run, and that the yacht would not leave without me.

The bayadere's robe had been packed the previous evening, just in case.

I threw a shawl over my shoulders and put rouge on my lips. Already I could hear the sound of the gate opening and the footsteps of the palanquin-bearers on the gravel of the path.

Ad at the exact moment when, sitting in the midst of cushions, I raised my hand to order the departure, a sweating Hindu child who had no garments save a loincloth and a red turban, showed his head at the window. The porters began to run. He threw on to my knees a piece of paper folded in four. I opened it. There were words traced in French in topsy-turvy handwriting that seemed deliberately disguised:

You must not go to Chillambaram.

I looked back through the window of the palanquin. Far away, on the avenue, there was a little Hindu running as far as he could in the opposite direction to that of the palanquin. As my porters had set forth very rapidly, a few seconds had sufficed for the red turban no longer to be any more than an almost imperceptible dot.

I thought that it was too late to go back and attempt to catch up with the messenger. His flight indicated, in any case, that he had been instructed to give me the enigmatic letter and disappear without explanation.

I crumpled up the note with a hint of irritation, because I had no idea who could have sent it, and for me, unsatisfied curiosity is analogous to a mental burn.

But what a desire I had now for that night of opium at Chillambaram! All the gods of India emerging from the mystery of their pagoda and extending their innumerable arms toward me would have stopped me when I launched myself forth along the interminable landing-stage of Pondicherry. The enigma of an unknown danger summoned me with as much force as the enigma of Mir's dark eyes. Oh, the beauty of that which one does not know, and that which might be revealed to you, whether it be good or evil!

The wind made my dress flap. An odor of rotten plants alternated with the intoxicating breath of the open sea. And on the launch that took me to the yacht, to the regular beat of the oars, amid the tedious and limited faces of English sailors, I imagined that I was sailing toward dangerous pirates, who had captured me by means of an incomprehensible ruse and whose prey I was about to be.

The Bayadere Cammatatchi

I believe that all events can always be deduced in advance, read in the atmosphere, by a clairvoyant person who knows how to cast her intuition artfully around her.

I ought to have understood and foreseen. Everything was irrevocably settled in the minds of the three men tormented by desire and the woman with the face as wrinkled as an apple burned by the sun.

First of all there was the unusual insistence they put into making me drink during the lunch on deck; then the fashion in which they all repeated that Mir had preferred to make the journey on horseback in spite of the heat of the day and that he would join us at Porto Novo, where we were to disembark. There was Comtesse Aurelia's laughter, as sharp as a rapier—laughter that she rapidly veiled when she remembered that it was necessary to disguise her perfidy. She then put on an expression of bonhomie and strove to become similar to a smiling apple, devoid of all acidity.

There were words whose meaning I didn't understand and which caused a great deal of laughter. There was a question of a game of cards, a stake, a fortune won or lost, but I couldn't understand what the prize was or even whether the game had already taken place.

Prince Vanini told Comtesse Aurelia and me, in fragments, stories about the antiquity of Chillabaram, its fabulous riches, its thousands of priests and its vanished splendors. He spoke with a certain mystery in his voice, as if everything he said had the character of a secret. Everything he knew he had from the Rajah, who nodded his head in approval from time to time. For the Rajah almost never spoke when several people were gathered together, and said himself that it was only possible for him to express himself before a single interlocutor. Prince Vanini, on the contrary, was only loquacious before a numerous audience.

And there was also the story of the bayadere Cammatatchi, which should have alerted me. The Prince's voice, when he spoke about her, became even lower, and Lord Portman, who was walking back and forth smoking a cigar, stopped, and I saw his fleshy lips agitating nervously in a fashion so repulsive that I was obliged to look away.

The bayadere Cammatatchi was a priestess of Siva the destroyer, the third god of the Hindu trinity. She was so beautiful that her renown extended throughout India and pilgrims came from the most distant parts of the Deccan to contemplate hr. But she had an expression in her face that drove men to despair. An incitement to death was in the lines of her body. Many pilgrims who had seen her offered their lives to Siva.

The Rajah of Tanjore, an ancestor of the one who was smoking a cigar beside me and never took his eyes off me, fell in love with the bayadere. By caprice, the marvelous Cammatatchi, who, by virtue of her profession as a sacred bayadere, gave herself to all those who brought important offerings to the pagoda, refused herself to the Rajah of Tanjore.

"The ancestor of our excellent friend," said the Prince, designating the Rajah, who lowered his eyes, "was a singularly cruel man. He resolved to have the bayadere in spite of her refusal and to punish her for it. It was the day of the feast of Sidambara...I'm not mistaken?" the Prince asked, turning to the Rajah, who made a negative sign with his cigar. "On the day of that feast,

Sidambara, who is an incarnation of Siva, appears to his initiates."

"And then?" I said, or the Prince had stopped.

The yacht had just rounded the rocky banks of Cooleroon, and we were in sight of Porto Novo.

Lord Portman, who was leaning over the side, shouted: "I think I can see Mir on the jetty. He's arrived before us."

Everyone got up. I looked in the direction of the coast. I distinguished the torsos of a few Hindus sitting on the sand. I saw a man with a staff in his hand pushing three zebus before him, but there was no trace of a horseman.

Prince Vanini, having looked in my direction and exchanged a glance of complicity with the Rajah and the Comtesse, murmured in a low voice: "Yes, I believe that Mir has arrived first." And he started to laugh in a servile fashion, turning to Lord Portman: the excessive laughter that is not commanded by merriment but the desire to flatter someone for a mediocre joke whose value one wants to heighten by approval.

He added: "I'll conclude the story of Cammatatchi this evening."

Lord Portman had indeed been joking, or mistaken. Mir was not waiting for us at Porto Novo. No one was astonished by that, and his father declared lightly that he would doubtless join us at Chillambaram.

The afternoon was not yet approaching its end, but we still had eight kilometers to cover overland in order to reach the first gopuram of the pagoda, built some distance from the village on the edge of the jungle.

Palanquins, horses and an escort were waiting for us. Comtesse Aurelia and I were to make the journey in a palanquin. I offered, out of politeness, to climb into the same magnificent palanquin as her, in which, in the midst of a stream of cushions, four people could easily have been accommodated. To my great surprise, she refused. She protested the great heat, a slight headache that she felt around her temples, and that thought she might cure by sleeping a little. Then, there were two palanquins, and she preferred to have one to herself. And when I persisted she turned her back on me, installed herself in the first palanquin and closed the door rather abruptly.

What a disagreeable woman! I thought, privately, unable to understand that manner of acting, which was not habitual to her.

We left.

There was still time to go back. Had I not been warned? Without being very perspicacious, it required no more to see things clearly. But it is noticeable that, when we fall into a trap, it is by virtue of a faculty of blindness that is of our own making, and which blindfolds our eyes for a while.

Palanquin-bearers intone a rhythmic chant, full of vague poetry, which initially invites melancholy, and afterwards slumber. My blindness and my quietude combined so well with the changing voice of the telingas and the sway they imparted to the palanquin, that I fell asleep.

When I woke up the palanquin had stopped. I had been asleep for nearly an hour. Prince Vanini and the Rajah were in the process of dismounting and Lord Portman, standing beside the window, was considering me with his empty eyes. His lips were trembling slightly, and they appeared to me so red, so thick and sensual that I felt my stomach rise in disgust.

"It's said that a good sleep is the sign of a tranquil conscience," he said. And as I opened the door to get down he added, in a low voice: "You who are the cause of all my nights of insomnia."

I was confused and surprised. I looked around. We were at the bottom of a steep slope. I distinguished at the summit an enormous red wall, towers, successions of gopurams covered with sculptures whose ensemble formed the pagoda of Chillambaram, as vast as a city...

To my right, quite some distance away, was the village, with a single two-story house dominating the palm-thatch roofs, which must be the travelers' bungalow. A large number of Hindus were watching us fearfully. To the left, Lord Portman's servants formed a respectful circular group. Behind us a saw the road we had followed paling between coconut palms and cacti. But I searched in vain for the second palanquin, the one bearing Comtesse Aurelia.

In interrogated the Prince, who was beside me.

"How well you must have slept," he said, laughing. "We'd only covered a few hundred meters when the Comtesse felt her headache worsen. An hour's sleep always cures her in such cases. Lord Portman went to install her in a cabin in the yacht, and he rejoined us before we had arrived. Comtesse Aurelia will arrive for dinner, doubtless at the same time as Mir, who can't be much longer now."

Could I now refuse, without being absolutely ridiculous, to visit the pagoda, take part in a dinner long prepared and accepted by me, under the pretext that I was the only woman in the company of three men? I should have done. A false shame prevented me from doing so.

We climbed the hill on foot. A few Hindus clad in yellow and black robes conversed with Lord Portman. I assumed that they were the Brahmin guardians of the temple. I distinguished in their attitude the deference and the scorn that one has for those one believes one has duped by an excellent bargain.

The sun was about to set and projected a red wave over the great stone wall, more than ten meters high, mute and inalterable, as eternal as the religion whose mysteries it encloses. We were at the foot of one of four fabulous portals formed by a truncated rectangular pyramid with seven steps. Sculpted on that portal were divinities of all sorts, maleficent Boutas, elephantine Ganeshas, Vishnus with nine arms, and faces and animal limbs that were superimposed and interlaced, and made a kind of animal forest of stone.

Prince Vanini drew closer to me and I felt his warm breath on my cheek.

"The antiquity of the monument renders the intoxication of opium or hashish more profound. You'll see."

I turned away, but the Rajah took my arm lightly while walking and said to me: "It's here that my ancestor made love to the bayadere Cammatatchi, who must have resembled you. Scarcely will I have crossed the threshold than I shall imagine that I'm my ancestor and that you are Cammatatchi."

Servants passed at a run, carrying carpets, boxes and torches: the final preparations for the dinner and the evening.

Lord Portman, who had remained in rear, advanced toward us joyfully.

"Even the Brahmins won't be sleeping in the enclosure," he said. "They'll spend the night in the village.

Chillambaram belongs to us until tomorrow, and I'll have the door locked behind us."

He made us a sign to follow him.

I would have sworn that at that moment, in the monsters and gods sculpted on the mass of the gopuram and covered with a vegetation of cryptogams, there was a sort of living stir, with facial grimaces, the quivering of horns and rumps, the advancement of snouts and elongations of claws. At the same time I was traversed by a mad, desperate, panic terror. The immensity of my folly appeared to me clearly, Mir had not been invited and would not arrive on horseback. Comtesse Aurelia was in the pay of the rich Lord. She had long been the procuress and accomplice of his pleasures. It had been agreed between them that she would spend the night on the yacht. I was delivered without defense to three men who nurtured against me the same wounded self-esteem and unslaked desire. I had fallen into a trap. I was about to be at their mercy in the confines of that redoubtable and unknown place, where I could neither call for help nor flee.

While reflecting, and almost involuntarily, I had passed through the shadow of a vault alongside Lord Portman. I was in a second enclosure, bathed by twilight. I turned round. There was a noise behind me. It was the iron-bound wooden door that had just closed.

The Pagoda of Chillambaram

As if in a dream, the ruined magnificence of Chillambaram extended before my eyes.

We crossed an enclosure strewn with isolated statues and pavilions. We passed under porticos, went along galleries, descended staircases. We sometimes encountered a marble elephant of natural size, a white bull under a mandapam with four columns, or a solitary cross-legged idol. We traversed uncultivated walled gardens, more enclosures, further rooms surrounded by colonnades, courtyards paved with stone slabs worn away by time and ordered with bas-reliefs representing mysterious scenes. Deformed statues gazed at us from niches or emerged from an upper floor of stone. We were suddenly in the presence of a hideous figure with an enormous mouth, sharp teeth curved back like tusks, pointed ears, and two long horns on the head.

We had just traversed a kind of quincunx strewn with monoliths under the dense shadow of an enormous tower with pyramidal step when, having come through an obscure portico, I saw a wide staircase extend at my feet and I was inundated by green light.

It came from a reflection of the sky in the waters of the sacred pool. The pool was in front of us, in a square of sculpted colonnades, hexagonal towers and silent temples. It sparkled like an emerald; it was alive, like an immobile body.

But I did not have the possibility of admiring the harmony of the monuments, those looming up around me and their doubles reflected in the depths of the waters. I was listing in my mind all the reasons for rancor that the three men walking beside me had.

I saw once again the earthen color that the Rajah's face had taken on, the day when he had seized me by the waist and tried to approach his lips to mine. That was in the drawing room of my villa one evening when my husband had invited him to dinner. I had detached myself from his grip without difficulty and as he looked at me, simultaneously surprised by his own audacity and my resistance. I had contented myself with showing him the mirror that was beside him. He had looked at it without understanding, and had looked at me with astonishment. Then I had said to him:

"It's a French mirror of special fabrication. If you care to examine it with a little attention, you'll see therein that the number of years that separate us would permit you to be my grandfather."

The Rajah had remained silent, looking at the tips of his feet, and he had murmured: "I've been deceived. I thought you were a true Frenchwoman."

I could not tell whether that was an insolence directed at all the women of my country or the natural expression of his disappointment.

I saw was again the episodes of the struggle that I had had to sustain with Prince Vanini—for it is the destiny of every slightly attractive woman who has a certain gleam in her eye; she cannot be alone with a man without the latter resuscitating the primitive beast dormant within him and attempting to tip her over, like a male animal blinded by desire in the presence of a female.

In the depths of the governor's garden, under palm trees where there were no longer any lanterns, at a party one night, I had made the error of going with him. The orchestra was playing a languorous waltz, my dress was too low-cut and perhaps he had extracted from his pill-box the frenzy by which he was suddenly possessed.

He had grabbed me by the hips and lifted me off the ground, simultaneously plunging his head into the hair over my neck. In resisting, I had clung on to the plastron of his shirt, which I pulled with all my might. The plastron tore in two, causing the button holding his collar to fly off, so that the collar fell on to the pathway, with the cravat and the pearls of the plastron. He understood immediately the extent of the catastrophe, the difficulty of finding the pearls in the dark, the ridicule of traversing the illuminated part of the garden with his short in tatters. He had released me so abruptly that I fell.

"That's not sporting," he said. "You're a..."

He stopped abruptly. His voice had changed, and taken on a crapulous tone that I did not know; I divined a gross insult that he retained. I thought for a few seconds that his fist was about to strike me in the dark. Nothing happened. I had taken pity on him, however; I helped him find the pearls and readjust his collar. And as we walked back in silence toward the light I noticed for the first time that the hand posed on the rip in the plastron, the hand of the aristocratic Prince, was a hand with square fingers, singularly hairy: the hand of a murderer.

And I also saw again the scene in Madras, in a dance-hall for the usage of foreigners to which Lord Portman had taken Comtesse Aurelia and me, one evening of idleness, after my divorce.

In the midst of the smoke, among the cries of drunken sailors, to the sounds of a deafening tom-tom, a fake bayadere had danced a synthetic nautch on a little stage. As dancing is my passion, I was following the dancer with my eyes in order to discern the element of traditional art that there was in her movements, and the extent to which she was dancing a veritable nautch.

The place where we were was so cluttered with sailors of all nationalities that we were narrowly crowded together and I felt with an invincible repugnance the warmth of Lord Portman's shoulder against mine.

When the dancer had finished her dance, she scarcely bowed two or three times, descended the steps of the stage with an extreme rapidity and went to fall on the floor at the feet of a sinister hirsute individual who was sitting cross-legged and had watched her dance with a distant indifference, smoking a cigarette. With a delectably amorous gesture, the dancer placed her arms around his neck, murmuring in a sigh; "Oh, Miguel!"

Then the man, placing his hand on the nape of the woman's neck, plastered his lips to hers brutally, by way of recompense.

That little scene in the drunken sailors' tavern, was gripping. I turned to Lord Portman. His eyes were almost bulging out of his head; his lips were fatter; he looked by turns at Miguel and me, with an envious expression in his features. He leaned toward me and I nearly fainted because of the impression his proximity gave me, while he said to me: "I envy that man. I'd like you to dance before me, and put your arm around my neck afterwards. Tell me that that will happen one day."

"Never," I said, trying to laugh and consider it as a joke.

"I always succeed in getting what I want," he said. "I swear that you'll dance for me, that you'll come to put your head on my shoulder as that dancer did, calling me by my first name, and that with my hand on the nape of your neck, I'll kiss your lips as forcefully."

I started to laugh more loudly, and furthermore, as he often joked with great seriousness, I thought that perhaps he did not attach any importance to those words.

But he had reminded me of them a little later, and they returned to my memory now.

"That tower you can see over there is the most ancient of all," said Prince Vanini, and he embarked on archeological explanations, to which I only listened distractedly.

"That's the place, on the edge of the pool, where we're going to dine," said Lord Portman. "I hope that you'll be satisfied by my installation."

His face, turned toward me, expressed such a puerile fear of displeasing me, a solicitude so affectionate, that it suddenly changed the orders of my thoughts.

I perceived servants clad in white; some were in the process of extending mosquito nets, others were running around a laden table. They were numerous and would doubtless remain close by. Were not my three companions, in any case, showing the most respectful courtesy in my regard? How could three men belonging to the highest aristocracy, having a name and a rank in Madras society, infringe the laws of gallantry with regard to a woman who was their guest? Would not their number paralyze their evil intention, in the hypothetical case that they had one?

It was true that they had some rancor to satisfy. I might have inspired their spite. But I ought not to exaggerate the importance of my refusals. All three were seekers of amorous adventures who made attempts on all the women they met and were accustomed to refusals as well as victories. They had classified me in the category of women one has for a friend and not a mistress, that was all. I had, on the contrary, acquired an absolute authority over them. Comtesse Aurelia had a veritable headache and, supposing that they had not invited Mir and they had deceived me on that subject, that was only a petty jealousy of aging men with regard to a very young man.

Night gradually fell and my apprehensions dissipated as I saw torches illuminated alongside the pool, on the side where the dinner was prepared. Their flames made large red circles in the green tints of the dead waters. They danced and flared up before dying down, and reappeared as if with the insouciance of the twentieth year and the love of pleasure.

Several connected rooms that preceded the sanctuary of an abandoned temple had been entirely covered with carpets, striped fabrics and Bengal veils. Champaca and jasmine flowers spread an insipid and relaxing odor.

"This will be the smoking room," said Lord Portman. "There's the stage for the dances. This room is the one where the musicians are and this is the room where I've had the chest placed that contains your robes, and where you can dress without being disturbed."

I saw at a glance that the door of that room had been recently fitted and that there was a brand new bolt that would permit me to lock myself in. I was sensible of the delicacy of that attention and that took away my final fears.

I also noticed that there were six places set at the table and I heard Lord Portman, after having looked at his watch, give the order to remove two of them. He added, in the most natural tone in the world: "There'll be time to reset them if they arrive."

My fears changed into remorse. Was I not naturally inclined only to see the bad side of things? How many times had I spoiled my existence with futile suspicions? That flock of birds, those dominos, and the Brahmin with the squint were the cause of it all. What ridiculous superstitions!

"It's time for cocktails," said the Prince, holing out a glass to me in which the colors of the inflamed sky and the emerald pool between the porticoes were condensed.

The Prince's hand was much less angular that I had thought. It was an honest hand, only a little too hairy. The Rajah was gazing silently into space with an expression of immense mildness. Lord Portman seemed timid and embarrassed, like someone afraid of not having done enough things to receive his gusts.

How foolish I am! I thought.

But I almost dropped the glass that I had just emptied. A howl, or rather a low, heart-rending, terrible mewl had resounded, and its echo reverberated under the profound vaults and in the sonority of the stone temples.

My eyes must have expressed fear.

"It's nothing," said Lord Portman, laughing. "It's my panther, who needs to be given his dinner."

The Smoking Room

My security increased during the meal, where the frankest camaraderie reigned. Lord Portman drank enormously, but his gaze did not have the impressive emptiness that was customary to him and caused me such a disagreeable sensation. Only for a few moments did his large eyes recover that expression.

There was talk about amour, naturally, and women. The three men found that they had the same tastes. They could not tolerate the resistance that women thought themselves obliged to put up at a first encounter. They were in accord in thinking that what was delectable was consent, and in unanimously criticizing brutes who took women by force.

"Do you remember," Lord Portman said to me, "that dance-hall for the use of sailors to which we went together one evening in Madras?"

I made a vague gesture that signified that I scarcely remembered it.

"Well, I don't know anything more mysteriously troubling than the gesture of abandonment with which the woman who danced offered her lips to a frightful Portuguese named Miguel. I can't imagine any greater joy in the world that that of seeing the woman I love come to sit at my feet as that dancer did that evening."

It was then that his eyes reflected the infinity of the void. Scarcely had he spoken those words than the Rajah and Prince Vanini burst out laughing and pronounced two or three phrases in English, in spite of the fact that I did not understand that language and it had been agreed that they would only express themselves in French in my presence.

They apologized immediately for those involuntary exclamations. I had almost understood their meaning, or thought I understood.

The Rajah had said something that signified: "You have one chance in three, no more."

And the Prince had added a phrase in which there as mention of the Atharva Veda and a magical operation. I knew the name of Atharva Veda from my husband, who had told me once the Prince Vanini amused himself studying magic with a Bengali physician in that ancient Hindu book.

But I did not attach any importance at the time to those incomprehensible allusions. I was penetrated by a physical wellbeing what went from the tips of my toes to the roots of my hair, and to that wellbeing was added a sentiment of amity and perfect mental tranquility.

Dinner concluded and we went into the smoking room. Mats and leather cushions were disposed in a circular fashion around a little silver lamp with a red-painted glass set on a tray. Curiously, I handled the ivory pipes, needles and little metal pots containing a dark paste that I sniffed, but was disappointed by the absence of perfume.

"Opium is a hidden genius," the Rajah told me, "which needs fire to reveal the infinite powers that it contains. It is similar to our soul, which is almost always dormant and silent; but if one warms it up with the magical warmth of amour, it spreads perfumes and allows treasures of dream to flow that one did not suspect that one possessed."

Lord Portman had just emptied a large glass of fine champagne in a single draught, and he was holding the bottle in his right hand in order to pour himself a second glass.

"I don't like this wine," he said, "although it's the best one can find in all India. The whisky is far superior." He turned in my direction with his most fearful smile and, as if he were addressing a prayer to me, he said: "It's better if you put on your bayadere's robe right away. They you won't have to disturb yourself again and we can admire you in the costume for longer. You can dance whenever you wish, either before or after the intoxications to which our friends will initiate you; for myself, I'll remain faithful to the only intoxication that doesn't deceive."

He emptied his glass of champagne, made a grimace and went it exchange the bottle he was holding for a bottle of whisky.

I found that program very wise and I headed for the door. Lord Portman called to my attention with a gesture the fact that I could lock myself in, in order to be tranquil while I dressed, and I was surprised to hear him say: "We'll take advantage of your absence to play a hand of cards.

"I won't be very long," I said.

"A single hand will suffice," said Vanini.

He had taken a pack of cards out of his pocket and my surprise increased when I saw Lord Portman and the Rajah moved closer to Vanini eagerly, and prepare to play. I even remarked an unusual gleam of passion in their eyes. I thought that they were keener gamblers that I had supposed, and I left them. I thought there was no need to bolt the door.

My costume was the classic costume of the bayadere of southern India. It was composed of a short, tight corselet around the bosom, with a colored veil over the shoulders, and bright transparent silk trousers embroidered with silver, with a bright silk skirt above them, also transparent, embroidered with gold. As the corselet was high and the trousers low, a part of the body below the breasts was bare, but the ensemble of the costume remained modest nevertheless. I rolled up my hair and enclosed it beneath a broad headband of gold and diamonds which descended over my temples. I put the rings around my ankles whose metallic clink is indispensable to the rhythm of the dance, and light golden rings on my toes.

When I had finished I darted a satisfied glace into the large mirror that formed the back of the narrow room, which was illuminated by a high lamp, and I admired the ingenuity and the comfort that had presided over the organization of the improvised dressing-room, where nothing was lacking.

These Englishmen are extraordinary, I thought.

And I rummaged through the rouges, the creams and the perfumes.

Suddenly, I heard a cry of triumph from the next room. It was Prince Vanini who had uttered it. "It's me! It's me!" he repeated. "I've won!"

His voice was followed by a kind of dull groan uttered by Lord Portman.

I was amazed and slightly annoyed to think that my companions, who had come to Chillambaram to smoke opium in my company, were putting such ardor into a game of cards commenced a few minutes before.

I opened the door slightly, and it made no sound as it swung.

I perceived the Rajah at the extremity of the smoking room, lying on a mat. He had just picked up a pipe and was dipping a needle into a little pot. In the slope of his massive shoulder and the inclination of his wooly head there was something suggestive of ill luck and resignation to destiny.

Lord Portman and the Prince had their backs to me. Lord Portman had taken the Prince by the arm and as speaking to him in a low voice. He was insisting on something that seemed to impassion his heart. The Prince shook his head to say no.

"Well, ten thousand pounds!" said Lord Portman.

"Well, if you put that price on it...," Vanini replied. "But it's much more than it's worth."

"You accept?" said Lord Portman, feverishly.

"I accept," said the Prince, "but I don't guarantee the efficacy off the Atharva Veda."

An extraordinary grunt of satisfaction was the Lord's response.

"I'll take charge of that," he said.

I was confounded by astonishment. They turned round and I put on a semblance of making my entrance without having heard anything.

There was a concert of exclamations regarding my beauty and my costume.

"What can you have been playing for," I said, "to bring so much passion to your game?"

"A diamond—that was our stake."

"A marvelous diamond!"

"It's the Prince who won," said the Rajah.

"No," said Lord Portman, in a peremptory tone, "I've bought the diamond. It belongs to me."

And everyone installed themselves on the mats around the little silver lamp.

I had hardly touched the cocktails and had drunk very little during the meal, sensing the necessity of maintaining all my presence of mind. How is it that I accepted one pipe, and then another, and gazed with an infinite satisfaction at the swirls of smoke that I launched at the ceiling? Perhaps it was because of the words that the Rajah pronounced, perhaps because one is impelled ineluctably to certain acts, and because the events that were about to be accomplished were written in the book of my destiny.

"I smoke every day, just as I gaze at the sunlight every day," said the Rajah slowly, punctuating his words with the little gestures that the confection of a pipe requires, "because opium, which is the spirit of plants, brings us the wisdom of the vegetal realm, the wisdom of nature, the sentiment of fraternity, and impels us to conform, with neither revolt nor sadness, to the laws of the world. Opium lifts us above ourselves and I deem that one can only comprehend amour by means of it. The most sublime sensation that one can known on earth is that of smoking in the arms of a woman one loves. Life is so complicated, and everyone strives so hard to complicate it, people are so separated from one another by their stupidity, their passions or their prejudices what I've never been able to realize that ideal. I have, however er searched for it ardently and I've come so close to the realization once or twice that, when I think about it, I can't help trembling with emotion."

I noticed then that the bronzed hand of the Rajah, which was suspending a droplet of opium above the flame of the lamp on the tip of a needle, was agitated by a slight tremor, with the consequence that it bumped into the glass regularly, so as to make a music as light and sad as a regret.

"Those who believe in God can say that opium brings us closer to God, in the sense that it enables us to communicate by means of a more subtle comprehension with the soul of things. Those who believe in amour find, with reason, that opium is the sole path that permits two human creatures avid for closeness to embrace one another intimately and veritably, for the embrace of bodies only gives an incomplete possession that leaves us unsatisfied. With opium we awaken an unknown faculty, we provide an aliment that our invisible double animates, and there is then above the caress of the lips another caress, that of our subtle bodies, which is the last word and the highest state of amour."

I watched him while he was speaking, examining the wrinkles of his face, the thickness of his neck, and the vastness of his torso, and I imagined in his place the regular oval, the sloping shoulders and the slim waist of his son Mir. The mental creation that I made was so vivid that, driven by an irresistible sympathy, I made a movement of the hand in order to take the hand of the absent young man.

The Rajah must have read my thought, for he had a melancholy smile and I heard him murmur, while he handed me the pipe that he had just finished: "Yes, I'm old and I've lost my last chance."

"We only know some of the resources of nature," said Prince Vanini, "that permit us to rise above ourselves and attain unknown joys. Opium and hashish are all very well, but Panya, my Bengali physician, claims that there are many other plants, charged with secret powers, the knowledge of which might perhaps make us equal to gods. What does the Soma used by the Brahmins in their secret rites contain? What is the peyote plant of the priests of the ancient Mexican religion? What did the knights of the Holy Grail drink from the sacred cup? There are herbal juices that contain mental virtues and we can, by absorbing them, acquire courage,

279

clairvoyance, and even the science of the laws of the universe."

The Rajah lowered his eyelids in approval, and handed me another pipe. I smoked it in a single draught. I was possessed by an extraordinary sentiment of light wellbeing, and had the sensation that my blood was pulsing more rapidly in my veins. My imagination was more rapid. I was surrounded by charming friends of an intelligence greater than I had known thus far. The world was filled with harmony. And a time that it is impossible for me to evaluate went by in that softness.

"Personally," said Vanini, again, "I take the Gurago that Panya prepares for me. It's a complex mixture into which a little hashish also enters and a little pulverized tobacco, for there are in simple tobacco, in addition to the poisons it contains, many fecund forces of which people do not know how to make good use. Gurago transforms dreams into reality. When one has taken a sufficient dose, the light imaginary tableau of thought becomes the veritable life: the illusion of life, but an illusion so clear, accompanied by so many sensations, and embellished with such magnificence, that I find that illusion more real than reality. Gurago will be useful to me this evening.

Lord Portman uttered a burst of disdainful laughter and shrugged his shoulders. He lifted a full glass and said: "Even if I were offered Soma or the cup of the Holy Grail, I'd trade it for a glass of whisky with as much pleasure as I've traded ten thousand pounds for..."

He stopped suddenly, and then continued, raising his empty glass again.

"I have a particular horror for your Gurago. Personally, I'm in favor of the real reality, not the illusion. The only pleasures that exist are material pleasures, those one perceives with one's nostrils or one's palate, those one touches with one's hands. My philosophy is that there is no spirit, nothing but material forms, avid with the desire for enjoyment. What I love in a woman is the diversity of splendid matter, the ivory of the teeth, the tissue of the hair, the velvet of the skin, sanguine warmth, and the movement of the form. Outside of the possession of that physical wealth, everything else is lies."

While he was speaking his eyes were bulging from his head and his mouth was almost making the motions of eating. At that moment he appeared to me more repulsive than ever

"I only desire," he said again, "one single manifestation of spirit in a woman: her consent."

He suddenly started laughing, and cried as he fell backwards: "And one can even substitute for that, thanks to the Atharva Veda."

I was about to ask why there was such frequent mention of the Atharva Veda when Lord Portman, who, while drinking, had the attitude of a man waiting impatiently, remarked that the moment had come to take advantage of the orchestra that was in the next room, as well as the dancing girl from Madras that he had brought.

"You can dance when you please," he said to me, "but it seems to me that it will be better for us to contemplate that which is imperfect before that which is perfect, and that we remain for the remainder of the night under the impression of your beauty.

I nodded my head. He got up and went out, but from the doorway he darted a glance of intelligence at his two friends and addressed a remark to them in English in which I thought I understood that there was mention of an oath. But my bliss was too great and I was no longer capable of astonishment.

The Magical Dance

I almost uttered a cry of surprise when I saw the dancer from Madras climb the steps of the stage. She wore exactly the same costume as me, with the same embroideries of silver and gold, the same shade of shawl, the same rings and the same headband descending over the temples, and as she was the same height as me, with something analogous in the carriage of the head, I thought for an instant that it was me, and that I was about to watch my double dance.

Lord Portman was watching my face for the impression I experienced.

"That's the dancer we saw together in Madras," he told me. "I noticed, that evening, that she had some of your movements. So I had the costume of the bayadere Cammatatchi, which is yours, copied exactly.

"What costume can a bayadere wear here," said Vanini, closing his pill-box, "except that of the unfortunate Cammatatchi?"

"Why unfortunate?" I asked. "You didn't finish your story."

"That's true," said Vanini. "Well, the terrible ancestor of our placid friend took pleasure in making the marvelous Cammatatchi dance in the same place where we are. I told you that the capricious creature had refused the Rajah, out of pure coquetry, for experience informs us that the majority of women have neither appetite nor disgust, and if they affect to make a choice it isn't by virtue of their elective preference, as they would like to make people believe, but by virtue of interest, whimsy or, often, for no reason at all."

I protested, for form's sake, having been familiar with Vanini's paradoxes for a long time.

"So, it as the day of the festival of Sidambara—but isn't it the day of the festival of that god today?"

"Precisely," said the Rajah. "But the old customs have fallen into desuetude, and Sidambara has ceased to be honored.

"Having watched Cammatatchi dance, the Rajah made thereafter the gesture of taking her in his arms. She turned away, laughing, as was her habit. Instead of persisting, the Rajah told her to return to the habitation of the sacred dancers, which was situated on the other side of the pool. When Cammatatchi had gone out, the Rajah had a ferocious panther released behind her. The bayadere fled along the stairways that you can see over there...."

"And then?"

"The bayadere was eaten," said the Rajah, tranquilly, "and my ancestor watched the scene through a loophole."

"That's a frightful story."

"Such was the punishment of coquettish women in that distant epoch," said Vanini. "Impunity is unfortunately assured to them nowadays."

Lord Portman leaned toward me and murmured, as gently as a lamb: "I hope that you won't hold it against me for having revived the evening in Madras and having made that dancer a poor imitation of you?"

At any other moment I would have found that pleasantry absurd and out of place, but in spite of the story of Cammatatchi, a river of benevolence and tranquility was flowing through my soul. I made a sign that I did not hold it against him.

The Massalchi, or torch-bearer, who illuminates a bayadere while she dances, had came to take his place behind her, in accordance with custom. The musicians' talam and mahatalam resonated at a signal from Lord Portman with a muted tonality, and the bayadere commenced her dance.

From the start, she gazed with the fixity of a magnetized bird at Lord Portman, and never took her eyes off him. The dance is an amorous coming and going, and alternation of approach and retreat, accompanied by undulations of the arms and movements of the legs, miming by turns hope, regret or the pleasure of amour. Only Lord Portman existed for that bayadere.

I made the interior reflection that that was scarcely polite for the Lord's guests, and I was about to make that reflection to the Prince, who was beside me, when I experienced a singular sensation. It was of myself that I was about to make a criticism, it was me who was gazing exclusively at Lord Portman, me who as dancing for him alone. Without my knowledge, I had identified myself with the dancer dressed like me; I was her.

I smiled at the absurdity of the sensation, of which I was fortunately conscious. By virtue of a curious duplication, however, I continued to watch the bayadere dance as if I were gazing at myself in a mirror, criticizing myself for certain faults in the dance, certain movements of the body that I found unseemly, certain thrusts of the breasts accompanied by passionate gazes fixed on a single man, which I judged as eloquent as a direct invitation to amour. I would have liked, above all, to retain the sort of chant commenced in a shrill tone, which ought to have been gentle on the ear, taking exception the dance continued because the bayadere from Madras

285

mingled with it passionate accents like appeals, as voluptuous as gasps of pleasure.

Suddenly, the dance concluded.

Then I saw the dancer descend the steps of the stage lightly, bound rather than run toward Lord Portman, and with the same spontaneous enthusiasm that she had had in Madras for a certain Miguel, she threw her arms around his neck, placed her head on his shoulder and said, sighing: "Oh, George!"

George was Lord Portman's forename, of which I never made use because it was antipathetic to me, without my knowing why.

Its resonance was as disagreeable to me as if I had pronounced it myself.

But I understood, or thought I understood, Lord Portman's intentions. In spite of my refusals he had had a dancer dress like me in order to have the illusion that it was me in his arms. And the words of the three friends that I had not understood came back to my mind, as well as the meaning of their card game. They had played for the dancer from Madras!

But how young they had remained to be able to be impassioned for the possession of a woman that could be had so easily in the port of Madras! I was invaded by an immense disgust for men, at the same time as a little anger. So only one thing existed for them: physical possession. They could not spend a single evening in pure amity, with conversation and ideal speculations. We had convened for amicable hours of dreaming and smoking. That had not been sufficient for them. They had still required the perspective of a whore, whose paid caresses one or other of them would possess.

The fears that I had had were completely dissipated, to be sure! They had been replaced by a sharp ill humor.

I experienced the need to exteriorize that ill humor, and I spoke to Lord Portman in order to reproach him for his vulgarity and that I would renounce dancing.

But, to my amazement, he had completely changed his attitude in my regard.

He replied to me by a shake of the head and he contented himself with making a little sign with his finger, a sovereignly imperious sign, to express that the moment had come for me to dance.

I sensed a blush of shame cover my face at that inconceivable gesture. Then something even more inconceivable happened, I stood up meekly, and even rapidly; I climbed the steps of the stage and I prepared to dance. At another sign from Lord Portman, the bayadere from Madras disappeared through the door to the left, and while my thoughts reeled, and I made a futile effort to recover myself, the talam caused its metallic sound to ring out, the muted sounds of the mahatalam resonated with an irresistible power, with a magnetic rhythm such as I had never heard, and I began to dance.

I did not know whether it was me who was dancing or whether it was the bayadere from Madras. But as soon as the first step I plunged my gaze into that of Lord Portman and I fixed it there. From the very first step, the chant that I intoned was a plaint of amour, an appeal to the man at whom I was looking, a humble chanted supplication. I was begging him to love me.

I took account of the insensate character of those amorous notes, but I could not prevent them from emerging from my throat.

I saw and judged my folly in a second consciousness. I intimated to myself the order to stop, but my will had abandoned me and I was not capable of going back.

And I did even more. I danced as I had never danced. I extended my arms with a bewildered vehemence, to fold them again suddenly with tenderness as upon a beloved individual. I mimed the poem of desire with the thrust of my breasts, I caused the nude part of my body to protrude with an abandoned immodesty, I offered myself in the inclination of my torso, I delivered myself in the reversal of my hips.

An interior and distant voice cried as if through a fog: "Stop, fool!" But it seemed to come from a consciousness that was foreign to me. I was still looking into Lord Portman's eyes, bewildered and fascinated.

And suddenly, the talam and the mahatalam expired. The massalchi lowered his torch; the dance was over. The final note had not finished vibrating when I bounded with an incredible lightness, I fell at Lord Portman's feet, I enlaced his neck with my arms, and I said, with a sigh of my extended lips: "Oh, George!"

Then Lord Portman leaned toward me, I felt the palm of his hand on the nape of my neck and he stuck his mouth to mine.

The Stone Cavalier

I don't know how many seconds or how many minutes I remained against Lord Portman's shoulder. I don't know whether or not it was him who, with the hand with which he was pressing my neck, inadvertently released the little chain by which the minuscule golden box was suspended.

After the intoxication of the pipes and the fatigue of the dance I was in a state of languorous torpor. I was awakened by the sensation of the chain opening and the box sliding between my breasts, over the naked skin.

I wondered at first what it was, and then I remembered that Comtesse Aurelia had given it to me that morning.

Mechanically, I seized the box, and opened it with my fingernail. A little object, of very ancient gold, fell into the palm of my hand. By the vague light that reigned in the room, I did not distinguish at first what that fragment of gold represented. Then I threw it away in disgust. It was a lingam, a minuscule obscene symbol of Mammaden, the southern Indian goddess of amour,

I had Lord Portman's head against my breast and I perceived his even and profound respiration, which attested his delight, and a clear reckoning of things returned to me.

The three men, in collusion with Comtesse Aurelia, had set a vile trap for me. They had used against me a magical operation learned from the Atharva Veda, the ancient Hindu book filled with extraordinary and absurd recipes for bewitchment, some of which must be authentic. The little gold box had been the point of departure, the talisman. Then there had been the dancer similar to me. I had heard it said that in certain conditions, a human being cannot prevent themselves from reproducing exactly the actions that they see accomplished by an individual like them, acting in their resemblance, who thus succeeds thus in exercising a power of suggestion over them. I had heard it said that a king of I know not what Indian country had been thus led to hang himself by a sorcerer clad in a royal costume who had hung himself before his eyes. The requisite condition had been fulfilled, in my case, by the opium that had weakened my will, and had permitted the singular duplication of which I had been the victim.

I saw all the elements successively combined, and how I had been duped. It was me for who they had played cards. I had been won by Vanini, who had ceded me for ten thousand pounds, finding that that price exceeded the value of the purchased object! I felt anger invade me. Fortunately, it was not over. Lord Portman had only obtained a kiss. So long as the three men were united they were not to be feared. I would tell them what they had done and demand that they take me back to Pondicherry without delay.

I stood up and took two or three steps, energetically and ostentatiously wiping my mouth with the gauze of my robe. I darted a glance around. But the room was empty, Vanini and the Rajah had disappeared, taking away the tray, the little lamp and the pipes.

"They've gone to smoke somewhere else," said Lord Portman, "in a room at the other end of the pagoda. I have their word. We're alone for the rest of the night."

He smiled triumphantly and moved his jaws, making his teeth click, doubtless with the thought that he was about to bite my flesh.

He too was standing, and as I took a step toward the door he added: "Our solitude is absolute. The servants and musicians had orders to quit the pagoda, and my panther has been released around the temple that we occupy, in order that no one will disturb us. Above all, don't take it into your head to go out. Remember the story of Cammatatchi!"

I saw that his eyes had lost all light. He was trembling with desire. My presence against him had thrown him into a kind of physical ecstasy, into which he wanted to plunge again. He did not doubt, moreover, that I was ready to obey him. With his two extended hands he made the gesture of capturing me as one captures an inoffensive moth blinded by the light.

Perhaps I might have been able to make him ashamed, to threaten to divulge his conduct. It's improbable that that would have done any good. He believed himself to be too close to the realization. He could, in any case, have replied to me that society would hold at fault a woman who had had the imprudence to render herself nearly naked, under the pretext of dancing as a bayadere, in front of three men in a solitary pagoda.

I looked at my costume. I measured the transparency of the trousers and the skirt, the tightness of the corselet, the nudity of my arms and a part of my body, and the sentiment of the folly that I had committed in delivering myself without defense to a man who was repulsive to me caused me to lose all prudence and sacrifice the only chance that might have remained to me, which was to appeal to his good sentiments.

My anger redoubled when I saw the gesture of his arms, which he was holding out with a tranquil certainty of success and a basely lustful cynicism imprinted in his features.

With all my strength I slapped his face, and the blow that I truck was so forceful that I felt a pain in my hand and wondered whether I had not sprained the fingers or the wrist.

Lord Portman had never received such a slap in the face in his entire life. His immense fortune, the cares with which he had surrounded himself, must have set aside from an early age any possibility of combat. Something so new left him completely stupefied. He had the expression on his face of a man witnessing an action that tends to prodigy.

He remained motionless for a few seconds, gazing with his enormous eyes at the cause of the prodigy. But the prodigy was painful and humiliating. His chest swelled, the expression of stupefaction gave way to an expression of hatred terrible to behold.

It was my instinct that dictated my conduct. I was impelled, so great was my anger, to give him another slap similar to the first. A struggle would have followed of which the outcome as certain.

Almost without reflection, I launched myself toward the only candelabrum whose lighted candles were illuminating the room, I lifted it up and turned it upside-down. Then, with the same bound I ran into the dressing room and bolted the door.

But that would only give me a few seconds. He did not negotiate. I sensed that he was hurling himself toward the door in order to break it down. I darted a circular glance around me; there was no door that would permit me to flee, and no window. I had a moment of despair. Without having any fixed plan, I moved the tall mirror in which I had looked at myself before with such dangerous complaisance, and I hid behind it. Perhaps I thought about letting it fall on Lord Portman when he rushed me. But as I moved it I felt a violent current of air that refreshed me and inclined the flames of the expiring candles by which the room was illuminated. The mirror had been set up against a tunnel, the masking of which had been completed by pieces of fabric. That tunnel did not seem to be very long, and I distinguished a vague lunar light at its far end. As the fragile bolted door cracked under a new pressure, I blew out the candles rapidly and launched myself into the tunnel.

I traversed it in a few seconds. A prodigious lunar fresco appeared before me. The green pool, the sacred pool, was reflecting a luminous trail of moonlight in its immobile waters. I had before me an immense sheaf of widespread, shiny, animated gold spangles. In the midst of the enchantment of columns, domes and porticoes, the moon had negligently placed over the pool that living bouquet of magic crystals, which seemed to end at my feet at the moment when I surged forth from the interior of tenebrous stones, beneath the yellow and green light of the world.

But I stopped, open-mouthed. It was not one panther—the panther with which Lord Portman had threatened me—it was two panthers that had been set on sentry duty for me, which were watching the entrance to the tunnel, standing to the right and left of its entrance, in a frightful immobility.

I held my breath, and, through my mind, with a vertiginous rapidity, all the horrible stories ran that I had hard since my arrival in India of men surprised and devoured by wild beasts,. Nothing had ever terrified me as much as the thought of dying between the paws of one of those giant cats with fetid breath, Lord Portman's kiss was better. But did I have the choice?

I heard a noise of breaking glass at the end of the corridor, which made me suppose that Lord Portman, after having broken down the door, was in the process of discovering the opening of the tunnel.

I had held my breath, but it was necessary for me to respire a little air. I remarked then that the panthers were not breathing; and I also remarked that they were much larger than panthers; they were tigers, and tigers larger than natural. They were not breathing because they were made of stone, because I only had before me one of the thousand reproductions of animals with which the Hindu religion populates its temples.

I slipped between them and, with an infinite satisfaction, I gave one of the inoffensive muzzles a little pat. At that same moment, footsteps resounded at the other end of the tunnel.

I launched myself at hazard alongside the pool. I had no idea how to direct myself within that formidable succession of gopurams, holy places, courts and porticos. On reflection I ought not to fear the panther. It had only been a threat to prevent me from fleeing. One does not leave a panther, even domesticated, at liberty in a place where there are a large number of servants. English law is rigorous on that subject, even for rich lords. We were no longer in the times of Cammatatchi. But where could I go? Ought I to try to find the place where the Rajah and the Prince were doubtless smoking peacefully? They now inspired me with a horror almost as great as Lord Portman.

"It's much more than it's worth," Vanini had said.

My arrival in my bayadere's costume, in the midst of musicians and sleeping servants, appeared to me to be the ultimate in ridicule.

My only hope was to be able to get out of the enclo-sure of Chillambaram, reach the village and obtain hos-pitality in a Hindu house, What welcome would be re-served for me there? How could I explain myself, given that I did not know the local language, or English?

All those difficulties appeared to me while I was running, and I could not see any practical way out of my situation. But I ran, because the essential thing, first of all, was to escape Lord Portman's embrace.

I had quit the edge of the pool, crossed an enclosure planted with coconut palms, and was going past the col-onnades of a temple. The opium and the terrors I had experiencing might have been acting on my imagination, but I thought I saw in passing the coconut palms begin to move and the columns running by my side, with their capitals on their thin shoulders.

A singular life took possession of things. An enor-mous solitary Buddha sitting under a cylindrical dome stood up ceremoniously as I passed and bowed as if to salute me. A tower performed a pirouette in front of me and I thought that it was about to deposit at my feet a bizarre ball covered with ornaments, which surmounted it. On the threshold of a door less temple all sorts of di-vinities with several heads and numerous arms came to watch me pass by. I saw Brahma, I saw Vishnu, I saw Siva. I saw many others whose names I did not know.

I emerged in front of the chapel of the sacred bull and fell at the foot of one of its four pillars, unable to do any more, indifferent to the movements of the pillars and the strange coming and going of the bull's head.

I seemed to hear a voice in the distance calling me. It was the abhorred voice of Lord Portman. Was he ex-horting me to come back? Was he threatening me with the panther again? The thought of his fat lips, his empty eyes and his hateful face sufficed to render me the courage necessary to flee.

I had recognized the pagoda of the sacred bull, which I had visited on my arrival. There could not be many of them. The only difference between the pagoda that I saw in the moonlight and the one I had seen at dusk was that the latter was motionless, with a stone bull solidly fixed to its pedestal, while this one was agitating feverishly and sheltering an animate bull that never ceased moving its head to the right and the left. And I was possessed by a bizarre agitation myself.

I recalled that, by going around the enormous monument that was to the right—which was the temple containing the Holy of Holies, on the altar of which the ineffable deity reposes, which is above the universe and the gods—I would find the boundary wall. I slid along the wall, plastering myself against it, making myself as small as possible. I darted a timid glance inside as I passed before the entrance to the temple. I had once gazed without dread, and had even smiled when I was told that the supreme divinity of the Hindu religion is worshiped on an empty altar. Now, scarcely a glance in passing, and I shivered on glimpsing, in the uncertain light, a great black stone on which nothing was set.

The enclosing wall was enormous. We had come through it by the western portal, but I knew from Vanini's discourse that there were four portals. I knew that in India, everything is dilapidation and ruins, and that doors that fall often remain for centuries without being replaced.

I went along the wall, and I perceived that I was not mistaken. I was at the eastern portal, the portal of serpents, framed by a tangle of sculpted serpents, coiled, suspended and intermingled—and the door was no longer anything but a few worm-eaten planks held together by lianas.

All the serpents—at least, I had the illusion of it—were stirring, advancing their flat heads and their bespectacled eyed, stretching toward me. But I was beginning to get used to that universal movement. I thought, with a good deal of reason, that there was more to fear from a tiny invisible snake living in the grass that the entire swarm of the snakes of the immense portico.

I removed one of the planks without much difficulty, slipped through the opening and, with a great sigh of relief, emerged from the enclosure of Chillambaram.

In the moonlight, I saw that all around the gate, in a large open space, disposed in a semicircle, there was an entire cavalcade of stone elephants and horses, with their riders. They were marvelously white and I would have admired their form and the harmony of their disposition if I had not been wandering anxiously in which direction the village might lie and what was going to become of me in the night.

Beyond that mute army, I thought I could see the while line of a road between the coconut palms, coming from I know not where to end at the eastern portal. I thought that the best thing for me to do was to take that road.

I took a few steps in the moonlight and behind me, the serpents of the portal, and the high and somber wall, agitated. In front of me the elephants were waddling, shifting their trunks, and the stone cavaliers leaned over in their saddles. I even heard the whinnying of a horse. But had I not seen the columns running, the sacred bull stirring between its four pillars, and astonishing idols appearing on the thresholds of temples? The effects of the opium were familiar to me now and their phantas-magoria could not stop me.

I advanced with a firm tread between the elephants and the cavaliers. There was one that was not wearing the same costume as the others and not standing in the same alignment. He leaned over to the point of falling, and I thought I was about to hear the sound that a block of marble makes when it breaks.

How surprised was I when he uttered a cry of joy with a human throat, when he enlaced me in his warm arms and deposited me, palpitating, in his saddle, against his young man's breast!

The Return to Pondicherry

Having lifted me from the ground, Mir did not replace me on the ground for explanations. It was only
afterwards that I told him about my adventure in the pagoda of Chillambaram, and how he had been able to find
me in the threshold of the eastern portal in that unexpected costume. I took care, in any case, to transform the
truth slightly in order not to make his father play the
odious role that I left exclusively to Lord Portman.

It was only afterwards that he explained his provi-
dential appearance to me. The day before, he had received a laconic note enjoining him depart without delay
for Chillambaram, where I was in danger. He had only
found the note in the afternoon and had spent the night
en route.

For the moment, I did not seek to discover who had
written that letter, as well as the one that I had received,
who the protector was who had watched over me and
was endowed with sufficient penetration to judge Mir
capable of crossing forty-nine miles at a single stretch
solely on the indication of a danger threatening me. In
fact, I never knew for certain. But when I learned that a
liaison of sorts had been created between Vanini and
Juliette Romano, I supposed that the latter had received
from Vanini the confidence of the Chillambaram project.

Vanini must have believed that Juliette Romano
hated me and that he would give her pleasure by describ-
ing the trap that had been set for me, and my imminent
humiliation. Vanini knew the admiration that Mir had
for me and the latter, in spite of his reserved nature,
might perhaps have confessed his sentiments to him.
Juliette Romano must have experienced to a high de-

gree—at least, I supposed so—the patriotism of the weaker sex that sometimes urges women to unreflective revolts and impels them to aid one another against the egotism and bestiality of men.

She had only warned me by means of an anonymous note, not wanting to quarrel with anyone, but she had also warned Mir, whom she must have supposed to be my lover. In formulating the last hypotheses she was, in any case, only mistaken by a matter of hours.

But while Mir carried me away along the road to Pondicherry, there was certainly no question of all that. There was only a question of the thirst that was devouring both of us—or even all three, for the forty-nine miles crossed by night had exhausted the horse on which Mir was hugging me with more timidity than desire.

The night ended and a light pallor spread over the spread over the landscape, outlining the clumps of palm-trees, the bare hills and the monotonous alignment of rice-fields. Muir remembered that after Gondelour he had passed over a bridge and had had the sensation that the bridge was extended over a flowing stream and not a dried-up bed, as is often the case.

We traveled a long distance in the hope of that bridge. One of Mir's hands maintained me in the saddle, wrapped around my midriff, which was the part of my body not covered by any garment.

We finally reached the promised stream, dismounted, drank several draughts and enabled the horse to drink. When our thirst was slaked we used the pretext of the water we had spilled, he over his neck and I between my breasts, to laugh together for a long time, because of the joy we were each secretly experiencing in finding ourselves together in a solitary landscape, bathed by the delightful freshness of the morning.

The horrible danger that I had run, and the difficulty of getting back to Pondicherry without scandal, were effaced from my mind at the same time, to give way to a puerile, almost sportive pleasure, the kind one experiences when one departs early for an excursion, and the unconscious elements of which are the wealth of one's own health and a odor of damp earth.

We started walking along the river; a great insouciance was in us. We agreed that the wisest thing to do was for me not to show myself during the day in my bayadere costume, which would not have failed to pique the curiosity of anyone who saw me. The best course of action was to find a refuge for the day, and only go back by night. By going back late we had every change of not encountering anyone. We immediately adopted that plan, which had the advantage of permitting us to remain together for quite a long time.

The day had concluded and the bad omens of the day before were no longer exerting their action. I was certain that, if I had looked into the sky, I would have seen white birds flying from right to left, that it would have been impossible for me to discover the smallest spider in the longest grass, and that if I had leaned over the pebbles of the stream, I would immediately have seen a minuscule pink stone shaped in the form of a heart by gods desirous of informing a favored creature, by means of a sign, that amour is close at hand.

But I did not have the leisure to gaze at the sky, the grass and the pebbles; I was too fully occupied with the silence that had just suddenly fallen on Mir and me, and by the thousands of words with which we were communicating silently.

Finally, a cabin was offered to our eyes. It had no door, and was composed of badly-jointed planks. It must have served as a shelter for peasants when they came to work in the nearby rice-field. We decided to rest for a while there, and go on later.

Mir tied up his horse to one side and examined the grass-covered ground of the cabin carefully, in order to get rid of the snakes if there were any.

We lay down side by side. Mir's timidity led him to leave rather a large gap between us, but the chill of the morning, further augmented by the proximity of the water, had gripped us since we had dismounted from the horse. I shivered, and instinctively put both hands over my bosom, with the movement that one gives to one's shoulders to narrow them when one is cold. I think, to be sincere, that I was deliberately exaggerating my sensation of cold. Mir was also shivering, perhaps also with exaggeration.

I do not know whether it was him that made the first gesture of drawing together. I believe that it was me, and that I legitimated it immediately by shivering again. But the sun was rising rapidly; it warmed up the planks of the cabin very quickly, and if we had needed a pretext to be close to one another that of cold would no longer have been valid. But we had no need of a pretext.

Late at night, a bayadere whom a young man was holding tight on the saddle of his horse passed through the mute streets of Pondicherry. She was very weary, half-asleep, but she was smiling at her strange adventure, especially in thinking that the most marvelous intoxication of her life she did not owe either to opium or hashish, but to a day spent fasting in a wretched cabin of planks, on the bare ground.

SF & FANTASY

Adolphe Alhaiza. *Cybele*

Alphonse Allais. *The Adventures of Captain Cap*

Henri Allorge. *The Great Cataclysm*

Guy d'Armen. *Doc Ardan: The City of Gold and Lepers; The Troglodytes of Mount Everest/The Giants of Black Lake; The Abominable Snowman*

G.-J. Arnaud. *The Ice Company*

André Arnyvelde. *The Ark; The Mutilated Bacchus*

Charles Asselineau. *The Double Life*

Henri Austruy. *The Eupantophone; The Olotelepan; The Petitpaon Era*

Barillet-Lagargousse. *The Final War*

Barbot de Villeneuve.*The Naiads/Beauty & The Beast*

Cyprien Bérard. *The Vampire Lord Ruthwen*

S. Henry Berthoud. *Martyrs of Science; The Angel Asrael*

Aloysius Bertrand. *Gaspard de la Nuit*

Richard Bessière. *The Gardens of the Apocalypse; The Masters of Silence*

Chevalier de Béthune. *The World of Mercury*

Albert Bleunard. *Ever Smaller*

Félix Bodin. *The Novel of the Future*

Pierre Boitard. *Journey to the Sun*

Louis Boussenard. *Monsieur Synthesis*

Alphonse Brown. *City of Glass; The Conquest of the Air*

Émile Calvet. *In a Thousand Years*

André Caroff. *The Terror of Madame Atomos; Miss Atomos; The Return of Madame Atomos; The Mistake of Madame Atomos; The Monsters of Madame Atomos; The Revenge of Madame Atomos; The Resurrection of Madame Atomos; The Mark of Madame Atomos; The Spheres of Madame Atomos; The Wrath of Madame Atomos* (w/M. & Sylvie Stéphan); *The Sins of Madame Atomos* (w/M. & Sylvie Stéphan)

Jean Carrère. *The End of Atlantis*

Félicien Champsaur. *Homo-Deus; The Human Arrow; Nora, The Ape-Woman; Ouha, King of the Apes; Pharaoh's Wife*

Didier de Chousy. *Ignis*

Jules Clarétie. *Obsession*

Jacques Collin de Plancy. *Voyage to the Center of the Earth*

Michel Corday. *The Eternal Flame; The Lynx* (w/André Couvreur)
André Couvreur. *Caresco, Superman; The Exploits of Professor Tornada* (3 vols.); *The Necessary Evil*
Gaston Danville. *The Perfume of Lust*
Camille Debans. *The Misfortunes of John Bull*
Captain Danrit. *Undersea Odyssey*
C. I. Defontenay. *Star (Psi Cassiopeia)*
Charles Derennes. *The People of the Pole*
Georges Dodds (anthologist). *The Missing Link*
Charles Dodeman. *The Silent Bomb*
Harry Dickson. *The Heir of Dracula; Harry Dickson vs. The Spider*
Jules Dornay. *Lord Ruthven Begins*
Alfred Driou. *The Adventures of a Parisian Aeronaut*
Odette Dulac. *The War of the Sexes*
Alexandre Dumas. *The Return of Lord Ruthven; The Man who Married a Mermaid* (w/P. Lacroix)
Renée Dunan. *Baal; The Ultimate Pleasure*
J.-C. Dunyach. *The Night Orchid; The Thieves of Silence*
Henri Duvernois. *The Man Who Found Himself*
Achille Eyraud. *Voyage to Venus*
Henri Falk. *The Age of Lead*
Paul Féval. *Anne of the Isles; Knightshade; Revenants; Vampire City; The Vampire Countess; The Wandering Jew's Daughter*
Paul Féval, *fils. Felifax, the Tiger-Man*
Charles de Fieux. *Lamékis*
Fernand Fleuret. *Jim Click*
Charles-Marie Flor O'Squarr. *Phantoms*
Louis Forest. *Someone is Stealing Children in Paris*
Arnould Galopin. *Doctor Omega*; *Doctor Omega and the Shadowmen* (anthology)
Judith Gautier. *Isoline and the Serpent-Flower*
H. Gayar. *The Marvelous Adventures of Serge Myrandhal on Mars*
Louis Geoffroy. *The Apocryphal Napoleon*
G.L. Gick. *Harry Dickson and the Werewolf of Rutherford Grange*
Raoul Gineste. *The Second Life of Doctor Albin*
Delphine de Girardin. *Balzac's Cane*
Léon Gozlan. *The Vampire of the Val-de-Grâce*
Jules Gros. *The Fossil Man*
Jimmy Guieu. *The Polarian-Denebian War* (2 vols.)
Edmond Haraucourt. *Daah, the First Human; Illusions of Immortality*
Nathalie Henneberg. *The Green Gods*

Eugène Hennebert. *The Enchanted City*
Jules Hoche. *The Maker of Men and His Formula*
V. Hugo, P. Foucher & P. Meurice. *The Hunchback of Notre-Dame*
Romain d'Huissier. *Hexagon: Dark Matter*
Jules Janin. *The Magnetized Corpse*
Gustave Kahn. *The Tale of Gold and Silence*
Gérard Klein. *The Mote in Time's Eye*
Fernand Kolney. *Love in 5000 Years*
Paul Lacroix. *Danse Macabre; The Man who Married a Mermaid* (w/Alexandre Dumas)
Louis-Guillaume de La Follie. *The Unpretentious Philosopher*
Jean de La Hire. *The Fiery Wheel; Enter the Nyctalope; The Nyctalope on Mars; The Nyctalope vs. Lucifer; The Nyctalope Steps In; Night of the Nyctalope; Return of the Nyctalope*
Etienne-Léon de Lamothe-Langon. *The Virgin Vampire*
André Laurie. *Spiridon*
Gabriel de Lautrec. *The Vengeance of the Oval Portrait*
Alain le Drimeur. *The Future City*
Georges Le Faure & Henri de Graffigny. *The Extraordinary Adventures of a Russian Scientist Across the Solar System* (2 vols.)
Gustave Le Rouge. *The Dominion of the World* (w/Gustave Guitton) (4 vols.); *The Mysterious Doctor Cornelius* (3 vols.); *The Vampires of Mars*
Jules Lermina. *The Battle of Strasbourg; Mysteryville; Panic in Paris; The Secret of Zippelius; To-Ho and the Gold Destroyers*
Maurice Level. *The Gates of Hell*
André Lichtenberger. *The Centaurs; The Children of the Crab*
Maurice Limat. *Mephista*
Listonai. *The Philosophical Voyager*
Jean-Marc & Randy Lofficier. *Edgar Allan Poe on Mars; The Katrina Protocol; Pacifica 1, 2; Robonocchio; Return of the Nyctalope;* (anthologists) *Tales of the Shadowmen 1-13; The Vampire Almanac* (2 vols.)
Ch. Lomon & P.-B. Gheuzi. *The Last Days of Atlantis*
Charles Malato. *Lost!*
Maurice Magre. *The Marvelous Story of Claire d'Amour; The Call of the Beast; Priscilla of Alexandria; The Angel of Lust; The Mystery of bthe Tiger; The Poison of Goa*
Camille Mauclair. *The Virgin Orient*
Xavier Mauméjean. *The League of Heroes*
Joseph Méry. *The Tower of Destiny*

Hippolyte Mettais. *Paris Before the Deluge; The Year 5865*
Louise Michel. *The Human Microbes; The New World*
Tony Moilin. *Paris in the Year 2000*
Michael Moorcock's *Legends of the Multiverse*
José Moselli. *Illa's End*
John-Antoine Nau. *Enemy Force*
Marie Nizet. *Captain Vampire*
Charles Nodier. *Trilby and The Crumb Fairy*
C. Nodier, A. Beraud & Toussaint-Merle. *Frankenstein*
Henri de Parville. *An Inhabitant of the Planet Mars*
Gaston de Pawlowski. *Journey to the Land of the 4th Dimension*
Georges Pellerin. *The World in 2000 Years*
Ernest Pérochon. *The Frenetic People*
Pierre Pelot. *The Child Who Walked on the Sky*
Jean Petithuguenin. *An International Mission to the Moon*
J. Polidori, C. Nodier, E. Scribe. *Lord Ruthven the Vampire*
P.-A. Ponson du Terrail. *The Immortal Woman; The Vampire and the Devil's Son; The Police Agent*
Georges Price. *The Missing Men of the* Sirius
René Pujol. *The Chimerical Quest*
Edgar Quinet. *Ahasuerus; The Enchanter Merlin*
Jean Rameau. *Arrival; in the Stars*
Henri de Régnier. *A Surfeit of Mirrors*
Maurice Renard. *The Blue Peril; Doctor Lerne; The Doctored Man; A Man Among the Microbes; The Master of Light*
Restif de la Bretonne. *The Discovery of the Austral Continent by a Flying Man; Posthumous Correspondence* (3 vols.); *The Fay Ouroucoucou* (2 vols.)
Jean Richepin. *The Crazy Corner; The Wing*
Albert Robida. *The Adventures of Saturnin Farandoul; Chalet in the Sky; The Clock of the Centuries; The Electric Life; The Engineer Von Satanas*
J.-H. Rosny Aîné. *Helgvor of the Blue River; The Givreuse Enigma; The Mysterious Force; The Navigators of Space; Vamireh; The World of the Variants; The Young Vampire*
Marcel Rouff. *Journey to the Inverted World*
Marie-Anne de Roumier-Robert. *The Voyage of Lord Seaton to the Seven Planets*
Léonie Rouzade. *The World Turned Upside Down*
Han Ryner. *The Human Ant; The Superhumans*
Henri de Saint-Georges. *The Green Eyes*

Louis-Claude de Saint-Martin. *The Crocodile*

Frank Schildiner. *The Quest of Frankenstein; The Triumph of Frankenstein; Napoleon's Vampire Hunters*

Nicolas Ségur. *The Human Paradise*

Pierre de Selenes: *An Unknown World*

Norbert Sevestre. *Sâr Dubnotal: Vs. Jack the Ripper; The Astral Trail*

Angelo de Sorr. *The Vampires of London*

Brian Stableford. *The Empire of the Necromancers (1. The Shadow of Frankenstein; 2. Frankenstein and the Vampire Countess; 3. Frankenstein in London); The Wayward Muse; Eurydice's Lament; The Mirror of Dionysius; The New Faust at the Tragicomique; Sherlock Holmes and The Vampires of Eternity; The Stones of Camelot* (anthologist) *News from the Moon; The Germans on Venus; The Supreme Progress; The World Above the World; Nemoville; Investigations of the Future; The Conqueror of Death; The Revolt of the Machines; The Man With the Blue Face; The Aerial Valley; The New Moon; The Nickel Man; On the Brink of the World's End; The Mirror of Present Events; The Humanisphere*

Jacques Spitz. *The Eye of Purgatory*

Kurt Steiner. *Ortog*

Eugène Thébault. *Radio-Terror*

C.-F. Tiphaigne de La Roche. *Amilec*

Simon Tyssot de Patot. *The Strange Voyages of Jacques Massé and Pierre de Mésange*

Louis Ulbach. *Prince Bonifacio*

Théo Varlet. *The Castaways of Eros; The Golden Rock.; The Martian Epic* (w/Octave Joncquel); *Timeslip Troopers* (w/André Blandin); *The Xenobiotic Invasion*

Pierre Véron. *The Merchants of Health*

Paul Vibert. *The Mysterious Fluid*

Villiers de l'Isle-Adam. *The Scaffold; The Vampire Soul*

Gaston de Wailly. *The Murderer of the World*

Philippe Ward. *Artahe; Manhattan Ghost* (w/Mickael Laguerre); *The Song of Montségur* (w/Sylvie Miller)

Victor Margueritte. *The Bacheloress; The Companion; The Couple*

www.ingramcontent.com/pod-product-compliance
Lightning Source LLC
Chambersburg PA
CBHW060428030726
47495CB00003B/780